LOVE BLOOMS AT HOLLYHOCK FARM

GEORGINA TROY

Boldwood

First published in Great Britain in 2025 by Boldwood Books Ltd.

Copyright © Georgina Troy, 2025

Cover Design by Lizzie Gardiner

Cover Images: Adobe Stock and Shutterstock

The moral right of Georgina Troy to be identified as the author of this work has been asserted in accordance with the Copyright, Designs and Patents Act 1988.

Every effort has been made to obtain the necessary permissions with reference to copyright material, both illustrative and quoted. We apologise for any omissions in this respect and will be pleased to make the appropriate acknowledgements in any future edition.

A CIP catalogue record for this book is available from the British Library.

Paperback ISBN 978-1-78513-778-5

Large Print ISBN 978-1-78513-779-2

Hardback ISBN 978-1-78513-777-8

Ebook ISBN 978-1-78513-780-8

Kindle ISBN 978-1-78513-781-5

Audio CD ISBN 978-1-78513-772-3

MP3 CD ISBN 978-1-78513-773-0

Digital audio download ISBN 978-1-78513-775-4

This book is printed on certified sustainable paper. Boldwood Books is dedicated to putting sustainability at the heart of our business. For more information please visit https://www.boldwoodbooks.com/about-us/sustainability/

Boldwood Books Ltd, 23 Bowerdean Street, London, SW6 3TN

www.boldwoodbooks.com

To my uncle, Nigel Sweeny MBE. For always being there for me.

1

SKYE

Skye stared out of her bedroom window across the expanse of the wide bay with its pale gold sand, rolling waves and Elizabeth Castle perched neatly on a small islet in the sea. The sun was setting and because her first day had been cut short when her flight to Jersey was delayed due to a mechanical issue with the plane, she now needed to get a move on if she was to see much before it got too dark.

'You were right, Gran,' she said, turning her phone so her grandmother could see for herself. 'The view from my hotel window is incredible. Thank you so much for treating me to this.'

'It's my pleasure, sweet pea. You deserve this long weekend away.' Her grandmother paused and Skye suspected it was because she worried about the outcome of her visit to the island. 'Hopefully you'll find a way to trace him, although I doubt you'll have time to do very much on this occasion.'

Skye agreed. 'But it's a start,' she said, picking up the worn, red hard-backed notebook her grandmother had recently given to her.

'It's Annie's,' Gran had said, surprising Skye who immediately flicked through some of the pages, her heart racing as she read snippets of her mother's life in her familiar spidery handwriting. 'This is amazing, Gran. Thank you.'

'I've only recently found it,' Gran had said. 'When I was having those two squeaky floorboards fixed in the spare room where your mum used to sleep. It was then that the chap discovered this book.'

'Have you read any of it?' Skye had asked, almost certain her grandmother would have been too intrigued to be able to resist.

'I did. Some of those things were a revelation, I can tell you. There are notes in there that I believe will help you trace your father and that's why I suggested treating you to this trip to Jersey.'

Dragging her thoughts back to the present, Skye said, 'It's going to be exciting visiting places where Mum worked.' She sighed happily. 'I can't quite believe I'm looking at a view she must have seen at some point while she was here in the late nineties.'

Skye heard her grandmother's sing-song doorbell.

'Blast, there's someone at the door. Go and have fun. I'll speak to you again soon. Much love.'

'Thanks, Gran.'

Skye ended the call but continued to gaze at the sea. Even though her mother had died ten years before when Skye was fifteen, it had only been recently after she and Gran had watched an episode of a show about people searching for lost relatives that she had felt a strong enough need to start looking for her own father.

'I wonder if you're still here,' she murmured, opening the window further to let in the sea air. 'Do you even know I exist?'

It had been a niggling thought of hers ever since her mother had told her just before her death from cancer that she had met Skye's father while working a season at one of the island's hotels. If only she had been brave enough to ask for more information while she had the chance, Skye mused regretfully. Her focus had been on simply being there for her mother during those short months while they and Gran struggled to cope with the tumultuous change in their lives.

Back then she hadn't cared much about an absent father, only that she was about to lose her amazing mother who had brought her up by herself. At least they lived with Gran so the pair of them could continue to support each other in the dark days, weeks and months after Annie Sellers died.

She would have a shower first to freshen up and then go out and have a walk along the seafront before returning to the hotel to grab some dinner before bed.

Feeling refreshed, Skye towel-dried her hair and put on fresh underwear. She was pulling a cotton top over her head when an alarm began blasting outside her bedroom door, giving her a fright.

'Not now,' she grumbled, quickly dressing in a short skirt and pushing her feet into her trainers.

Someone banged loudly on her bedroom door. 'We are evacuating the hotel immediately,' the voice called.

'Coming.'

Skye grabbed her bag and, slipping the strap over her head, took her door card and left the room. She had been travelling around Asia for six months and thought it ironic that in all the times she had spent sleeping in hostels and cheap hotels nothing like this had happened before. Following the rest of the guests, she passed the hotel staff indicating the way out, and she wondered how long this might take.

'Do we know what's happened?' a man carrying a small, terrified-looking child asked the person behind him.

'No idea.'

'I think it might be a fire somewhere,' someone else announced as they reached the top of the staircase. 'I spotted two fire engines outside my window.'

At the thought of a fire, Skye realised she had left her notebook with all the information her mother had written in it. Skye had no intention of losing such an irreplaceable treasure. She turned and went to retrace her steps past other guests.

'Excuse me,' a firefighter said, putting his arm out to bar her way. 'You can't go back inside until the all-clear has been given.'

'I've forgotten something valuable,' she said, looking over at the hotel and not seeing any smoke. The place was clearly not about to burn down. 'I won't be a moment.'

'You're still going to have to wait here with everyone else until you're allowed to go back.'

She glared at him, desperate to argue, but seeing the steely look in his blue eyes, realised he wasn't going to change his mind. 'Fine.'

Seeming satisfied that she was going to do as he asked, the firefighter left to speak to someone else. Checking his back was turned to her, Skye hurried back to the hotel entrance and ran up the stairs to the first floor. She reached the room, wishing the alarm would stop blaring out.

'Hey, you can't go in there,' a deep voice called, giving her the second fright of the evening.

Damn, he must have spotted her going back inside, Skye realised. Hand shaking, she held her room card against the lock and, relieved when it clicked, opened the door and stepped inside. Before it could close he entered the room behind her.

'You cannot be in here,' he said, sounding thoroughly irritated with her.

Understanding his annoyance, but unwilling to leave without the notebook, Skye scanned the room and seeing her precious book on the dressing table, crossed the floor to grab it. Her fingers grazed it, when he spoke again.

'You must leave now.'

Skye picked it up and turned to see a tall, broad-shouldered firefighter in full uniform. Even as she battled to make sense of what was happening it dawned on her that, at any other time, this might be quite exciting. Then she noticed the grim expression on his handsome face.

'Now.'

'One minute,' she said, pushing her book into her jacket pocket.

'You don't have a minute,' the firefighter said, his voice clipped as if he was trying hard to keep from losing his temper.

Aware he had her best interests at heart and was only doing his job, Skye nodded apologetically and left the room. 'Sorry, I promise I won't do that again.'

He didn't reply, just gave a nod and a sideways glance as if he didn't trust her to do as she had said. He followed her silently until she was back outside with the other guests.

2

JOE

Joe removed his uniform and hung it up ready for the next emergency. His adrenalin was still pumping after the fire in the hotel kitchen. No one had been hurt and they had managed to contain the fire to the kitchen, which was a relief. His thoughts returned to the woman in the bedroom who had insisted on fetching a book. A book, of all things. Who would risk their life, and potentially his, for a book? He thought back to the fire in the village soon after he and his mother Faye had moved to France when he was fourteen, and to the shock he still felt when he recalled watching the building with neighbours in the village square, waiting for the three people trapped on the top floor of a hotel to be rescued.

The bravery of the *pompiers* – especially the one who had climbed the ladder and carried down a traumatised woman with partially burnt clothes, saving her life – had stayed with Joe since then. The heroic actions of the firefighter had been the reason he had chosen to do the same job.

Joe was glad he hadn't seen the woman he had taken from the hotel bedroom after leading her to join the final few hotel staff as they left the building again. The temptation to tell her how silly she had been would have been intense, and it wasn't for him to lecture anyone.

He couldn't think straight with all the chatter from his colleagues, so Joe finished putting his things away and realised he should go home. The thought of returning to his home, to his mother and her new husband Roger, was not something he was looking forward to. They had only been staying with him for two weeks but it already felt more like a couple of months. If only it wasn't so early and the café was open; he could do with wasting an hour eating one of their delicious breakfasts right now.

'I'm off,' Joe said.

'Me, too,' his good friend and fellow firefighter Paul said, joining Joe as he left the building. 'You OK, mate?' Paul asked as they strode towards their cars. 'You seem a bit down lately.' Paul stopped by his car. 'It's not woman trouble, is it?'

Joe shook his head. 'Not unless you're thinking of my mother,' Joe replied, keeping his voice light.

Paul slapped him on the back. 'Good luck with that.'

Joe knew Paul had been referring to a recent conversation when Joe had admitted his last relationship ended badly. He had then insisted, despite Paul's assurances to the contrary, that he had no intention of becoming involved with anyone romantically for a very long time. 'Thanks, I'm sure it'll all work out somehow.'

'I'm sure it will.' Paul smiled. 'And let's hope it's a quieter shift next time.'

Joe thought of the guests and staff at the hotel and was glad they had all been able to return to their accommodation after the fire had been contained and extinguished, and he couldn't agree more.

He took the scenic route back towards Noirmont where he had lived alone, barely having a chance to settle into the bungalow his paternal grandfather had left him before his peace was shattered when his mother had pitched up on his doorstep with her suitcase and husband in tow, acting as if this was going to be a great family reunion.

'Why didn't you let me know you were coming?' Joe had asked the morning they'd arrived. 'I could have at least prepared a room for you both.'

'We wanted to surprise you,' his mother Faye had insisted, handing Joe her cabin bag and walking past him into his hallway, leaving Joe to introduce himself to her latest husband.

'Hi, I'm Joe,' he'd said, assuming his stepfather already knew but unsure what else to say. 'Come in.'

'Thank you.' The man had held out his hand for Joe to shake. 'I'm Roger. Faye insisted you could put us up for a bit.'

'Of course,' Joe had agreed, wishing his mother had thought to at least ask him first. 'I'd be happy to.'

Now though, two weeks later, having moved into his spare room when his mother claimed it was only fair that she and Roger took the larger of the bedrooms as there were two of them, Joe was tired of her things being strewn everywhere and never having a moment's peace. His mother and stepfather were either rowing or tiddly from drinking each evening, and Joe wanted space from them.

Deciding to stop off at the store to buy one of their takeaway coffees and a doughnut, Joe parked his car and went inside.

'Well, if it isn't Joe Marett. I haven't seen you for months. Where've you been hiding?'

Recognising the voice, Joe turned and smiled at the local vet. Brodie had returned to the island to take over the village veterinary practice and the pair of them had become good friends in that time.

'Hi, mate. Here and there.'

Joe thought of his beloved grandad who had left the bungalow to him after his death the previous year. Joe wondered when the pain of losing his grandad would ease. He thought of how much his grandad had done for him. Joe had often returned to the island to stay with him after his mother had taken him to live in France when his parents divorced when Joe was fourteen.

The decor was dated but somehow that only added to his cherished memories of time spent there. As for the tiny shed in the garden where all the old but well-maintained garden tools were neatly stored away, he decided that was his favourite part of the property. Joe pictured coming to the bungalow after school when he was young to spend time with his grandparents until his mother finished work and sitting on a small stool next to his grandfather in front of the shed as they drank lemonade and stared out over the sea below them in Ouaisné Bay. His grandmother had died while he and his mother had been living in France for a decade, but it still felt odd not being able to see his grandfather.

'I moved in a few months ago. Slowly settling in.'

Brodie rested a hand on his shoulder and Joe struggled for a couple of seconds to keep control of his emotions. 'If there's anything you need help with, just let me know.'

'Thanks, Brodie. I'll bear that in mind. How come you're up this early?' Joe said, tapping his watch. 'It's barely seven-thirty. Not had an emergency at your veterinary practice, I hope?'

Brodie shook his head. 'No, thankfully. I couldn't sleep too well last night so took Derek out for an early walk.'

Joe grinned as he pictured the strange-looking black rescue

Brodie had adopted the previous year when Lettie Torel, Brodie's now fiancée, had found him by the side of a road. 'How is he doing?'

'Well, thanks.' Brodie frowned. 'Better than poor Lettie.'

Concerned for his friends, Joe asked, 'There's nothing wrong with the pregnancy, I hope? She must be, what, seven months along by now?'

Brodie nodded. 'Thirty-four weeks.' He sighed. 'She's been overdoing it running Hollyhock Farm. We had a bit of a scare last week.' He looked around, then lowered his voice. 'We haven't told anyone but Lettie has something called placenta praevia.'

'Sounds nasty,' Joe said, wondering what it was.

'It isn't ideal.' Joe frowned. 'It's where the placenta attaches in the womb lower than normal and can cause haemorrhaging during delivery.'

'Poor Lettie.' Joe wished there was something he could do to help. 'And she's allowed to work with that?'

'She's been getting twinges over the past few days, which is worrying. Lindy and Gareth are away on another cruise, as you probably know, and it was planned so that they would be back a few days before the baby's due date. The doctor has now insisted she give up work as soon as possible, at least until the baby's born.'

'Lettie won't have liked that, I imagine.'

Brodie shook his head. 'She wasn't impressed but the doctor warned us that as soon as she goes into labour she must get to the hospital, just in case there are issues. Now he's concerned she might have the baby early, and I'm panicking a bit about it all.'

'I'm not surprised,' Joe said, resting a hand on his friend's shoulder. 'You do know that you can call on me for anything you need, I hope.'

'Thanks, Joe. I might have to take you up on that offer.'

'Then do.' Joe thought of the recent conversation he'd had with his supervisor about taking the four weeks' leave he had carried over from the previous year. Joe had thought he had hidden his grief well from his colleagues by focusing on his work and taking on extra shifts whenever they were available. He was still surprised by what he had been told.

'You need time away from the station,' his supervisor had said. 'And you have the next few weeks to decide when to take it, otherwise I'll decide for you.'

Joe shrugged now. 'Don't think too long. I'm due four weeks off work and had been putting off taking it because I wasn't sure what to do with myself. You'll be doing me a favour too.'

Brodie sighed. 'You don't know how relieved I am that I bumped into you this morning. Chatting to you has taken a weight off my shoulders. Lettie and I had planned that I would help out at the farm. I'm only a short drive away in the village in case of an emergency, so wouldn't be far if she needed me.'

Joe thought back to how hard his friend had been working for the previous ten months to make a go of the place, and wasn't surprised Lettie was upset about stepping back from the farm.

'I would have asked Zac but he's still away on tour. And although I'm sure her parents would come back immediately if Lettie needed them to...' Brodie crossed his arms.

'Let me guess,' Joe said narrowing his eyes. 'Lettie won't hear of you disrupting their holiday?'

'That's right. She said they've worked hard all their lives and she has no intention of ruining their enjoyment of their well-earned retirement at the first hiccup.'

'I would hardly call it that.'

'That's what I said.'

'Typical Lettie,' Joe said fondly. His friend was too kind for her own good sometimes, but it wasn't his business to say so.

'I've spoken to her Uncle Leonard, who has promised to send in his own workers to harvest the potatoes. I offered to spend any free time feeding and tending to the animals, but you know how busy my practice has become now that I'm the only vet in the village, so I won't have the capacity to do all I need to for them.' Brodie shook his head wearily.

Joe recalled the delicious buttery taste of the small Jersey Royal potatoes the island was so famous for, after the Jersey cow.

'I can't help feeling that it's my fault we're in this predicament.'

Unsure why he would think that way, Joe asked, 'How is this your fault?'

Brodie puffed out his cheeks. 'Well, she wouldn't be pregnant without me, would she? The baby, as much as we are excited to welcome it, would have been better coming in a couple of years when Lettie was more established at the farm.'

Joe understood his friend's sentiment, but had no intention of letting him blame himself for something neither of them could help. 'Hey, that attitude isn't going to help either of you and it certainly won't resolve the farm issue. Anyway, this is something involving the pair of you, so stop blaming yourself.'

'I suppose you're right.' Brodie shrugged. 'I just wish I could give her some reassurance that there's a resolution to this, but I'm not sure what yet. I only popped in here to buy a tasty treat for Lettie's breakfast and don't want to still be out when she wakes up. She's had a pretty tough night worrying herself silly about the farm.'

'Look, try not to worry too much. Let me speak to my boss about taking leave so I can help out on the farm.'

'Really?'

'Of course. I'm sure he'll be delighted if I finally give in and take time off from work. I'll let you know as soon as I have something confirmed.'

'Thanks, Joe. That would be incredible.'

'It would be my pleasure.' A thought occurred to him. 'Why don't you leave Derek with me at the farm, too? You'll be busy with your veterinary practice and will surely want to spend your free time with Lettie before the baby is born. Derek will be fine with me and Spud.'

Brodie frowned thoughtfully as he considered Joe's suggestion. 'That does sound like a sensible idea.' He watched Brodie picking up a pair of plastic tongs and putting two croissants into a brown paper bag. 'Thanks, Joe. I appreciate that more than you know.'

Breathing in the smell of the pastries, Joe decided he could do with eating a couple too. He put four into a bag and walked over to the counter to ask for a coffee. 'I'll catch up with you as soon as I can,' he called to Brodie as his friend turned from the counter, having paid for his purchases. 'Please send Lettie my best.'

'You're a star,' Brodie called before smiling and leaving the store.

As Joe paid for his things, then stepped aside to wait for his coffee to be made, he couldn't help worrying about his friends. Poor Lettie had worked long hours to keep the farm running. She was such a hardworking and lovely person, giving up a life in fashion in London to take over the farm when her father was forced into early retirement. He thought back to their one and only date before she and Brodie had got together. Joe might have liked her, but he was glad to see her happily making a life with Brodie. They were well suited with their love of animals and similar humour.

He took his coffee and, after thanking the assistant, left for his short drive home. Maybe he wouldn't be so irritated by his mother and Roger if he could put some space between them? If he was able to help out with the animals at the farm, then maybe Lettie might be agreeable to let him stay in one of the rooms she kept for guests.

It was a thought and one that cheered him up enormously.

Feeling his mood dip again as he parked his car outside the bungalow, Joe braced himself to go and face his mother and Roger. He found them sitting at the kitchen table niggling at each other, yet again, about something.

Joe forced a smile and held up the brown bag. 'I have fresh croissants for breakfast,' he announced, relieved when the pair were distracted enough to stop their sniping.

'How thoughtful of you, darling,' Faye said, giving Roger a look as if to say, *look how thoughtful my son is*, as she got to her feet. 'Sit down and I'll fetch some plates.'

Joe had no intention of being drawn into their arguments. 'No, you stay there; I'll get them.'

Finally seated, Joe focused on keeping the mood light while they each ate their pastries. 'So, what have the pair of you got planned for today?' he asked, hoping they would be going out somewhere and leave him to catch up on his sleep. He didn't mind night shifts but coming home and spending a peaceful few hours in bed seemed to be a thing of the past since Faye and Roger's unexpected arrival. He spotted the pair of them exchanging glances and his mood dipped. He recognised that expression on his mother's face and knew he wasn't going to like what she was about to say.

3

SKYE

Skye heard a familiar ringing from somewhere nearby. It took a couple of seconds for her to be awake enough to recognise the ringtone on her mobile. She peeled her eyes open but apart from the bright light of her phone screen everything else was in pitch-blackness.

She reached out to pick up her phone, and one look at the screen told her it was Melody and that it was nine-thirty. She answered the call.

'You're calling later than you usually do,' Skye said, her voice gravelly from sleep. How long had she been sleeping, she wondered, to sound this bad?

'Late? It's the morning.'

'Is it?' She looked over to the curtains, realising they must be black-out ones. Skye sat up and rubbed her eyes lightly with her free hand. 'Sorry. Is everything all right?'

'Fine, thanks. I was wondering about you.'

Skye told Melody about the fire the previous evening. 'I think the firefighter was annoyed with me for coming back to my room to fetch Mum's notebook.'

'Skye!'

She heard the disapproval in her friend's voice. 'What? Wouldn't you have done the same?'

'Maybe.'

'Apart from that episode, I know I've only been here one evening, but I am loving it so far. I'll be sad to leave.'

'Really?'

Skye sensed there was something else Melody was calling about. 'Yes. Melody, is there another reason you're calling me?'

Skye listened as Melody explained about her friend Lettie who ran a farm, was pregnant and in dire need of someone to move in and take care of her animals for a few weeks.

'How many animals?'

'A few cows, some sheep, chickens and three rescue alpacas. Oh, and a dog called Spud. He's adorable.'

'Is this where you and Patsy stayed last summer?'

'That's right. Just like when we were there, the accommodation will be free. You'll also have time to see the island and get to know the place. The farmhouse is a beautiful granite place and has loads of colourful hollyhocks growing either side of the front door and some of the windows every summer. Unfortunately you'll be there too early to see those.'

Skye laughed. 'You seem very confident that I'll agree to go and look after this place.'

'Why wouldn't you?' Melody asked. 'Unless you've found a job already, or made plans since I spoke to you last.'

She hadn't. 'No, nothing new.'

'Look, I know what you're like when you've just woken up. I'll leave you to have a think. Lettie is a wonderful person and I know she would be very grateful. I also know you'll adore staying on the farm and spending time with the animals. I'd do it in a heartbeat if I didn't already have commitments here.'

The idea did sound intriguing. Skye swallowed. 'Let me have a cup of tea and I'll get back to you with my answer.'

'Great. Chat later.'

Skye threw back the duvet, got up and walked over to the window, and drew the curtains. She blinked as the bright sunshine flooded the room. When her eyes had adjusted, she opened the window and gazed out at the stunning blue sea. There was barely a cloud in the sky and she wondered what it would be like to spend more time on this pretty island.

She put on the kettle and took a shower while it boiled, then dressed and sat with her cup of tea to call her grandmother and see what she thought about Melody's suggestion.

'It would give you more time to search for your father, Skye,' Gran said thoughtfully. 'And you are already on the island, so that makes things easy. It's not as if you have any other plans yet either, is it?'

'No, Gran,' she said, deciding that if her grandmother and best friend both thought it a good idea then it probably was the right thing for her to do. 'I'm going to give Melody a call before I have a chance to talk myself out of it.'

'That's my girl. You go and enjoy yourself and tell me how it goes.'

Maybe this was just what she needed, Skye mused. Time spent somewhere new, doing something a little different. 'Will do, Gran.'

4

JOE

'Roger and I are going to need to borrow some money from you, Joe.'

Joe never minded lending people money, but he'd been here far too often in the past with his mother. Her knack of spending was on another scale to anyone else and he suspected it was the reason Roger had run out of funds. But how could he refuse? Despite their differences and her insisting everything was done her way, regardless of Joe's feelings, she was still his mother and he loved her.

'Can I ask if it's to rent a place of your own?' he asked, hoping Faye was ready to move on.

She laughed. 'Don't be silly. Why would we waste money on another property when we're all perfectly happy here? No, I've decided we're going to help you redecorate our room.'

Their room? Joe took a mouthful of his croissant and chewed before swallowing, determined to remain calm. 'Why?'

'Darling, you must admit the decor is terribly old-fashioned. Tired, even. It's depressing to wake up to the bland walls.' She turned to Roger. 'Isn't it?'

'It is,' he agreed.

Joe knew his mother wouldn't want to spend too much time in the house looking the way it did and had half-hoped it might encourage her to find a job and move on to a modern flat, or somewhere that suited her better. He noticed how awkward Roger seemed about the suggestion and knew his mother had told him how to react.

Joe groaned inwardly. 'So, you're planning on staying for a while then?' He had no idea why he was even asking the question when it was perfectly clear that if his mother was going to the effort of decorating the room, in her mind she had already taken over his home.

She beamed at him, causing Joe to feel guilty. 'Yes. I thought you'd be happy having me living back on the island again.'

He wasn't sure why she would think this way. The pair of them had always struggled to live together with him finally leaving France when his ex had been unfaithful to him and his mother had questioned why he couldn't move past something trivial like Aurélie sleeping with his boss at the station where he then worked.

She hadn't explained why she and Roger had left France, and Joe wondered if now was a good time to discover more about their reasons for moving back to Jersey after she had seemed so happy living in France all these years.

'You know I'm happy to see you,' he assured her. 'Although I had presumed you might find your own place. In fact, I still don't know why you're both here, or why you came with so little stuff.'

She gave him a soulful glare. 'You're making me feel very unwelcome, Joe.'

'Sorry, I don't mean to,' he said guiltily. 'I just don't understand what's happened. Something must have done, for you to leave your home, and I can't help wondering what it could be.' Joe finished his coffee and sat back in his chair, waiting for Faye to speak.

His mother glanced at Roger then shrugged. 'It was my fault really,' she said. 'I persuaded poor Roger to invest in my business when it began struggling last year.'

'Your clothes shop,' Joe recalled, having only visited the place once on his last trip to see her.

'I loved that place,' she said miserably, her eyes filling with tears. 'And it still went under.' She reached out and took Roger's hand in hers. 'He lost his entire life savings,' she said, pouting at her husband. 'And mine into the bargain.'

Joe's heart ached for her. She had always insisted she and his father divorced because he was mean-spirited and selfish. Maybe he was being unfair. She couldn't help how she was.

Joe stood and walked around the table to give her a hug. 'I'm so sorry, Mum. I know how much you loved that place.'

He thought back to how he had tried to persuade her that maybe a boutique selling high-end fashion in a small out-of-the-way village probably wasn't the most ideal business plan, but she had refused to listen, insisting that a firefighter with little fashion sense couldn't possibly be qualified to give business advice about selling women's clothes.

'Thank you, darling. I promise I won't waste a penny this time.'

Returning to his seat, Joe picked up his plate and cup. 'Where are the rest of your things then?'

'They're in a storage unit at a friend's farm,' Roger replied. 'They said we can leave our furniture and the rest of our clothes with them for as long as we need to.'

That was something, Joe mused. He considered his mother's request to redecorate the bedroom they were staying in, aware that once she got going she would expect to redecorate the entire house. He hadn't thought to redecorate yet, wanting to keep anything that kept his grandfather alive for him, but the style was dated. How could he ruin another day for his mother by refusing to let them redecorate? He couldn't be that mean, although, he thought, he did need to catch up on some sleep.

'I need to go to bed for a few hours,' Joe said. 'Why don't you both go and buy whatever paint or wallpaper you need while I do that. Then I'll help you start the prep work on the room. How does that sound?'

It was his mother's turn to come to him. 'You are the best son in the world,' she said, flinging her arms around his back and hugging him. 'I knew you'd understand.'

Joe kissed the top of her head and left them to eat the remainder of their breakfast. As he showered and dried himself, he decided that he needed to rethink his living arrangements. Clearly his mother and Roger weren't going anywhere, and as much as Joe loved his mother he knew from experience that the two of them got along better when they weren't under each other's feet.

He transferred some money into her account, then yawned and closed his eyes again, relieved to give in to sleep.

* * *

He woke a couple of hours later to the sound of another argument. Groaning, Joe rubbed his eyes and sat up. He leant against the pink headboard and sighed.

'If you didn't want to return to live in England again, you should have said so,' Faye yelled from the room next door. 'Nobody forced you to come with me.'

'This isn't England though, is it?' Roger retaliated. 'This is a small island and I don't know a soul.'

'You know me. You know Joe, too.'

'It's not the same, Faye,' he shouted, sounding frustrated at her lack of understanding. 'And you know it.'

'Not again,' Joe grumbled, glancing at the clock. He might not need too much sleep but he needed more than three and a half hours if he was to be alert enough for his shift later that night. He realised they had gone quiet and, feeling hopeful that the pair of them were about to make up, slid back down on his bed and closed his eyes.

A door slammed and woke Joe with a start. He peered at the clock, relieved to see he had enjoyed another three hours' sleep. He closed his eyes and hoped his mother and Roger might have gone out and left him alone in the house.

'Roger!' Faye shouted. 'Why haven't you brought in both pots of paint from the car?'

They must have gone out to a hardware store while he slept. No wonder he hadn't been woken earlier. He decided he may as well get up because clearly there would be little reason for him to stay in bed now, not if Roger and his mother were about to start decorating.

He heard them bickering again in the bedroom, this time about her spending most of the money Joe had given them for the decorating on a pair of red leather shoes.

'Why shouldn't I treat myself occasionally?' he heard Faye snap.

Irritated to hear that it had taken no time at all before his mother spent the money he had sent her on something frivolous, Joe listened as their quibbling continued.

'But you do treat yourself, Faye,' Roger snapped. 'And often.

It's why we're living in this tiny bungalow with your thirty-year-old son as our landlord.'

'How can he be our landlord when we're not paying him anything?'

Joe sighed as he got out of bed and wondered as he showered whether his mother had married Roger because she felt guilty about spending his savings, or maybe they did love each other and just didn't get along all that well. Whichever reason was behind their marriage, it was a tumultuous relationship and not one he could live with for much longer.

He shampooed his hair and tried to figure out what to do about his living arrangements. He was unable to come up with anything useful. Maybe he needed another coffee to help wake him up a bit. The thought of coffee reminded him of bumping into Brodie that morning and then what Brodie had told him. Lettie needed to step back from running the farm.

He could move in and help her out, while resolving his own living situation, at least for the time being.

He picked up his phone and, deciding to meet up with her to discuss the matter further, gave Brodie a call.

5

SKYE

Skye tucked her hair behind her ears, wishing she hadn't uncharacteristically succumbed to the trend for wearing her hair in a French bob. She knew others loved the style and she did too, on someone else, but she was finding it more difficult than expected to keep her hair out of her face and it was getting on her nerves. She made a mental note to buy hair clips so that she was better prepared next time she went out.

Picking up her phone, Skye called Melody.

'So you've thought about my suggestion then?'

'I have. Tell me more about Lettie and Hollyhock Farm so I can make up my mind.'

Skye listened as Melody told her about her boyfriend Zac's family home on the island of Jersey and how his pregnant sister was in desperate need of help. 'It's coming up to harvesting time for those tasty little potatoes we get at the supermarket,' she explained. 'You know the ones Gran always tries to get as soon as they are stocked in the shops.'

'I do,' Skye said, recalling her surprise at the excitement for a bag of tiny potatoes, then the delicious taste when Patsy served them up to her and Melody. 'But I don't know anything about harvesting.' Maybe this wasn't such a good idea, Skye thought.

'Sorry, I've given you the wrong idea. Apparently Lettie and Zac's Uncle Leonard will be taking charge of all that. What you'll be needed for is to look after the animals. You know, let them out to the field, bring them back inside the barn, feed them, make sure they have enough water, that sort of thing.'

'Sounds simple enough,' Skye said as it dawned on her she had only ever had to look after a family cat Gran once had. 'Not that I have any experience doing that though.'

'That's the thing. Brodie, Lettie's fiancé, is the village vet and will only be down the road. Any issues and he'll be there straight away.'

Knowing that she would have backup in case of an emergency helped. 'How long will it be for though?'

'Well, Lettie is due to have the baby in about six weeks, I gather. But her parents are due back in four, so it'll only be from now until they return from a trip. Lettie is lovely,' Melody said. 'And don't forget she'll be around to show you everything you'll need to do and answer any questions. The farm is amazing too and I know you'll love it there.'

Skye did like the sound of it. 'It sounds simple enough and as long as there'll be time for me to search for my father, I suppose I don't see why I shouldn't do it.'

Melody gasped. 'Really? You wouldn't mind?'

Skye smiled, hearing the delight in her friend's voice. 'No, of course not.' She laughed. 'It's not as if I have a job to return to Edinburgh for, is it?'

Skye heard voices in the background. 'Did I catch you at the gym?'

'Yes, sorry. I'm about to give my next yoga class. Look, shall I give you Lettie's number? Then you can give her a call and make whatever arrangements you need to. I'll send her a quick message letting her know you'll be contacting her. And, Skye?'

'Yes?'

'I know you'll love it there. You'll be kept busy, but the island is beautiful with stunning nearby beaches and lots of restaurants.'

'You don't have to keep trying to sell it to me, Melody.' Skye laughed. 'I've said yes.'

* * *

To give Melody a chance to message Lettie, Skye decided to speak to her grandmother.

'I'm so happy for you, sweetheart,' her grandmother said. 'And as you know, Annie worked there in a hotel for a summer season. I believe your father was one of the barmen there, or was it a porter, or concierge? Unfortunately she didn't ever share his name with me. I always felt guilty that she didn't feel she could discuss more about your father with me.'

'You shouldn't, Gran,' Skye said, hating to think her kind grandmother could ever feel badly about her mother's choices. 'I asked her a couple of times about him while I was growing up but she always became sad when I broached the subject, so I stopped asking in the end.'

'Can I ask what she did tell you about him?'

Skye didn't have to think long before answering. 'Only that he was handsome and dark. She did say once after a few drinks that he had been the love of her life, which I think is really sad, don't you?'

'I do,' Gran replied thoughtfully. 'I wonder what went wrong between them.'

'Or why he never bothered to make time to meet me.'

Skye thought back to her five-year-old self, realising for the first time that most of her friends had daddies. When her grandmother took her to Santa's Grotto at the local shopping centre, she said she wanted her daddy to come to their house, when Santa Claus asked her what she wanted for Christmas. She remembered her disappointment then and for all her birthdays and Christmases when she still held on to hope that even if he didn't come to see her he might send her a card. None had ever arrived, and by the time she was a teenager all she had for him was anger that she meant so little to him.

When her gran didn't say anything, Skye continued, 'I know we both agreed that I should try to look for him while I was here, but I'm not really certain how to go about it. Not when we don't know his name.'

'I suppose you do know you look more like him than you do Annie,' Gran said. 'With your dark hair and brown eyes, you're so much darker than anyone else in the family, so I presume you must take after him with your looks.'

'I always assumed that too,' she admitted, miserable not to have any idea of the other side of her family. 'Where would I start looking though?'

'The hotel where they worked, of course. Where else?' Her gran mentioned two hotels where her mother had worked.

Skye took a sip of her cooling tea. 'A lot could have changed since 1998. What if they're now blocks of flats or housing estates?'

'I know you're worried about this going wrong. But what if it doesn't, Skye? Tell me that. If you don't find him then you're no worse off than you are now. If you do, well, then you at least know who he was.'

She was right.

'I know this is daunting,' Gran said. 'But this is an amazing opportunity for you. It can't be scarier than travelling solo across the world for the past six months.'

Skye laughed. 'I think it's far scarier than that, Gran.'

'But you'll do it anyway?'

'You know me, Gran. I'm a sucker for a challenge.'

'Good girl.'

'Right,' Skye said, staring out of her bedroom window at a couple of small boats, their white sails the same colour as the few clouds in the blue sky. 'I'd better give Lettie a call.'

6

SKYE

Skye stepped out of the hotel entrance and immediately spotted a woman about her own age, maybe a couple of years older, with light brown hair, blue eyes and a spattering of freckles over her nose, waving at her next to a car.

'Sorry, there aren't any more parking spaces otherwise I would have come in to greet you,' she said proffering her right hand. 'I'm Lettie, if you hadn't already guessed, and I'm delighted you've agreed to come and look after Hollyhock Farm for the next four weeks or so.'

Skye shifted her bag onto her left shoulder and shook Lettie's hand. 'I'm happy to be able to help out.' She glanced at the woman's rounded stomach. 'How are you feeling?'

Lettie shook her head and indicated the passenger door. 'I'm fine, thanks, but we'd better get going. I can see a member of staff coming our way.'

As they drove, Skye recalled her plane journey as she flew over the sunny island. She remembered looking out of the plane window and seeing what looked like a long breakwater, then soon after passing over an impressive castle on a hill, and she wondered whether they would be passing either of those locations now. She hoped so. It would be exciting to see either of them close up. She already knew she was going to like it here. Before the plane had even landed, she'd already fallen in love with several beaches covered with golden sand.

She waited for Lettie to join a row of cars before a roundabout and thought how amazing would it be if her father still lived on the island. Although realistically there was probably little chance of that being the case. She didn't even know where he was from. He could be Australian and enjoy travelling, which may be where she got her urge to travel from. Or he could come from somewhere in Europe. She wished she had some idea. Even a small clue would be nice.

If only her mother had thought to tell her something in case she ever did want to track him down. She wondered, not for the first time, if her mother kept everything from Skye for a reason. If that was the case, then she would have to face whatever it was that had bothered her mother when she got to it. She was an adult and, as far as she was concerned, fairly worldly. Skye was confident she could handle anything that came her way in this quest to track down the man whose genes she carried.

'That's better,' Lettie said as the car picked up speed along a dual carriageway. 'This is the Esplanade, and that,' she said, pointing to their left, 'is the bay you probably saw from your hotel room.'

'It's so beautiful,' Skye said dreamily, barely able to quell her rising excitement about what the next few weeks might have in store for her.

'I'm glad you think so. I hope you'll be happy at the farm, too.'

'I'm sure I will. I can't wait to see it. Melody and Patsy have both raved about the place since they stayed there last year.'

'I'll show you around as soon as we get you settled. We should be there in fifteen minutes.'

Skye loved that the island was so small and everything seemed close by.

'Is this your first time to the island?'

'It is. I love it and I'm really excited to have an excuse to extend my stay.'

'Well, it's very kind of you to offer your help.'

Skye laughed. 'Not that kind. I don't exactly have anything else planned.'

'That works well for both of us then.'

Skye gazed out of the window as they drove through a small village and relaxed further. She was looking forward to getting to know everyone. Lettie soon turned into an entrance off a lane, and Skye noticed a small sign saying, 'Hollyhock Farm'. On the opposite side of the entrance was a stall displaying brown bags in which Skye presumed must be vegetables they grew at the farm.

'That's our honesty stall,' Lettie explained. 'I know I said to Melody that I only need you to look after the animals, but I was wondering if you could add another job to that.'

'No problem at all. You mean to pick vegetables and pack them up?'

'Yes. It shouldn't take too long. I'll show you what I do. Basically choose the veg, bag it up and weigh each one to check they're about right.' She laughed. 'And collect the money each night before you close it.'

Before Skye had a chance to answer, Lettie pointed through the windscreen. 'Oh look, there's Brodie. I hadn't expected him to come to the farm this early.'

Skye peered at the tall sandy-haired man. 'He's a vet, I seem to recall Melody saying during one of her chats about her time at the farm.'

'That's right. His practice is in the village we passed through a couple of minutes ago, so if you're ever worried about any of the animals and I'm not around, he'll be the one to call. He can be here in no time.'

'That's good to know.'

Skye noticed a dark-haired man get out of the passenger's side of the old Land Rover. He looked as if he had stepped out of a *Wuthering Heights* movie. 'Who's that?' she asked, wishing her voice hadn't sounded quite so breathless.

Lettie grinned. 'That's Joe. He's a good friend of ours.' She didn't speak for a moment as she turned her car into the driveway and parked. 'Although I'm not sure why he's here.'

Skye saw the men look over at them. Joe smiled and waved. Brodie frowned briefly before smiling. They walked over to the car as Lettie and Skye got out.

'Who have we here?' Brodie asked, reaching out to shake Skye's hand as a shabby black dog jumped out of his vehicle.

She looked at Joe and wondered the same thing. She was sure she recognised him from somewhere, but where? This was only her second day on the island and she hadn't been to that many places.

'This is Skye,' Lettie said.

Brodie's smile faltered and Skye wondered why. He seemed bothered about something but was trying to hide it. Why?

Joe stepped forward and she realised he was staring intently at her. What was going on? she wondered. There was definitely an undercurrent but she wasn't sure whether it was between Brodie and Lettie, or because of her being at the farm. Very odd.

Lettie put an arm around Skye's waist. 'Skye is from Edinburgh. She's a good friend of Melody's and has agreed to come and stay at the farm to look after the animals for me.'

Brodie's eyes widened slightly and slid sideways to Joe. Skye was trying to work out why the men exchanged confused glances, then noticed Joe had a large bag with him.

'You going somewhere, Joe?' Lettie asked.

'Er, no,' Joe replied, scowling at Skye as it dawned on her there had been a mix-up.

Brodie gave an awkward grimace. 'Joe's come here to look after the place too.'

'You have?'

Skye was starting to feel awkward. At least Lettie seemed to know Joe. 'I can, er, always go back to the hotel if you don't need me.' She hoped her disappointment didn't show as much as she felt it might.

Lettie shook her head. 'No, I've promised you four weeks here.' Lettie bit her lower lip and frowned thoughtfully. 'That's so sweet of you, Joe. Thank you.'

Skye saw Joe's disappointment straight away and wondered why it meant so much to him to step in to look after the place. Then he gave her a look and she instantly knew where she had seen those eyes. He was the firefighter from the night before. She clenched her teeth. Why, of all the people, did she have to end up sharing the farm with him? She saw recognition in his eyes and understood why he had seemed so grumpy with her.

'Joe's taken four weeks off work,' Brodie explained.

Skye saw Lettie open her mouth to answer but before she had the chance, Brodie gave her a pointed look Skye didn't understand and added, 'He's finally taking that time off from last year.'

'Last year?' Lettie seemed confused, then her eyebrows shot

up and she covered her mouth. 'Oh, Joe, that was careless of me. I'm so sorry.'

'Hey, don't be silly. I'm fine, Lettie.' His entire demeanour changed when he addressed Lettie, and Skye wondered if the pair of them had some sort of romantic history. 'There won't be enough work for two people if your uncle is taking care of the produce. I'll go home.'

If he had a home, Skye wondered, then why was the mix-up such a problem?

'You OK?' Joe asked Skye without smiling.

'I am. It just took me a while to recognise you without your uniform on.'

Lettie raised a hand. 'You two know each other?'

'There was a small fire at the hotel Skye was staying in last night,' he explained.

'Yes,' Skye said without taking her eyes off him. 'And he wasn't impressed when I returned to my room to fetch something.'

'I see,' Brodie said, looking as if he understood Joe's reason for being unhappy with her. 'I'm sure once you get to know each other you'll be fine.'

Lettie nodded, a look of determination on her face; she had obviously come to a decision. 'You both have reasons for being here,' she said calmly. 'It's Skye's first time on the island, and you need time away from Faye and Roger, Joe. You also need this break from your job. Anyway, with the pair of you here I'll feel happier leaving the farm in your capable hands, so I can sit out the rest of this pregnancy at the cottage with Brodie.'

Brodie put his arm around her shoulders and gave Lettie a kiss. Skye couldn't miss the delight on his face. 'Perfect.' He looked at Skye and then Joe, smiling. 'I'm sure the pair of you will figure out who should do what chore, won't you?'

'Of course we will,' Skye said quickly before she had a chance to panic over having to share the farm with the grumpy firefighter.

Joe glanced at her before adding, 'Don't worry about a thing.' Joe gave Skye a smile that made her stomach flip over until she remembered he was probably doing this for the benefit of his friends. 'We'll work something out between us.'

Lettie sighed. 'That's a relief. OK, so why don't we begin with me showing you both up to your rooms? Then I'll give Skye a tour of the farm and go through the animals' needs with each of you.'

7

JOE

Joe followed Lettie and Skye up to the top floor of the farmhouse. Of all people to have to share the farm with, why did it have to be the annoying woman from the hotel? He still couldn't believe she'd made so much fuss over a book. So much for having a peaceful four weeks away from work. Never mind that, he thought, he had already had a taste of how difficult this woman could be. Dividing up the workload between them was, he imagined, going to cause a few problems.

He heard Lettie chatting to them both as she led the way upstairs to the attic and decided to worry about Skye later. As they climbed the stairs to the second floor, he thought how he had been inside the house many times but never up to the bedrooms. Skye seemed pleasant enough, but unfortunately he knew better. Thankfully though Brodie seemed happy enough, as did Lettie, with how things had turned out, so there shouldn't be any upset over them not discussing their plans about finding someone to move into the farm.

'This is such a beautiful house,' Skye said.

Joe puffed out his cheeks, wondering how he was going to

find a way to get along with this woman. Ever since telling his mother about moving out for four weeks he had been looking forward to having time by himself to think and process his grief a bit. He couldn't help feeling disappointed that things had already changed and he now had to navigate living with a stranger. He may as well have stayed back at the bungalow. He thought back to his mother's last row with Roger – well, maybe not, but this wasn't ideal.

'It's not much, I'm afraid,' Lettie said as she waited for Joe and Skye to view the two attic bedrooms. 'Choose whichever one you prefer.' She smiled at Skye. 'Melody and Patsy said they were very happy when they stayed up here and both said it was comfortable.'

Joe wanted to put her out of her misery as quickly as possible. 'It's perfect,' he insisted. 'You choose which room you want, Skye. Either one is fine by me.'

'Me, too.' She shrugged. 'I suppose we should take the rooms we're standing closest to?'

'Good idea.' Lettie stood on the landing, waiting for them to take their bags inside. 'This is beautiful,' he heard Skye say. 'And the view is, well, it's perfect.'

Joe walked over to his window and stared outside at the paddocks and fields beyond. There was the largest barn, with the smaller one next to it and several smaller outbuildings to his left, but straight ahead was even prettier from this viewpoint than it was from the ground. 'It is incredible.'

'And of course our priority is to look after the animals?' he said, wondering what he and Skye would find to do the rest of the time.

'That's right.' She took a hand in each of hers as Joe joined Skye and Lettie on the landing. 'I believe things happen for a reason. I know it probably seems a little unnecessary having you both here at the same time, but you'll no doubt find ways to fill the time.' She gasped. 'Maybe you could show Skye around the island a bit, Joe. Although you should also take the time to chill while you're off work.'

Lettie already had enough to worry about and he had no intention of adding anything more. 'We'll be fine, won't we, Skye?'

He noticed the look of surprise on Skye's face. 'Er, of course we will. Don't worry about us two. I'm sure we'll get along fine.'

'And with both of us looking after the animals they'll be spoilt for attention, so I'm sure they'll be fine.'

The look of relief on Lettie's face was unmistakable. 'You two are amazing, fitting in like you have.' Joe felt guilty that Lettie assumed he was doing this solely out of the kindness of his heart. How could he let her feel this grateful to him when he was only too happy to do this for her? 'You're doing me a favour too, if I'm honest. Mum is driving me nuts with her constant squabbling with Roger, and the thought of moving to this peaceful farm is almost too good to be true.'

'I don't think I've met your mum, have I?'

He shook his head, aware that if Lettie had done she would probably like Faye. Most people did and he often wished he and his mother didn't clash. Then again, he mused, they got along far better than they had done when he was a teenager and she had taken him away from his friends and the island to move to France. He now realised she had done what she thought right. A fresh start away from his father had been what she needed. If only his father hadn't blamed Joe for choosing to live with his mother despite being constantly away on business. It was all in the past now, thankfully.

'I remember the first time we met.' Lettie laughed, reminding him about when she stopped on the lane down the road from the farm, believing he needed help with his broken-down tractor. 'I thought I was helping you that day.' She looked at Skye. 'I had no idea he knew his way around a tractor.'

Thinking he should explain a little further, Joe added, 'My uncle has a farm and I help out when I'm free and he needs the extra staff. I enjoy it.'

'I see.' Skye smiled. 'So you know your way around farm-work as well as tractors.'

He smiled. 'I do. Not so much the animals though. My uncle grows produce, so you and I will probably know as little as each other.'

Lettie grinned. 'Don't forget I can still do the lighter jobs around the house and help with things like feeding the chickens; I just need to be careful not to do the heavier work. At least for the next few weeks.'

He walked over to her and, resting a hand on each of her arms, gave her a reassuring smile. 'If you do that, then what will we do here? I think you should do what your doctor told you and take things easy. Don't you agree, Skye?'

'I do.'

'Anyway, doing this will probably save my sanity and stop me from overthinking about what I should do with regard to Mum and Roger going forward.'

She sighed and gave him a hug. 'Aw, Joe, you really are the loveliest guy,' she said. 'How you haven't been snapped up yet I don't know.'

He tried to hide his embarrassment, not wishing Skye to think he was some sort of loser, even if he probably was where relationships were concerned. 'I did ask you out before you realised Brodie was the one for you. Mind you, I think we both realised pretty quickly that although we were fond of each other it wasn't in a romantic way.'

She placed her hands on her hips and narrowed her eyes in amusement. 'Yes and I'm grateful to have you as a friend.'

'Me, too.' He took her by the shoulders and turned her to face the bedroom door. 'Now, why don't you show Skye around the farm while I nip home and speak to my mum.'

* * *

'Let me get this right,' Faye said sarcastically as soon as Joe told her about moving out temporarily. 'You're saying I've pushed you out of your home – is that it? Because if that's the case, we'll find somewhere else to live immediately.' Joe knew this was an idle threat. His mother didn't have the money to pay for a place and didn't have any local friends left since she hadn't kept in touch with any of them since moving to France over a decade before. 'I don't want people thinking you're having to move out of here.'

He had half expected her to react in this way. He loved his mother but living in the same house as her again reminded him how difficult she could be when everything wasn't going her way. He suspected that if she was honest with herself she would be relieved to hear his news. This was clearly one of those times when she liked to play the martyr.

'You know that's not what I'm saying at all, Mum,' he argued. 'I've already explained Lettie needs me to help her out and I'm very happy to do that for her.' He didn't mention Skye being there too because it would only make his mother argue with him even more. He left her and Roger staring at him and went to his room. 'I'm going to pack a few things for now and will be leaving as soon as that's done,' he continued.

After throwing a few things into a sports bag, Joe went to the bathroom and picked up his shaving kit and toothbrush and popped them into his bag, zipped it up and carried it back to his mother's room. 'Right, that's me. I'll see you in a few days and don't forget, if you need anything just give me a call. I'm only twenty minutes away at the most.'

'But Joe—'

He bent to kiss her cheek. 'It's fine, Mum, I promise. I'd better get a move on, I don't want to keep Lettie waiting and I only have a few hours until my next shift starts.'

He hurried to his car and drove away, relieved to have somewhere else to go and a good excuse to move out of his home for the next four weeks. Maybe his mother and Roger might have settled down together a bit better in that time, he thought hopefully. Or, they might even find somewhere else to live, or move back to France. He had no idea, but was grateful that for the time being, at least, his situation seemed much rosier than it had done. Right now, he needed to contact his supervisor and agree dates for his time off from the fire station.

8

SKYE

'This is the larger barn,' Lettie said as they stood outside a huge granite barn with metal double doors that were open, letting the sunlight stream inside. 'We stable most of the animals here at night, or during bad weather.'

Skye followed her inside. It was empty of animals but she could see where most of them would be brought at the end of each day.

'Over there is where we keep the food,' Lettie continued. 'As you can see, I've written up a list for when Melody and Patsy stayed here last year as to who gets fed what and how often.' She indicated the large bins. 'Each one has been labelled and the scoops are hanging from the side.'

'It seems very straightforward,' Skye said, relieved. She followed Lettie, listening as she explained about the bedding, pointed out the halters for the alpacas if needed and various other pieces of equipment.

'I think that's everything for in here,' Lettie said. 'I'll show you how I bring them all in at the end of the day.'

'I look forward to it.' She couldn't wait to get started. She had been home from her travels for a few weeks and was desperate to work again. As they walked out of the barn, the sun glinted on the front windows of the farmhouse. 'You're incredibly lucky living in such a beautiful home,' Skye said half to herself. 'Melody mentioned the hollyhocks either side of the front door and I'm sorry I won't be here long enough to see those.'

'You can always come back for a visit,' Lettie said, smiling. 'And I can send you photos, if you like.'

'I'd love to come back again,' she said without hesitating. 'But photos would be wonderful.'

After showing Skye the smaller barn and outbuildings, Lettie led her out of the yard. 'This is the lower paddock where the retired Jerseys are today.'

Skye looked a little way in the distance and saw four cows. 'Oh, they're so pretty,' she said, loving the dished faces and smiling as they slowly ambled towards the gate as Lettie and Skye walked through it into the field.

Lettie laughed. 'They think they're going to be fed.' She called out to them, 'It's not time for your food yet, ladies.' Then to Skye she said, 'We'll go this way and climb between the fence rails. I want to show you the wild meadow and the stream; it's my favourite place here on the farm. Then I'll introduce you to the alpacas.'

As they walked, Skye breathed in the scent of fresh earth, flowers and something else. It took a moment but she realised it must be the sea air. 'It's so peaceful here, as well as beautiful,' she said.

'Thank you, I'm glad you think so. This place means the world to me.' They reached the stream, which Skye noticed was running quickly. Lettie stopped and rested both hands on the top of her rounded stomach. 'I'm sorry about the mix-up.' When Skye didn't reply, not quite sure what to say, Lettie added, 'About you and Joe being here at the same time. I hope it's not going to be difficult for you.'

'Not at all,' Skye assured her. 'I'm sure we'll soon get to know each other a bit better and we'll both settle in.'

Lettie sighed. 'You don't know what a relief it is for me and Brodie to know I can take a step back, at least until this little one has made an entrance.'

'You mustn't worry about a thing. We'll be fine, and as you said, we can always call you, and Brodie is close and will come if ever we need him to.'

'Thank you.'

Lettie went to say something else then hesitated. 'What is it?' Skye asked, concerned.

Lettie pressed her lips together briefly before speaking. 'As I mentioned before, Brodie feels the only way I'm going to truly rest is to move into the cottage with him where he can keep a close eye on me.' She grimaced. 'Would you be happy being left alone in the house with Joe?'

Skye shook her head. 'I think it's lovely that he wants to make sure you take things easy.' She grinned. 'I've spent the past six months travelling, and most of it was by myself. Please don't worry about me – I'll be fine. Anyway, Joe seems like a nice bloke.'

'He is, otherwise I'd never even consider leaving you here.'

'Then that's settled,' Skye said. She pictured the tall, handsome and clearly fit guy and wondered whether they would find a way to work comfortably side by side.

Too bad if he wasn't as pleased about having her around. The feeling was mutual, especially if he was going to be difficult. Anyway, she mused, just because he looked like he had stepped from a movie set didn't mean she was going to fall for any of his charms. If he had any, that was. So far, all she could see was a moody misery who had been rebuffed by Lettie. Maybe he still had hidden feelings for her, Skye thought.

Whatever his issues, she had no way of letting someone's resentment ruin this golden opportunity for her.

Skye had no intention of letting her guard down with Joe or any other man for that matter. She had learnt her lesson the hard way, not to put all her trust in another person before she was aware of what it meant. If it hadn't been for her grandmother being there for her after her mother had died, she didn't know what she would have done. It wasn't even that tragedy that had taught her to be self-sufficient. Her mother was beautiful and charismatic but life hadn't been easy for her – that much Skye did know. Having spent most of her childhood with her mother going away for long periods of time and suffering from long bouts of depression, Skye knew to make the most of the happy times when they did come along, and being here at Hollyhock Farm was, she was sure, going to be one of those times.

She thought of her ex. The last time she had let her guard down had been for him, believing him when he told her how important she was to him. She sighed. She had believed him only too readily until she had discovered what a liar he was. But she had learnt a lot since then, she reminded herself. She had travelled a lot and visited many places and had made a living as a travel writer for a magazine until it closed down a couple of months before. She knew better now. No one would make a fool of her again – of that she was certain.

Hearing a car arriving, Lettie looked up. 'I'm going to see who that is,' she said. 'You take your time and join me in the kitchen for a cuppa when you're ready.'

Happy to be left alone to enjoy her beautiful surroundings, Skye agreed.

'I won't be long.'

Ten minutes later, Skye walked back into the farmhouse and heard laughter coming from the kitchen.

'There you are,' Lettie said, her friendly smile welcoming her. 'Come and join us. We were just trying to work out how best to split the workload here between you and Joe. Weren't we, Joe?'

'Really?' How typical of his type to get in there first and grab the best jobs for himself, Skye mused, trying to hide her annoyance.

'We were, but you and I can always adapt things, so nothing's set in stone.'

Slightly appeased, Skye nodded. Maybe she had been too hasty to think the worst of him. Although as far as she could tell there wasn't too much for them to split between them. She doubted she would get bored though, especially if she made the most of her time off to start the search for her father.

Joe poured milk into a mug and stirred it, then, turning, brought two mugs of coffee over to the table and placed one down in front of Skye. 'I hope that's OK. If not, I can always make you another one.' He pushed a sugar bowl towards her. 'In case you need sweetening up.'

She stared at him, taken aback for a moment, then, gathering her thoughts, she saw the glint in his dark blue eyes and realised he was joking. 'I'm sweet enough, thanks,' Skye said, smiling.

Lettie laughed. 'I can see you'll both get on fine.'

Skye was glad Lettie had misinterpreted her reaction to Joe and she suspected his to her. She might have an issue with this man, but most importantly she was here to take the pressure off Lettie, not cause more stress for the poor woman.

'I'm sure we will,' Joe said, catching Skye's eye and waiting for her to break their stare.

Skye wasn't sure whether he was trying to reassure Lettie, or send her some subliminal message that whatever Skye assumed, she was the interloper here. She looked forward to getting to know him better, so it would be easier to read him.

Having eaten slices of cake, drinking another cup of coffee and much discussion, Lettie made a list of all the jobs they needed to carry out each day, and others that had to be done once or several times a week.

'I know there's another list in the barn, but this one is broken down in more detail.' She chewed the top of the pen. 'There are a few things that need seeing to, if you don't mind. Like the broken gate to the middle paddock, Joe. If you could do that first, I'd be grateful. The rest of the extras down here—' she pointed to the lower half of the list '—are for when you have time to fit them in. None of them are too urgent though, so mostly it's the day-to-day work you'll need to keep on top of.'

'No problem at all,' Joe said. 'We'll soon get our bearings.'

Skye noticed Joe watching her.

'It's fine,' he said. 'No need to worry unduly. I've booked a bit of time off work, so I'll be here with you. I'm sure we'll manage.'

She realised he had misunderstood her concerns but decided not to correct him. 'We will.'

They went over the list Lettie had written for them and, over another cup of tea, agreed that while Joe was on the farm he would take the lead in deciding things and do whatever manual labour needed to be carried out. Skye, on the other hand, would follow his directions, but when he was at work she could make whatever decisions she deemed necessary at the time. They both promised to call Lettie with any questions before Brodie insisted that he should be the first point of contact if those issues were to do with the animals.

'You're not to worry about anything here,' Joe said, going to stand next to Skye's side. 'The two musketeers – that's us.'

'You see?' Brodie said. 'What did I tell you?'

Lettie laughed. 'Good. That's settled then.' Lettie's smile vanished. She winced and her hands flew to her rounded stomach.

Stifling a gasp, Skye tried not to show her concern. 'Er, is everything all right?'

'Lettie?' Brodie moved in front of her, holding her by the shoulders. 'What's the matter?'

'I'm fine.' Lettie raised her hands in the air and gently pushed Brodie back a couple of steps. 'Firstly, you can all stop fretting about me. The baby kicked,' she said, directing her comment to Brodie. 'It caught me unawares – that's all.'

'I think you've done enough for today though,' Brodie insisted. 'I think it's time I took you back to the cottage to put your feet up for a few hours.'

Skye heard the insistence in his voice. Lettie nodded in agreement and Skye realised she mustn't feel all that well.

'Yes,' Skye said. 'You two go. Joe and I will be fine here now, won't we, Joe?' She gave him her sweetest smile.

Joe, clearly guessing what she was doing, reciprocated. 'We certainly will, so no arguments from you, Lettie Torel. Off you go now and leave us to get to know each other better and start doing what we're here to do.'

Looking relieved, Lettie stood. She went to pick up hers and Brodie's mugs and plates, but Joe leant across the table and took them before she could do so.

'No. I can tidy up.' Joe waved Lettie away. 'Please take her to your cottage, Brodie. She's going to be insisting on digging the fields soon if we don't get her away from here.'

Brodie laughed. 'I know you're joking but I don't trust her not to do exactly that.'

Lettie puffed out her cheeks and rolled her eyes. Smiling at Skye, she said, 'They don't trust me at all, do they?'

Amused, Skye laughed. 'Somehow, I suspect they have good reason not to. As Joe said, we'll be fine. You go and rest while you can. From what friends tell me you'll have little time on your hands to do that after the baby's born.'

Lettie grimaced. 'Don't remind me.' She shrugged. 'Fine. I give in. Come along, Brodie, let's leave the pair of them to get on with things.' She made two steps towards the kitchen door before stopping and turning back to them. 'But, if there is anything—'

'We'll call you,' Joe and Skye said in unison. They looked at each other and Skye saw Joe was as surprised as her that they had reacted in the same way. Then forcing her gaze from his, turned to Lettie.

'We will. I promise.'

Skye and Joe followed Lettie and Brodie out to the yard. They waited while Brodie gave Derek a hug and took out his dog bowls, a bed and some blankets, handing them to Joe and Skye.

They waved as Lettie and Brodie got into the Land Rover and drove away. Skye stroked Spud's head, concerned the dog might be upset to see Lettie leave, but he turned and walked back into the house.

'Don't worry about these dogs,' Joe said, following them. 'As long as they're at the farm together they'll be happy. I think he believes this is his place and that everyone who comes here, including the Torel family, are merely his guests.'

Skye laughed. 'I like that idea. Good for Spud.'

Back in the kitchen she waited for Joe to clear the table and start washing up the crockery while she packed away the remaining couple of slices of chocolate sponge cake into a tin then back into the larder and then wiped the table.

That done, she leant back against the worktop, wondering what to do next. Deciding she could help by drying the dishes, she picked up a tea towel hanging from one of the drawer handles and began wiping.

'I think we'll be fine left to our own devices,' Skye said thoughtfully.

Joe stopped what he was doing and looked at her. 'I'm sure we'll be fine.'

His words were perfectly neutral, but Skye was certain she sensed a tone in his voice that belied his words. Whether he admitted it or not, she believed Joe was unimpressed about sharing the farm and duties with her. Well, she mused, that was just too bad.

9

JOE

Joe pinned Lettie's list onto the noticeboard in the kitchen. 'I'm putting this up here to be sure we don't lose it.'

'Good idea.'

Skye seemed a little uncomfortable and Joe wondered guiltily whether he could have been a bit more welcoming to her on her arrival. Maybe, though, she was as anxious as him about their first couple of days.

For now though he would help Skye settle in. The better the pair of them got along the more chance they had of working well together. This wasn't about him or Skye, this was about Lettie and helping her when she needed him most.

'I thought we could go and see to the damaged gate on the upper field, then feed the animals, if you're up for it,' Joe said, wanting to get some of the work out of the way before he needed to start his next shift in a few hours.

'Sure.'

He fetched the tools he expected to need to fix the catch on the gate and, as they walked up the field, he explained that he would be out for most of the night. 'I hope you won't mind being here alone on your first night,' he said. 'I know it's not ideal but you will have Spud and Brodie's rescue Derek with you, and it's a safe place.'

'I'll be fine,' Skye insisted. 'I'm used to travelling alone and I've got Brodie and Lettie's numbers if I need to call them.'

'I'll give you mine, too,' Joe said. 'I won't be able to answer if I'm out on call but will always phone you back as soon as I can.'

They reached the gate and, after checking what exactly needed to be done, Joe picked up two new heavy screws and a battery-operated heavy-duty screwdriver.

'You weren't pleased to see me here,' Skye said as soon as he finished fixing the damage. 'I'm not sure why, but I hope there's no hard feelings now we're stuck here together for the next few weeks?'

Surprised that Skye was voicing her concerns so directly, he put down the tools and folded his arms. 'I have to admit you're right,' he said, feeling badly for making her feel this way. 'And it was wrong of me. All I can say in my defence is that I had just woken up and was still tired from a long shift at work.'

She went to say something, but Joe continued, 'I know that's no excuse for bad manners.'

'I wouldn't call it that exactly,' she said, and he wasn't sure whether she now felt guilty for bringing the matter up in the first place.

'I would,' Joe said. 'I'm not usually unfriendly and I'm sorry that I came across that way.' He rattled the gate. 'Shall we take this lot back to the barn?' he said, indicating the tools at their feet.

As they carried everything down the hill to the yard, Joe did his best to explain the situation with his mother and his need for some peace and quiet. 'None of which is your fault, of course.'

Skye sighed. 'I see. Well, that explains a lot.' She laughed. 'Your mother sounds a bit of a character.'

Joe groaned. 'That's one way of describing her.' He felt mean talking about his mother in a derogatory fashion. 'I shouldn't be unkind. Faye is lovely really, but she mostly sees things from her point of view and can be a little overbearing at times.'

They walked on for a few steps and Skye bent down to pick up a lone daisy. 'Did you live in France with her for long then?'

'A long time, yes. I loved it there, but needed to go and do my own thing.' He didn't mention his relationship breaking down being a bigger part of wanting to get away and return to Jersey. He'd had several relationships, but Aurélie was the one he thought would be his wife. She had said that was what she wanted many times during their relationship. It still hurt to think that she had told him those things while secretly having an affair with the man she eventually left him for. 'I love it here and, like I mentioned before, I spent some time assisting my uncle on his farm when he needed the extra help, so coming here seemed like a no-brainer.'

'I see.' She thought for a moment and he wondered whether Skye was going to share a little about herself.

When she didn't say anything, he decided to ask her. 'So, what brings you here then?'

He listened while she explained about being away travelling, how she and Zac's fiancé Melody were best friends and how she and her grandmother had been there for each other when her mother had died when she was fifteen.

'You've been through a lot,' he said feeling bad for her.

She shrugged. 'No more than most people,' she said.

He didn't agree, but it wasn't for him to say so. He could tell Skye didn't want his pity and he understood that. Hadn't he felt the same way after his relationship ended? Wasn't that a big reason for leaving France and returning to Jersey?

He checked the time on his watch and saw he had just over an hour before he needed to leave for his shift at the fire station. 'Shall we go and start feeding the animals now?' he suggested. Skye nodded. 'We can start by bringing in the ones who are kept in overnight.'

'Good plan,' Skye agreed. 'Shall we start with the alpacas?'

Joe laughed. 'Because they're easier to round up than the chickens?'

She shrugged and grinned at him. 'I've no idea. I've never even seen a real alpaca before coming here today.'

'I've seen these three many times but I'm not sure I've ever had to do much with them.' He thought back to Lettie's instructions. 'I suppose we should put some food out in their shelter and then take their head collars and lead them back inside.'

'I agree,' she said. 'I know Lettie said they'll come if you call them and they know there's food, but I think they probably need to become more familiar with us first.'

'And learn to trust us a bit,' he suggested, wondering if that's what needed to happen between him and Skye. He noticed Skye watching him silently as if she'd had the same thought as him. 'We'll be fine here together, once we get to know each other better.'

Skye smiled. 'I was thinking the same thing. It's not either of our fault that we've been pushed together and have to live and work in close proximity for the next four weeks, I guess.'

'It isn't. I'm sure we'll make the best of it. We'll soon get into a routine.'

'We will.' She narrowed her eyes. 'And if you turn out to be a snorer then I'll bang on the wall to shut you up.'

'Er, me? How about you?'

She opened her mouth in shock. 'I don't snore, thank you very much.'

'As far as you know.'

She rested her hands on her hips, a slight lift on either end of her lips to show she wasn't really cross. 'I do know.'

'Fine then.' Maybe being here with Skye wasn't going to be quite as bad as he had at first thought. Joe hoped not. He supposed the next few days would be enlightening, for both of them.

10

SKYE

Joe had kindly shown her around other parts of the farm that Lettie hadn't covered. While they walked he had explained about his time off.

'My supervisor was relieved when I finally agreed that some time off was probably what I needed. I know my grandfather died last year, but instead of allowing myself to grieve I threw myself into work, taking on as many shifts as I was allowed, which in hindsight probably wasn't the right way to go about things.'

Skye recalled only too well how losing her mother had felt like being slammed in the gut by a train. 'Sometimes it's easier to try and focus on anything else other than what's happened,' she said knowingly.

He looked at her and her stomach did that annoying flippy thing it tended to do when she caught his eye. He didn't speak immediately and she was about to fill the silence when Joe said, 'I think being here and out of the bungalow he always lived in will make things a little easier. At least I'll have other things to focus on apart from my feelings.'

'That's understandable.' She gazed at the pine trees at the edge of the huge lawn at the back part of the house. 'And you couldn't really be in a more magical place than this if you don't want to dwell on sad things.'

He laughed. Confused by his reaction, Skye turned to him. 'What did I say?'

He smiled and she saw a softness she hadn't noticed before. 'If you think this is beautiful, wait until I show you some of the other places on the island.'

'I like the sound of that,' she admitted. 'What, bays and cliff paths you mean? I saw quite a few stunning places when I looked the island up on the internet.'

'You'll have to wait and see.' He gave her a wink and began walking again before stopping and looking at his watch. 'Hell, I'm going to be late for my shift if I don't go and change now. Sorry to cut this short.'

'It's fine,' she said, thinking that maybe he wasn't that bad after all. With Joe away from the farm, Skye came up with the plan to make the most of his absence to familiarise herself with everything. That way she could go over everything and feel more confident that she could carry out any of the work without his help. 'I'll go and feed the chickens.'

'Great, I'll see you in a bit.'

Joe ran inside and she walked around the side of the house to the large coop near the lower meadow fence. The coop had its own water supply, so there was no need for her to worry about that, so she fetched the scoop Lettie had shown her and filled it with their feed and then walked over to them, calling out for the cute birds.

'Here, chickens. Dinner time.'

She went into the coop to check if any of them had laid eggs and, finding two, was just crouching to leave the coop.

'How's it going?' Joe asked.

Startled to hear his voice, Skye she stood up straight, hitting her head on the wooden bar at the top of the entrance and dropped one of the eggs. 'Bugger.'

'Sorry, I didn't mean to surprise you like that.'

'It's fine, I thought you'd left for your shift, that's all,' she said, turning to see him stride across the driveway from the yard to join her. Skye's voice caught in her throat at the sight of Joe in his trousers and shirt, which although it wasn't tight still outlined his muscular arms, and for a moment all she could do was stare at him.

'Anything wrong?' He frowned, misunderstanding her expression, which was an enormous relief. She tore her eyes away as he quickened his pace.

She rubbed her sore head and pointed to the broken egg. 'That's a great start, isn't it?'

'It was my fault. Anyway, don't worry about it. I'll clean this up.'

'No, you'll be late. I'll do it,' she said.

'I should check there's no damage to your head first.'

'No, it's fine,' she said, mortified. So much for appearing capable. 'It's just a bit of a bump.'

He stared at her for a couple of seconds. 'You've got the right feed, if that's what's bothering you.'

Relieved Joe had assumed her stunned silence was related to what she was doing, she decided to go along with it. 'Thanks. I started feeding them then worried that you might have already done it, or that I was about to give them the wrong food.'

He frowned. 'No, I haven't fed them yet, so you're all right there.' Joe then picked up a handful of the pellets and corn and let it run through his fingers. 'Nope, this is the right stuff.'

She continued feeding them, aware he was still watching her. 'You'd better get going,' she said, hoping he would leave and give her a chance to gather herself. When he didn't speak she looked up at him again. 'What?'

'It's just that... Well, are you sure you'll be fine here tonight? I know it's a safe place, but it's probably a good idea if you lock the front door. If you take the key out, I'll let myself in with the spare one Lettie handed to me.'

It hadn't occurred to her not to lock up before going to bed, but it was good to know he had a key to get in when his shift ended. 'I'll do that then.'

'Great.' He smiled. 'I won't be back until the early hours of tomorrow, but when I am we can probably have breakfast together.'

'Yes, sure. I'll see you in the morning then.' She smiled, only too aware of his close proximity and the appealing scent of whatever soap he had used to shower, only minutes before, going by the dampness of his hair. 'Really, I'll be fine. I'm used to looking after myself. You go and don't give me another thought.'

He shrugged. 'Will do.'

'I hope you have a peaceful shift,' she said, hoping that was the right thing to say. 'I'll see you for breakfast in the morning maybe.'

He gave her a nod, then walked back to the house. He might be a bit annoying at times but it still took all Skye's control not to watch him. Minutes later she heard him drive away but didn't look up to wave in case she made things any more awkward than they already were.

After finishing with the animals, Skye fed Spud and Derek, then made herself a cheese and tomato omelette from two of the eggs Lettie had collected that morning. It was a treat to have eggs this fresh, she thought happily as she ate the first mouthful. Spud was lying in his bed snoring, with Derek dozing nearby. She couldn't help thinking how lucky she was to have landed such an exciting new job, especially in such a beautiful place. She couldn't wait to go for a wander around the nearby area and to the beach. Maybe she could take the dogs for a walk in the morning after getting some of her chores out of the way. She would have to see whether she had time.

After finishing her food, Skye tidied the kitchen and washed up the pan and utensils she had used to make her supper. Yawning, she decided that it would be a good idea to get an early night and, having checked she had removed the key after locking the front door, Skye then refilled the dogs' water bowls. She left the kitchen door open for them to wander around the house, not sure whether that was the right thing to do but not wanting to close him in the kitchen overnight in case he wasn't used to being shut in there.

After showering and changing for bed, Skye went into her bedroom, closed the door and got into her bed. It was incredibly comfortable, she was relieved to discover. The downy pillows and duvet were soft and dreamy. Realising she had left the window open and hadn't drawn the curtains, she decided to leave everything that way and make the most of being woken naturally with the dawn.

Skye lay down and stared across the room through the window at the night sky. She wasn't used to seeing the sky so inky black, nor so many stars. She closed her eyes and after a few seconds wondered what the slight rumbling noise was in the background. It didn't sound like thunder, but it wasn't like anything else she had ever heard.

She sat up and then getting out of bed walked over to the window and leant out slightly, straining her ears to try and fathom what it could be. Deciding it was far away and that neither Spud nor Derek were barking and didn't seem distressed in any way, she went back to bed and closed her eyes. She would ask Joe when he got back to the farm after his shift, she mused before falling into a deep, blissful sleep.

11

JOE

Joe drove straight back to the farm as soon as his shift was over. It had been a quiet night with no incidents and he was glad of it. At least he would have more energy to help Skye on the farm, although he sensed she was happy when he left her in peace to get on with things. He still wasn't sure how the pair of them would be kept busy enough with just the animals to look after. There weren't even that many of them. They were going to have to agree to certain jobs so that they didn't get under each other's feet. He sighed. He would have preferred to be kept busier and have less time to think. Maybe he could find some other way to keep himself occupied?

As he drove through St Peter's Valley it occurred to him that he was looking forward to seeing Skye again, which was unexpected after his initial disappointment at discovering he wouldn't be alone on the farm. During his shift, when he'd had time to reflect on the day's happenings, Joe decided the only thing he could do was try to make the best of the situation.

After all it was a good feeling being able to do something for Lettie and Brodie, who really were two of the nicest people he knew. He also reasoned that it was hardly Skye's fault that Melody and Zac had asked her to step in at the farm. She was clearly as disappointed as him to have to work alongside someone else and it would be easier all round if they could find a way to live at the farm and keep things going while Lettie was otherwise engaged with her pregnancy and new baby and recovery afterwards.

Thinking of Skye at Hollyhock Farm, Joe hoped her first night there alone had gone without a hitch.

He drove into the yard and parked his car, spotting Skye up in the top field with the alpacas. Then, reminding himself that now was as good a time as any to change how he behaved, Joe left his things by the front door and ran up to see her.

'Hey there,' he shouted, giving her a wave and hoping he came across as friendly as he intended. 'I was going to do that?'

She looked over at him, frowned briefly. 'I wasn't sure what time you'd be back so thought I'd do it for you.'

He frowned and resisted the urge to say anything else about it. 'Everything else OK?'

'Fine, thanks. Just letting these three out before seeing to the girls.'

By 'the girls' he knew she meant the elderly cows Lettie's father, Gareth, hadn't wanted to part with when he sold on the herd a decade before to move his farm to grow organic crops instead.

Joe was glad that Skye seemed to be taking her cue from him. He was slightly out of puff when he reached her. 'I thought I was fitter than that,' he joked.

'You're still fitter than me, so I won't tease you about it.'

She seemed refreshed and happier than she had the previous day, he was relieved to note. Maybe they could find a way to make their time here go smoothly? 'Did you sleep well?'

Skye nodded. 'Very, thanks. Although I've been wanting to ask you about something I heard.'

Intrigued to discover what, he asked, 'Shall I guess what it might be?'

'You can.' She smiled and her face lit up. 'But I'm not sure you'll get it.'

'Let me try.' He tried to recall sounds that had seemed unusual to him when he first returned to live on the island. For a moment he was stumped, then it dawned on him. 'Was it the waves?'

'Sorry?'

'Like a rumbling in the distance?'

She nodded. 'That can't have been the sea, could it? Surely it's too far away.'

'It's about a five-minute drive from here, but that's still close. And we're high up here on the farm.' He recalled his surprise on hearing this sound for the first time several years before. 'I'm not sure how loud it was last night, but it can be very loud on occasion when you live on this side of the island.'

'That's amazing.' She listened, looking disappointed. 'I can't hear it over the cars on the road.' She cocked her head in the direction of tractors working the next-door farm. 'It's impossible to hear the sea when there's noise.'

'Don't look so disappointed,' he said. 'You'll more than likely hear it again tonight.'

'I do hope so.'

Joe yawned. 'I'm going to try and get a few hours' sleep, then I'll come and join you.'

'No rush on my account,' Skye said. 'I've got loads to keep me busy and I'll be fine. I'll see you a bit later.'

* * *

Several hours later, showered and dressed, Joe made himself a piece of toast and a coffee and went to find Skye on the farm. He walked up to the fields and studied the potatoes. They looked almost ready, as far as he could tell. He had missed a call from Lettie while he was sleeping and, not wishing to disturb her, he messaged her to apologise for not picking up and saying he was free whenever she liked to call.

As he was studying the crops covering two fields, he heard Skye's voice. Turning, Joe saw her coming towards him, smiling. She gave him a wave.

'I hope you managed to get some sleep,' she said, reaching him. 'You're up much sooner than I expected.'

'Me, too,' he admitted. 'But once I woke I couldn't fall back to sleep, so thought I'd be more useful if I got up.' He explained about missing Lettie's call. 'I haven't heard back from her so I presume she's resting, which is a good thing.'

He had only just finished speaking when Skye grinned and pointed in the direction of the driveway. 'Is that her, do you think?'

Looking at the car, Joe sighed. 'It is. She's probably come to check that we're not at loggerheads and to make sure we haven't mislaid any of her animals.'

'I doubt that very much.' Skye laughed. 'She probably just wants to see how we're getting on with the work and offer sage advice.'

'We should save her walking up here and go to the yard to speak to her,' he suggested, finishing his coffee. 'Sorry, I should have thought to bring you one of these.'

Skye raised her hand. 'I'm fine, thanks.' She held up a metal bottle. 'I usually carry this water bottle with me.'

'You're good,' he said, impressed.

'I do my best.' She smiled. 'I suppose I'm used to keeping

hydrated in hot countries and just got into the habit of carrying water with me.'

'Don't come down,' Lettie bellowed. 'I'll come to you.'

'No, it's fine,' Joe argued, not wanting her to overexert herself.

'I need to see the state of the crops,' she replied. 'Wait there for me.'

She reached them a few minutes later, slightly out of breath but seeming happy to be there. Joe and Skye accompanied Lettie as she walked along the top of the first and then the second field. They waited for her thoughts.

Lettie stopped and folded her arms. 'I've just come from Uncle Leonard's farm. He took me to visit another farmer's field in the next parish. He's also growing this crop and his look the same as these. He's going to start harvesting the week after next, so I suggested he aim to do the same thing here as soon as his fields are finished.'

'Shouldn't they be done at the same time?' Skye asked, presuming all crops took the same length of time to grow.

Lettie shook her head. 'His fields were planted up a couple of weeks before mine.'

'Was there a reason for that?' Skye asked, looking intrigued.

'Some of his fields are what we call cotils.'

Joe nodded. 'Steep sloping fields facing south or west that get the winter sun. They are the tastiest ones.' His mouth watered at the thought of those first Jersey Royals of the season.

Skye grinned. 'That's right. Also, Uncle Leonard's team of farmworkers came straight here to help me after finishing planting his crop.'

'That makes sense.' Skye's cheeks reddened and Joe sensed she felt embarrassed for asking the question.

Not wishing her to feel silly, Joe said, 'I was wondering the same thing.'

He felt her look at him but kept his focus on Lettie. 'How are you feeling?'

She shrugged. 'I'm fine. Missing this place a bit, and Spud. I was thinking about taking him to the cottage but Brodie worried that Spud might find it a little restrictive after living on the farm.'

'I promise you there's no need to worry about him,' Joe assured her. 'We're taking very good care of both dogs. Aren't we, Skye?'

'We certainly are.'

As if on cue, Spud and Derek raced outside, wagging their tails, and ran up to Lettie, nudging her thigh for a cuddle. She bent down to oblige.

'You do look happy enough, boys,' she said, kissing their furry heads.

Lettie stood upright and beamed at Joe and Skye. 'I do hope you won't be too bored with just the animals to take care of, but I couldn't have left you to deal with the harvesting because that would be taking advantage. Anyway, I can't tell you how grateful I am to the pair of you.'

'I'm glad not to have to worry about the potatoes,' Joe admitted, aware how important harvesting the crop was to island farmers.

Lettie hugged them both and thanked them again before leaving to return to Brodie's cottage.

'I've been thinking,' he said to Skye as Lettie's car disappeared down the drive. 'We should prepare a rota rather than just agreeing who does what job.'

'Good idea,' she said as they began to walk back into the

house. 'I would hate for one of us to not do something presuming the other had carried out the work.'

'Exactly. I'd never forgive myself if we forgot to feed any of the animals.'

Skye shuddered. 'Oh, don't say that. OK, let's go and find some paper and a pen and sort this out straight away.'

Finally agreeing on who should do what around the farm, Skye put down the pen and pushed the piece of paper towards Joe. 'Please check it and then if you're happy I'll stick it up on the fridge under one of the magnets Lindy has there. At least that way we won't lose it.'

He sensed her watching him as he lowered his head and read her notes. 'Looks fine to me.'

She smiled, then stood and took the sheet and pinned it up on the fridge, looking satisfied with their work. Skye seemed unsure about something. 'I think I'll go to my room and read for a bit,' she said, pushing in her chair and taking her mug to the sink. 'I'll see you in a couple of hours?'

Relieved to be left alone and not having to think what to say next, Joe nodded. 'Sounds good to me.'

Joe was beginning to feel a little more comfortable being at the farm. Even though they still had awkward silences, Joe sensed Skye had resolved to do her best for Lettie, just like he had. She was diligent and, like him, wanted to do the work well. Most of all, she seemed to enjoy spending time in her own company. He supposed it was because she had spent six months travelling solo and only having herself to rely on in different situations.

Deciding to try and get to know her better, Joe decided to make supper and, hoping she liked lasagne and salad, drove to the village to do some shopping.

'Thanks for supper,' Skye said later as he carried through

their drinks and joined her in the living room after they had tidied the kitchen. 'It was delicious.'

He was glad she thought so. 'It wasn't too bad, was it?'

'Ooh, thanks,' Skye said, taking the glass from him and having a sip. 'I could do with this.'

'It's been a long day, hasn't it.' Maybe if he had spent more than three hours catching up on his sleep earlier he wouldn't feel so tired.

'No shift tonight?' Skye drank a little more.

He shook his head. 'No. I'm now off work for four weeks.' He still needed to find a way to keep himself busy.

'You must be looking forward to having some time off work.'

'Yes, I suppose so, although I'm used to keeping busy and with the pair of us taking care of the animals that isn't going to happen unless I find some other way to keep myself occupied.' Even as he spoke he knew he could fill a lot of that time helping his mother redecorate the bungalow, but removing wallpaper that reminded him so much of his grandfather was not something he felt he could cope with just yet. Maybe he would feel differently after his time off work?

They chatted for a bit longer but Joe was finding it more and more difficult to keep his eyes open. He yawned, covering his mouth with his free hand. 'Sorry, I don't mean to be rude.'

'No problem.' Skye frowned. 'You must be shattered after not getting any sleep after your shift.'

'I am a bit,' he admitted.

They finished their drinks and went up to their rooms.

'Sleep well,' Skye said. 'I'll see you in the morning.'

'You, too.'

Half an hour later Joe lay in his bed staring out of the window at the almost black sky. The stars were out in force tonight and the sea was louder than usual. He wondered if maybe that was what could be keeping him awake. He might live as close to the sea in St Brelade but the sound of the waves wasn't nearly as loud as it was from St Ouen's Bay, probably because it was a bit wilder on this part of the island.

Intrigued as to whether Skye might be awake listening to the sound, Joe got out of bed and walked over to his window. Looking to the right, he saw that her window was open too and was about to go back to bed when he spotted her hand resting on the window frame.

'Listening to the waves?' he asked.

Skye laughed. 'How did you guess?'

'Because I'm doing the same.'

'You should be sleeping.'

He heard the amusement in her voice and realised he was enjoying their banter. 'The sound of your waves is keeping me awake.'

She laughed again. 'My waves? You can't blame your insomnia on me. I'm not even from here.'

'I suppose not.' Stifling a yawn, he added, 'Maybe I should give it another go.'

'Good idea,' Skye said. 'We have a lot to do tomorrow and you won't have time to stop and take a nap if you're tired.'

'Yes, ma'am.' Feeling happy but sleepy finally, he stared out at the stars and listened to the waves, aware he was starting to enjoy being at the farm much more. 'I'll see you in the morning then. Night.'

'Goodnight, Joe. Sleep well.'

He walked back to his bed and got in. He hoped the experience of doing something completely different would satisfy his need to feel like he had achieved something, and helping Lettie out at such an important time could be the answer.

He closed his eyes, imagining Skye still staring out at the

window and wondered what had really brought her here. There was a loneliness about her that he couldn't help noticing. He turned on his side and moved his pillow until it was perfect. Could it be that he recognised the loneliness in her because he felt like he was missing out on something, or that perfect someone too? It was a bit presumptuous of him to think of her feeling lost, but what if he was right?

What if he was wrong though? He decided not to think about it any longer and cleared his mind. He was overtired and needed to sleep, otherwise he would be no help to Skye or Lettie tomorrow.

12

SKYE

Skye woke earlier than she had expected. It was still dark outside and the clocks weren't due to go forward an hour until the end of March. She much preferred the lighter mornings after the clocks changed each spring, and summer couldn't come soon enough. She sat up and stared out at the dusky pink and salmon coloured sky. She shouldn't wish away the days, because when the summer did come she would be back in Edinburgh or somewhere else. Either way she would no longer be here.

She thought of Joe sleeping soundly in the next room. She wasn't sure if it was because both their windows were open, or if his snoring was loud, but she rather liked hearing him peacefully sleeping nearby. He was a good man; she knew that much now. Kind too to offer to help Lettie so readily. Skye wondered if there had every been anything between the pair of them to make him want to help her so much. Or maybe Lettie was simply a good friend of his and he was determined to help out in a crisis.

Skye knew that she had her grandmother and of course her

best friend, Melody, there for her whenever she needed them, and for that she was grateful. It was lonely only having Gran left as family. She wondered what it must be like to have a large, close family you could call upon whenever you needed them.

Enough. There was little point in wishing for something that was impossible. It was time to get up and go and start feeding the animals while Joe let the cows and alpacas into their paddocks. She needed to check the sheep and goats and make sure their water was fine. After that she had stalls to muck out and wanted to do some of it before returning to the farmhouse and eating breakfast with Joe.

Dressing and hurrying outside with Spud and Derek in tow, Skye heard Joe calling to the alpacas as he let them out of their stall and took them to the lower meadow. She recalled the dream she'd had the previous night. It had been odd, as most dreams were, but in this one she had kissed Joe. She cringed remembering how in her dream she had been the one to insti-gate the kiss by getting up from the sofa in the living room where they had been drinking and going to sit on his lap, taking his bottle of lager from his hand and placing it down on the table next to him before kissing him hard on the lips. A tingle ran through her, just as Joe called for the alpacas once more.

She went into the barn and lifted the lid of the chicken pellets, picking up the scoop.

'What the hell?' She shook her head, patting Spud when she noticed him tilting his head, trying to understand what she was going on about. 'It's OK, boy,' she soothed. 'I'm just embar-rassing myself in my sleep now.' She led the way to the back of the barn and opened the small storeroom. 'Let's get those chickens fed, shall we?'

'You talking to me, or one of the dogs?' Joe said, striding into the barn.

Hearing his voice, Skye jumped. 'How are you here already?'

He frowned, looking confused. 'I was on my way back to get the girls when I heard you talking. I've put the coffee on ready for us when we go back inside.'

Skye realised she was blushing and focused her attention on filling the scoop with pellets for the chickens, so Joe didn't notice. It was bad enough having a dream about him without him finding out about it. They were starting to get along well, and she had no intention of ruining that.

'It's still early,' she explained, hoping he would think her not quite awake yet. 'I was in a world of my own then.'

'Talking to Spud here.'

She turned to look at Joe, seeing him crouch down and cuddle the dog who – by the way his tail was wagging – clearly loved him.

'He's my buddy, aren't you, mate?' Joe straightened up. 'Have you fed the dogs yet or would you like me to?'

Realising they had forgotten to add the dogs' mealtimes to their list, Skye made a mental note to do so. 'I was going to feed them when we went in to make breakfast but you can go feed them once you've finished taking the cows out and I'll join you both soon.'

He stared at her for a moment before smiling. 'Shall I make us a fry-up?'

His expectant look was so appealing that Skye thought her heart would leap out of her throat. 'Great idea,' she said, trying her best to sound cool. 'I won't be much longer.'

She watched him go to let out the cows with Spud and Derek running on ahead of him. How was that man single? Skye wondered. He was gorgeous to look at and once he let you in a bit was actually a nice bloke too. Maybe there was something untoward about him that she hadn't discovered yet. She hoped not.

By the time she reached the kitchen the smell of bacon and eggs filled her nostrils. Her stomach grumbled noisily, no doubt to encourage her to sit and eat just in case she hadn't been going to.

'Take a seat,' Joe said from the cooker. She did as she was told and watched him work, a tea towel slung lazily over his shoulder as he hummed something she couldn't place, happily to himself.

'You're used to doing this by the looks of things.' She wondered if she should make them both a drink while he was busy cooking.

'Coffee's ready,' he said, making her wonder if she had shared her thoughts out loud. 'Won't be a second.' He stepped back and indicated two pans, one with bacon sizzling in it and the other with four perfectly fried eggs. 'There's beans in there and I've also done us a tomato and some mushrooms. Anything you don't want?'

She laughed and shook her head. 'Nope. I can assure you I have a healthy appetite.'

He gave her a look she couldn't decipher then began serving up their food onto two plates.

Once the toast popped up in the toaster and they were both seated and ready to start eating, he smiled.

'This looks amazing,' Skye said happily. 'Thank you.'

'My pleasure,' Joe said, putting a forkful of food into his mouth and chewing. 'I like to see people enjoying their food.'

'Doesn't everybody?'

He shrugged. 'I think my mother's been on a diet her entire adult life.'

Skye continued eating and wondered if maybe the look he

had given her was more to do with relief that she wasn't going to be a picky eater.

'I was thinking,' Joe said after drinking some coffee, 'later, when we've done all we need to, I could take you for a drive.'

'Really?'

'Yes. You haven't left the farm yet. It doesn't seem fair, or right, that you shouldn't get to enjoy all this island has to offer.'

'I'd love that. Thanks.'

'We might as well take whatever chance we have to visit some of the places I think you shouldn't miss.'

'Like where?' she asked, intrigued.

'Well, some of the beaches for a start. Then there's the usual visitor haunts like Devil's Hole, Jersey Zoo, um, the cliff paths. There are many historical sites to visit too – the castles, for instance, and there's the museums.'

'Crikey. For a small place there seems to be a lot to take in.'

Joe seemed pleased with her observation. 'There is. I haven't even mentioned the restaurants and bars yet, but I doubt we'll get to see most of them. One of the things I do think you should see are the tides when they're very high. Spring tides are impressive for the most part and you shouldn't miss seeing one of those.'

She ate another mouthful of toast. 'I'm happy to let you be my guide. Anything you show me will be interesting, I'm sure.'

Joe smiled at her from across the table, making her insides do a little flip. 'I'd wait until I've shown you around before you say that. I might have a completely different idea to you about what's interesting.'

'Good point,' Skye said, pulling a face and making him laugh.

13

JOE

He was glad Skye had been open to going out with him and seeing parts of the island. As much as they might have been thrown together, neither of them had planned for this to happen. He loved the island and knew that Lettie would want him to look after Skye and show her around. Now that Melody and Zac seemed to be serious it made sense that Skye would also be on the periphery of the Torel family and, as he was too, to a certain extent, then he should ensure that he did all he could to help Skye make the most of every moment she was on the island.

After breakfast they finished the outstanding tasks from their list and now he was sitting in his car, and waiting for Skye to freshen up and join him.

'So,' she said, appearing at the passenger door, looking excited as she got in. 'Where to first?'

'I thought we should start on the other side of the island. I could drive you to a few bays and then around the north coast. We could stop at one of the places for a bite to eat for our lunch, then carry on making our way back towards St Ouen, ending up at the farm in time to take Spud and Derek out for a walk and check on all the animals. How does that sound?'

'Great fun,' she said, fastening her seat belt.

He drove off wishing they could take the dogs with them but aware that they would probably be happier left in the warmth of the kitchen. 'It's a bit nippy today, isn't it?'

Skye nodded. 'I guess so.'

Joe looked at her. 'You're not cold?'

'I'm from Scotland, Joe,' she reminded him. 'The weather here is incredibly mild. Almost summer-like.'

He saw the glint in her eye and knew she was joking. 'My blood must be much thinner than yours.'

'I suppose it's not surprising if you've lived here and in France all your life. I'm used to warm climates since I've been travelling but I grew up in Edinburgh and suppose I'm more comfortable with lower temperatures.'

'I can see you're going to think me a bit of a wimp,' he teased as it dawned on him he was enjoying spending time with her.

'Yes, I have a feeling I might.'

He wasn't really that cold but there was a nip in the air. Summer was his favourite season and as far as he was concerned it couldn't come quick enough, but they had a few months to go until then.

His phone rang and, always on alert for a call, Joe indicated as soon as they reached a safe place to pull over on the road. 'Sorry, I'd better see who this is.'

'No problem.' Skye picked up his phone from the cubbyhole in the dashboard and held it ready for when he had parked the car.

He took the phone from her. 'Thanks.' He looked at the screen and, seeing it was his mother, sighed. Faye had a knack of calling at the wrong moment and usually wanted him to do something for her. 'Hopefully this won't take a moment and then we can get back to sightseeing.'

He answered the call, aware from experience that Faye would continue to ring until he picked up unless she was distracted in some way.

'Hi, Mum, what's up?'

'I need you pick up a couple of bits for me at the village shop and drop them off at the bungalow.'

He thought of Roger with little else to do apart from Faye's bidding and had to swallow his irritation. 'Why can't you or Roger pop to the corner shop? It's only at the end of the road and sells most things you should need.'

'I know, Joe, but Roger's gone out for a walk somewhere and I've run out of tea and milk. You know how rattled I get when I can't have my tea.'

He did. 'I would have thought after all your years in France you'd be used to drinking coffee by now.' Before she could answer, unable to resist he added, 'Anyway, wouldn't you enjoy a short walk to the shop?'

Noticing Skye wave to get his attention, he raised his eyebrows and held his phone away from him. 'Sorry about this,' he whispered.

'It's fine. I was just going to say that I don't mind the detour if you don't.'

'It's not that,' Joe said, unsure how to finish his sentence without admitting he would rather not go to the bungalow with Skye and deal with his mother's excitement that he might have found a girlfriend. She seemed to have a mission to see him in a long-term relationship and as far as Joe was concerned he was happy as he was right now. Not that he wouldn't mind seeing someone again, he thought, just that he would rather the poor girl not have to put up with Faye's incessant questions when she did meet her.

'You'd rather I not be there,' Skye whispered.

He could see she was trying to hide her hurt, assuming he didn't want to see his mother with Skye in tow. 'It's not what you think.'

Skye smiled. 'Really, it's fine. It was just a thought.'

'No, it's just—'

'Joe?' Faye shouted. 'Are you still there?'

Aware Faye was calling for him, he rolled his eyes and brought the phone nearer to his face once again. 'Sorry, Mum. You were saying?' He had no idea what she had been talking about, but assumed it had something to do with why she was insisting he did her shopping at that moment.

'Well, I did wonder. I thought for a moment there I was talking to myself.'

'Sorry, Mum.' He didn't like to admit that she had been. 'I'm listening. Carry on.'

'It's my sciatica. Damn thing has flared up again and I'm in agony. If I was fine I would have been happy to go to the shop and get to know the people running the place. You know how friendly I always am. And I'd be out walking with Roger right now rather than stuck here in this miserable place.'

He didn't like to remind her that the house she was being so rude about was his and that he had moved out to let her and her husband have the home to themselves.

'Fine. Let me know what you want and I'll get it for you. I won't be able to stop for too long though because I'm out with a work colleague who's new to the island and I'm supposed to be taking her on a tour of some of the sights.'

'Her?' The one word was filled with his mother's intrigue.

He closed his eyes, desperate not to give in to his irritation.

'Mum, we work together, nothing more.' He smiled at Skye and, seeing she was staring out of the window, assumed she was lost in thought taking in the scenery.

'No need to give you a list,' she said, sounding overly cheerful all of a sudden. 'I'll call them and ask them to put everything by. I'm sure they'll do that for me.'

'I'm sure they will.' He didn't doubt it for a moment. Faye could be very persuasive when she was at her most charming. 'I'll be with you in about twenty minutes.'

'Sorry about the detour, Skye.' Not wishing to waste her time, he tried to think how to make the most of having to go out of their way. 'Although, there are a couple of places like Noirmont and Ouaisné that I'm sure you'd enjoy visiting, but we can do those another day.'

He caught Skye staring at him, an unreadable expression on her face.

'Would you rather go there today?'

She shook her head. 'Not at all. I'm in your hands. You decide what we see and when. It's not like I have a clue what's here anyway.'

He must have been mistaken. 'Great. East it is then. We'll go there as soon as we're done at Mum's.'

Mum's? That hadn't taken long for him to forget it was his house and now automatically think of the bungalow as his mother's home.

'Sounds perfect.'

They turned into the road and, relieved to spot a parking space just outside the store, Joe parked. 'Is there anything I can get for you while I'm here?' he asked.

Skye shook her head. 'I'm good, thanks.'

Joe hurried inside. 'Hi, Joe,' the shopkeeper, Mal, said cheerfully. 'Not like you to drive here?'

Joe sighed. 'I'm housesitting at a friend's farm while they're away,' he explained. 'My mother and stepfather have moved into my place. In fact, she was going to phone through an order for me to collect.' Aware not everyone would accommodate such a thing, Joe decided to apologise for any inconvenience. 'I'll understand if you decided it's not something you wish to do.'

The jovial man shook his head. 'Not at all. I was only too happy to oblige. Faye explained she now lives in Gerry's place.'

Hearing the man mention his beloved grandfather, Joe smiled. 'That's right.'

'Sorry, it's your place now.' He crossed his arms and leant against the counter. 'I suppose I've been referring to it as Gerry's place for decades and keep forgetting he's gone.'

Joe couldn't miss Mal's sadness at his grandfather's passing and somehow it helped ease his own grief slightly to be reminded how loved his grandfather was by so many other islanders. Joe listened as Mal reminisced while he checked through a bag of groceries Faye had requested and began ringing them up on the till.

'Great chap, Gerry was. Sorely missed around here and at pétanque. We won the league once with him on the team.'

'Really?' Joe didn't recall his grandfather ever mentioning playing pétanque.

'Yes, he was a good 'un.' Mal finished with the items and rang up the total. 'That'll be fifty-three pounds and seventeen pence, mate.'

Joe took his card from his jeans pocket and paid for his mother's food. He lifted the bag off the counter. 'Thanks for doing this. I appreciate it.'

'No problem at all,' Mal said. 'I told Faye that next time I can drop her shopping off if you or she can't fetch it.'

Joe wondered if his mother had thought to mention that she

did in fact have a husband who would usually be happy to do the shopping for her. Or, Joe mused, maybe he wasn't. It wasn't as if Joe knew much about him at all, he realised, apart from his first name.

He thanked Mal once more and took the shopping out to the car. 'Sorry for the wait,' he said to Skye.

'It's fine. I'm perfectly happy sitting here.'

'The house is only a little further along here,' he explained.

Joe drove down the lane to the bungalow and had to carefully pass a postal van parked in the narrow lane before he pulled up outside. He and Skye got out of the car and realised the man was leaning against the garden wall with his leg tilted at an odd angle.

'Is everything all right?' Joe asked, wondering if the man needed his help. Spotting his mother standing nearby for the first time, he asked her the same thing.

'We're fine,' Faye explained. 'Stan here was just showing me some exercises to help with my sciatica.'

'I was just delivering that parcel for Faye,' Stan said. 'And asked why she was having difficulty walking. I've been demonstrating a few exercises I learnt at Pilates. Going to lessons has been an enormous help to me since I got sciatica. I was telling Faye that once she's in less pain she should try doing this, gentle like. Then, when she's better she should come to the classes at the parish hall. It only costs a few quid each time and I can't tell you how much it's helped me. I'm always happiest on a Wednesday when I've finished a class.'

Liking the idea and thinking of this as a way for his mother and maybe Roger to make a few friends on the island, Joe hoped to encourage her. 'Sounds like a good idea to me, Mum. What do you think?'

She pursed her lips. 'I might give it a go. No harm in trying, I suppose.'

An elderly lady he recognised as Mrs de la Mare walked up to them. 'What's happening here then?' she asked. 'Oh, Stan. You've not hurt yourself again, have you?'

'No.' Stan laughed, lowering his leg. 'I was explaining to Faye here—'

'I'm afraid I'm going to have to go into the house and sit down. My leg is rather sore standing here. Thanks for your suggestion, Stan,' Faye said, smiling at them. 'I'll certainly give it some thought.' She turned to the neighbour. 'Nice to meet you.'

Joe gave a nod to the pair of them and followed his mother inside, standing by the open doorway to let Skye walk into the house. 'Sorry about this,' he whispered.

She seemed amused rather than annoyed, he noticed with relief.

As soon as they were in the kitchen, Joe put the bag of groceries onto the worktop. 'Here you go, Mum. All safely delivered.'

His mother didn't seem interested in what he had brought. He turned to see her smiling at Skye.

'Now, who is this friend of yours, Joe, and why haven't I met her before?'

* * *

Joe pulled an apologetic face at Skye as he drove them away from the bungalow an hour later. 'Sorry about that. Mum is lovely but she can be a bit nosy sometimes, especially where I'm concerned.'

Skye grinned. 'She only wants the best for you, I imagine.

Isn't that what most mothers would do if their child brought someone they don't know to their house?'

'I suppose you're right.'

'Anyway, I liked Faye.'

'You did?' Joe was surprised how happy her comment made him. 'I'm glad.'

'She's such a character. She reminded me of Patsy a bit. Don't you think they have some similar qualities?'

He thought about the strong, positive, fun woman who came to the island last summer with Melody. The grandmother and her granddaughter had made a massive impact on everyone connected to Hollyhock Farm.

'Yes, I think you're right,' he agreed, slowing the car to an almost crawl as they reached the end of the traffic jam near Beaumont.

Once past the filter-in turn, the traffic began moving more quickly. Eventually, they reached Gorey, and Joe hoped Skye was going to enjoy the places he had planned to take her.

'Look at that!' Skye pointed through the windscreen at the majestic castle rising high above them as they drove along the road from Gorey village.

'What do you think?' Recalling Skye was used to seeing the grandiose Edinburgh Castle, he added, 'I suppose you're used to seeing castles in Scotland. I imagine this is nothing compared to those.'

She laughed. 'In this instance I am impressed. That's a pretty castle and it's very imposing the way it stands so high above those lovely terraced houses below it on the pier.'

'We can go in if you like, but I thought today we could just stop on the road and take some photos. Maybe go down to the small bay behind the castle green.'

'I'm happy to do whatever you think.'

'Fine,' Joe said happily. 'Then we'll start our tour with that.'

Once down on the beach he recalled part of the movie that was filmed there in the fifties. 'Do you know Rock Hudson filmed *Sea Devils* in this very bay in the fifties?'

When Skye didn't respond he looked over his shoulder to check she wasn't having trouble following him down. 'You OK?'

'Fine,' she said thoughtfully. 'I was just trying to think where I'd heard that name before.'

He recalled his mother being shocked when he hadn't known who the actor was either when she first told him this snippet of information. 'There was a series about Hollywood. He was one of the actors depicted in it.'

She frowned and he could tell she was thinking about what he had said. 'That's it. I remember watching that a couple of years ago.'

They walked along the small beach and Skye made him stop for a couple of selfies.

'Smile then,' Skye said, holding up her mobile to take a photo of them with the rolling waves in the background.

'I thought I was.' Joe laughed.

She took the photo. 'Do you know when I first saw you at the farm and realised who you were, it never occurred to me that we could ever be friends.'

Her comment surprised him initially, then he thought back to how they had both reacted to each other when he had gone to her hotel room and tried to persuade her to leave the hotel. Disappointed to discover her opinion of him, Joe decided he would nonetheless need to respect them and keep any feelings he had for her hidden.

'Don't you agree?'

He looked down at her pretty face and wished she saw him differently. 'I do,' he fibbed, forcing a smile.

'This is fun,' she said, nudging him lightly on his arm. 'Although I can't help feeling a little guilty about leaving the farm when I'm only on the island to help look after the place.'

Not wishing the excitement of Skye's day to be ruined, he frowned. 'Lettie's not going to expect us to be there all the time,' he said. 'In fact, I'm sure she'd be surprised if I didn't show you around the island. She would definitely want me to make sure you have time to enjoy yourself away from work while you're here.'

'In that case, I won't worry so much, but we shouldn't be away too long.'

'I agree. To be honest, nothing is that far away from anywhere here and at the most it probably only takes twenty-five to thirty minutes to drive from one end of the island to the other.'

Skye stopped walking and stared out to sea. 'I forget it's only a small island. I'm used to it taking ages to travel from one place to another at home.'

She breathed in deeply through her nose, slowly exhaling afterwards. Joe noticed her eyes were closed and did the same. Even if she did only see him as a friend, this was relaxing and he decided he should take note of how someone who saw the island for the first time viewed everything. He would make the time to stop and appreciate the sights and sounds of the beaches more often. Skye was good company and he realised he could easily get used to days like these.

14

SKYE

'Thanks for today, Joe,' Skye said as she got out of the car as soon as he had parked up in the yard. 'I had fun.'

'I'm glad.' He stepped out of the car and walked with her towards the front door. 'Any time you wish to go out again, just let me know.'

'I definitely will.'

She unlocked the front door and had to grab hold of each side of the doorframe when Spud, then Derek ran into her, wagging their tails with delight.

'Someone is happy to see you back at the farm.' Joe laughed. 'You OK?'

Skye nodded, wondering why she felt so emotional after such a perfect time out with Joe. 'Just about.' Wanting to gather herself before saying anything further, Skye bent down to ruffle the dogs' fur, then she gave them a cuddle. 'I don't think I've ever had such a warm welcome before. I could get used to this, boys.'

There was an awkward silence between them she wasn't sure how to fill.

'Let's go and change,' Joe suggested. 'We can see to the animals and then plan what we're doing for supper.'

Grateful to him for changing the subject without questioning her, Skye nodded. She really had got the wrong first impression of Joe and was glad they now got along well. Feeling a rush of enthusiasm, Skye took the first two steps up the staircase. 'Last one up to the attic has to muck out the cow barn.'

'Hey.' Joe laughed. 'You cheat!'

She took off up the rest of the stairs, sensing him close behind her, enjoying feeling carefree for the first time since her return from travelling. As much as she loved seeing her gran again when she was in Edinburgh briefly, something had been missing for her. Skye wondered whether she would ever feel at home anywhere, or if she would need to keep going away to feel fulfilled. She pushed the thought aside, determined not to overthink at least for today. She reached the first floor, then, taking the slightly narrower stairs to the attic, she heard his footsteps right behind her and couldn't help laughing as she arrived slightly out of breath when she reached the top landing.

'I'll remember not to fall for that one again,' he grumbled, attempting to frown but failing miserably.

Skye went to her bedroom, unable to stop grinning. She sat on the bed getting her breath back. It really had been a pleasurable day and she hoped there would be several more before her time here at the farm came to an end in a little under four weeks. She heard Joe singing something to himself and tried to work out what it was. Unable to recognise the song, she walked over to her window, opened it and leant on the sill, gazing out at the glorious view of the fields with the animals grazing happily. She really loved it here and was grateful to Melody and Zac for thinking of her and arranging for her to come to Hollyhock Farm.

Hearing Joe leave his room, Skye thought she had better hurry and change to go and help him with the rest of their chores. As she slipped off her jeans and replaced them with an old pair of cargo pants she had brought with her, Skye wondered whether she would get to meet Lettie's parents, Lindy and Gareth, before she left. She would love to know the people who had spent their lives building up this beautiful place. How lucky they were to have spent their working life on land as beautiful as this.

She heard Joe calling her name. Smiling, she went back to the window and peered down to the yard, her heart fluttering to see him looking up at her, Spud standing next to him.

'Are you going to come and help, or should I do your bit too?'

She knew he was teasing but, pressing a forefinger up to her lips, pretended to give his question some thought. 'Let me see. Would I rather recline on my bed in my boudoir and read the latest book by my favourite author, or come and help you muck out stinky stalls in the barn?'

Joe laughed. 'I know I lost our unplanned race but you did make up the rules.'

'So I did. I suppose it was a little mean catching you unawares. Fine, I'll be down in a minute.'

'We'll get started while we wait.'

Skye watched amused as he and Spud ambled over to the barn. Joe hummed something and Skye couldn't help but watch him, admiring the way his sweatshirt, as loose as it was, still somehow accentuated his muscular arms. She sighed as he disappeared into the barn and turned away from the window. If only her time here was for longer than four measly weeks.

'Behave yourself,' she murmured, remembering she was trying to stay upbeat. Anyway she was here to work not drool after Joe, and as far as she knew he might have a girlfriend somewhere who would not appreciate the latest farmhand at Hollyhock Farm following her boyfriend around the place like a lost sheep.

Anyway, the last thing she needed to do was fall for him and end up having a fling and going home pregnant like her mother had done. Skye shivered at the thought. Not that she had any intention of sleeping with him or anyone else while she was here, and if she did she would ensure they used protection.

Why hadn't her mother been more careful about not falling pregnant? From what she'd gathered from the odd comment her mother had made, the relationship with Skye's dad had been brief, even though the one thing her mother had said about him was that she had loved him very much. Poor Mum, Skye thought, wishing she could spend just one day with her to hug her and ask a few questions about him. She didn't know all the facts about what had happened between her parents. Hell, she knew barely any at all. She had no intention of judging her mum for her choices, Skye just wished she had left some indication about who her dad was.

15

JOE

They had been working on the barn for a few minutes, when Joe looked over at the pretty dark-haired woman with the even darker eyes. Skye was a bit of an enigma, he decided. There was something mysterious about her and he couldn't help being intrigued and wanting to know more. Was he just being nosy? Probably, and he hated nosiness. There was something bothering her though; he was sure of it. But what? He noticed her lost in thought quite a few times that day and wondered if it would be rude of him to ask if anything was wrong.

She suddenly looked up at him. 'What's the matter? Am I doing something wrong?'

Shocked to have been spotted staring at her, Joe went to say no, then thought now might be the perfect opportunity to discover what was on Skye's mind.

'You've seemed a little out of sorts today, I noticed.' Damn, that wasn't what he had meant to say. He saw a look of annoyance cross her face and struggled to find the words he was searching for. 'Sorry, that came out wrong. More...'

'What do you mean? I've really enjoyed today actually.'

Wanting to rescue the moment, he shook his head and crossed the barn to where she was standing scowling at him.

'No. Nothing like that.' He winced. 'All I meant was that sometimes you seem thoughtful, sad sort of, as if you have a lot on your mind. I just wondered if there's anything I could to do help if there was something wrong.'

She stared into his eyes with such an intensity he wasn't sure if she was angry or simply trying to process his comment and decide how to answer.

Eventually Skye shrugged. 'I found out information about my parents before coming here. I haven't had time to decide what to do about it yet and it's thrown me slightly.'

So that was it. 'Ah, parents. I've had a few issues in that department too. Any new family information that changes your life always takes some getting used to.'

Skye frowned, seeming surprised. 'How do you know it was big news?'

Had he guessed wrong? 'Sorry, I shouldn't have assumed.'

She shrugged and leant back against the stall wall, folding her arms. 'You're right though. It was a little surprising and unexpected.'

He knew Skye didn't have anyone here to confide in and although they hadn't known each other long wanted her to feel she had someone to turn to should she need to.

'Do you want to tell me about it? I hope you know I'd always keep anything you tell me to myself.'

Her expression softened. 'Thanks, I appreciate that. Can I have a think about it?'

Joe nodded. 'Take all the time you need.' He laughed. 'It looks like you'll be stuck with me for a while here anyway.'

'Thanks, Joe. I appreciate the offer.'

He looked around them. 'While you're thinking, shall we carry on and finish this fun job?'

Skye groaned and picked up her shovel, ready to scoop up another load of animal poo to dump it in the wheelbarrow. 'When I agreed to come here,' she said, tipping some onto the pile, 'I pictured green meadows filled with wildflowers, strolls on the beach, eating comforting farm food.'

'Isn't that what you got?' he asked, happy to hear more cheer in her voice again.

'True, but it didn't occur to me that I'd spend so much time clearing up manure.'

'I imagine Zac forgot to mention that bit when he was trying to sell the idea to you.'

'It was Melody who persuaded me.' She grinned, stopping and resting her hands on the wooden handle for a moment. 'Then again, she seems to remember everything about this place fondly.'

'Not this, I imagine.' Joe looked over at her. 'It's not that bad though, I hope.'

He waited for her reaction, relieved when Skye immediately shook her head.

'Don't be daft. I've done far worse jobs than this, including cleaning out dog kennels during some of my school holidays and helping a friend's mum with her cleaning business for a few months. I wasn't very good. Anyway, at least the views and accommodation here are amazing.'

'They are a welcome treat for me too, I have to admit.' He wondered how his mother and Roger were getting on with the decorating now Faye was suffering from sciatica. Amused, Joe imagined her using the walking stick she had been leaning on when he visited her to point out any bits of painting Roger might have missed. 'I don't miss being at my place.'

'You mean it hasn't been all that bad staying here with me then?'

'Mmm, I'm not so sure about that.' It was an effort to hide his amusement at her expression.

Seeing Skye open her mouth pretending to be shocked, Joe laughed. 'Well, maybe it's not all that bad,' he teased.

'To be fair, after seeing me here the day after you had tried to get me to evacuate the hotel, especially when you had expected to be at the farm by yourself, I would have probably felt the same way as you.' She raised her eyebrows and gave him a pointed stare. 'Actually I did, didn't I?'

Joe waggled his finger at her. 'That's true. I noticed you were none too happy to find me here either.'

'Really? I thought I'd hidden my reaction well.'

'Not that well.'

Skye shook her head and pointed to the heaped wheelbarrow. 'I emptied the last one on the manure pile; it's your turn to do this one.'

'Fine.' He cocked his head to the right. 'Why don't you fetch a second wheelbarrow while I sort this one out, then we can get this muck cleared and lay fresh bedding for the animals and get out of here. It's too pleasant a day to miss too much of it inside.'

As Joe went to find a second wheelbarrow, he couldn't help thinking how much he was enjoying her company. He was warming to Skye. She was cute and sassy, but still tough, and he loved that combination. He doubted she would put up with any nonsense from a partner, unlike he had done with Aurélie, his previous girlfriend in France. He walked round the corner of the barn to one of the outbuildings, assuming he would find what he needed in there.

As soon as he had emptied the wheelbarrow, he pushed it back to the barn. As he passed the smaller barn, Joe decided how good it felt being single and making a new friend like Skye. Lettie was independent like Skye and had reminded him that most women were fun and kind, unlike Aurélie had turned out to be.

He sighed and pushed away the difficult memories of their break-up when she had mocked him about taking their relationship too seriously. He was still embarrassed about declaring his love for her over a meal at the restaurant in the village and her mocking laugh while other diners, most of whom knew him, tried to pretend he hadn't just been completely humiliated. He now knew it was her way of breaking up with him because she had met someone else, but Joe wished she'd had the decency to simply tell him while they were alone.

It was the reason he had sworn never to allow himself to fall in love again. It wasn't worth it especially when you didn't even understand what love felt like as he clearly didn't.

'Here, catch.' Skye's voice distracted him. He pushed his wheelbarrow back into the barn and saw Spud pick up a stick and trot back to her, dropping it at her feet for her to throw again.

'I think I've started something here,' she said, rolling her eyes.

Skye was different to Aurélie, he mused. He didn't know her well, but she seemed kind and certainly mucked in without any reservation. Maybe working with her would be a bit more fun than he had initially presumed, he thought, feeling better. Two singletons happy with their lot and prepared to work hard on a beautiful farm like this one was probably what they both needed right now.

16

SKYE

She still couldn't decide whether to share information about her family with Joe. She took a shower, hoping to clear her mind a little. It had been another amazing day at the farm and she was feeling more and more comfortable in Joe's company. Skye felt her energy being revitalised as the sensation of hot water cascaded refreshingly down her head and body. She shampooed her hair while she gave her conundrum more consideration. By taking Joe into her confidence, she was opening another layer of herself, something she hadn't felt comfortable doing with another man since her last relationship ended so badly.

She thought of her ex and how he had betrayed her, gaslighting her when she discovered he had been seeing an acquaintance of hers for several weeks by trying to make out Skye had been the one not trying in their relationship. The following six months away had been eye-opening and character building and she now knew that it was the best thing that could have happened to her. Although, she would have much rather them not break up for such an upsetting reason, because that had caused her latent distrust of most men her age. If only he could have had the courage to admit he had met someone else, instead of moving on before bothering to tell her and letting her find out for herself.

Skye soaped her body, then rinsed her hair and skin and stepped out of the shower, just as there was a single knock on the door before it opened and Joe stepped into the tiny shower room.

Skye shrieked as she made a grab for her towel, cursing when it slipped from her fingers onto the damp floor.

'It's fine,' Joe said, turning his back immediately and covering his eyes as he reached backwards to pick it up. Standing, he held it out. Skye snatched it from his hands, furious with him for bursting in on her. She wrapped it around herself as he hurriedly left the room. 'I'm so sorry about marching in like that,' he said from outside the closed door. 'I hadn't expected you to be in here.'

Mortified and hoping she had covered her boobs before Joe had seen anything but doubting it, Skye grumbled, 'Maybe wait for an answer after knocking next time?'

'Don't worry, I will.'

She heard him mumble something to himself as he walked down the landing. It sounded like Joe was as mortified as her. She felt a little mean for snapping at him for what had been an obvious mistake.

After tidying up after herself, she left the shower room.

'Shower is free now, Joe,' she yelled and gave a quick knock on his bedroom door in case he hadn't heard.

'Thanks.'

Skye hurried to her bedroom to dry herself and dress in her favourite tracksuit. There was nothing for it but to brazen it out and go to join him. Thoughtless man, she thought angrily as she dried her hair. She tried not to think about what had happened.

They had agreed to meet downstairs at seven o'clock to make supper and talk about their plans for the following day. Although she would rather not have to see him again that evening, she decided she had to face him sometime and may as well get it over with rather than feeling embarrassed. Anyway, she reminded herself, she wasn't the one in the wrong and she still needed to work out whether or not to confide in Joe about her parents.

Having roughly dried her hair and clipping it back from her face, Skye left her room and passed the shower room. All she could hear was water from the shower. For once Joe wasn't singing some tuneless song she didn't recognise.

She fed the dogs, filled their water bowls and then refolded the thick blankets on their beds, needing to keep busy until Joe came down. Skye washed her hands, filled the kettle and pressed it on. She desperately needed a cup of tea and couldn't recall the last one she had drunk that day.

'I'm so sorry I walked in on you like I did.' Joe strode into the kitchen, pushing a strand of his damp hair from his handsome face and making her stomach flip over. 'I've clearly spent too long living alone in my bungalow and must remember to knock before entering.' He frowned. 'You all right?'

Apart from being embarrassed to be seen without her clothes, Skye reminded herself it had been a mistake and seeing how mortified he seemed to be about the incident decided she was fine. 'I'll lock the door next time, just in case you forget again.'

'I don't think that will happen.'

Skye didn't want to ruin an otherwise happy day with an atmosphere between them and, she mused, he did seem horrified by what he had done.

'It's fine. No harm done.'

'You sure?'

'Yes.' Deciding to change the subject, she said, 'I was just thinking about something.'

'Anything I can help with?'

She saw the look of concern on his face and knew she wasn't ready to confide in him yet. 'No. It's nothing really.' She turned and pointed one arm to the fridge and the other to the pantry. 'What do you fancy eating tonight? There's a choice of a few things, and I'm happy with all of them.'

'Not a fussy eater then?'

Skye looked at him and grinned. 'No. Why, do I look as if I could be?'

He shook his head, looking amused. 'You don't.' He seemed unsure. 'Then again, what does a fussy eater look like?'

'Not me.' It dawned on her that Joe hadn't realised she was teasing him. And, not wanting to worry him at all, she told him.

'I knew that,' he said, looking relieved. Joe shook his head. 'I seem to be making a habit of saying or doing the wrong thing.'

'Only tonight.' She laughed, determined that their evening wouldn't be ruined by any unfortunate misunderstandings.

Joe looked at her gratefully for a moment before he walked over to the fridge and pulled open the door.

'Good plan. I'm sure there'll be more than enough topics for us to fall out over and argue about during the coming weeks. We need to choose our battles with each other if both of us are going to come out of this with any energy left at all.'

Skye laughed. 'My sentiments exactly.' Her stomach rumbled loudly and she went to stand next to Joe at the fridge door, staring into the compartments just like he was doing. 'Do hurry up and choose,' she moaned. 'I don't know how much longer I can wait and we still have to cook whatever it is we decide to eat.'

They finally settled on steak and chips for Joe and salmon fillet with chips and peas for Skye. As they ate Skye continued to reason whether or not to share her situation with Joe. On the one hand, he was bound to know people who remembered the summer seasons in the nineties – probably through his grandfather's friends or contacts through other locals. It was a small island after all, so a lot of people must know each other. On the other hand, by telling him about her father, she was opening herself up to him more than she had ever done with anyone else other than her grandmother and Melody, and she wasn't sure she was ready to do that.

But if she didn't accept Joe's offer to help her, then she might waste these next few weeks. How would she feel to return home never having such a good opportunity again to search for her long-lost father?

However unused to allowing others to see her vulnerability Skye might be, she was beginning to think that she needed to be brave and open herself up to him.

If Joe did turn out to be the man she suspected he might be and help her find her father, then surely that would be worth any embarrassment. And, if he didn't end up being someone worth trusting, then she would have learnt another valuable lesson. Not one she wanted to have to go through, but she had faced difficulties before and if there was one thing Skye knew about herself it was that she was resilient. Hadn't she needed to learn to be when she lost her mum, then her gran when she was younger?

She caught him looking over at her thoughtfully and could tell he was worried about her. Skye finished her last mouthful and set her cutlery down on her plate. Taking a sip of her tea, she swallowed. It was now or never before she lost her nerve.

'Joe, I have something I'd like to share with you.'

'I'm so pleased,' he said, his hands becoming still. 'I was hoping you'd decide to trust me with whatever has been bothering you.'

Skye sat back in her chair and folded her arms. This being vulnerable thing wasn't to her liking at all, but she had decided to give it one last go. 'It's about who my parents are.'

17

JOE

Joe listened enraptured as Skye told him about her parents working the summer season on the island in 1998.

'And you want to trace him, is that right?'

'That's the plan, but I don't know his name and Gran only had a vague idea about where the pair of them might have worked. Mum was obviously very secretive, so you can probably see why I'm not really sure where to start my search.'

He pondered her problem for a moment. 'You could put something on social media. Lots of people join Facebook groups for those who worked summer seasons here, especially in the seventies, eighties and nineties. I've come across them a few times and there's usually someone sharing a photo and asking if anyone has information on that person. Others are simply hoping to reconnect with old workmates or reminisce.'

'That is a good idea,' she said. Then pulling a face, added, 'But I don't have a photo of him or even his name, which is a little embarrassing, so I'm not sure how I could ask for information about him.'

He sighed. 'That does make things rather difficult.'

'Anyway, I'm still getting used to the thought of looking for him. I thought about doing a DNA test but the results might take weeks to come through. I was also concerned that if my father doesn't know I exist then I would hate for him or his family to find out about me from an online database.'

'I understand.' He would feel the same way about strangers online delving into his private family matters. Joe wasn't sure how she could possibly find her father with so little information though, especially if she also didn't put the feelers out for any snippets about him. 'Islanders are always happy to help though, if you do change your mind.'

'Thanks, I'll bear that in mind.'

'I love a good mystery,' Joe admitted. 'And I'm only too happy to help you wherever I can.' He cocked an eyebrow. 'It would help me feel better about what I did too.' The image of her perfect naked body stepping out of the shower sprang into his mind. He realised she was staring at him, eyes narrowed. 'What?'

'Did you see me naked?'

'Wh—?'

He barely had a chance to answer before she gasped. 'You did!'

'I didn't mean to.'

She glared at him as if trying to make up her mind whether to believe him or not.

'Anyway,' he added, trying not to panic. 'I thought you were fine about it.'

'That was when I assumed I had covered up before you saw anything. It's different now.'

Why had he brought up the damn shower incident when he hadn't needed to? 'Look, I really am sorry. I'll forget I ever saw anything,' he said, knowing it was going to be impossible, but desperate to at least attempt to appease her.

'Really,' she said doubtfully. 'You think you can do that?'

She clearly didn't believe him. He didn't blame her.

They sat in silence and Joe tried to think of something helpful to say. He wished he hadn't seen her naked. He already struggled to act as if he just saw her as a friend because that's what she had said she was happy for them to be. Now all he could think of was how she was even more perfect than he had originally thought.

Skye sighed, interrupting his thoughts. 'Look, it's done now and we can't do anything about that. I'd rather not refer to the matter again, if you don't mind.' She gazed out of the window for a few seconds before focusing her attention on him once again. 'I don't have long if I hope to trace my father during this visit to the island, so your offer to help me really is appreciated.'

'You're taking me up on it?' he asked, relieved to be able to get their friendship back on a level footing again.

'I am.' She shrugged. 'When I've worked out how, I'd like to take the next step to find him.'

Joe thought about Skye's father and whether he had an inkling that he had a daughter at all. Maybe Skye was the only child he had fathered? If so, surely he would be delighted to be located and meet up with her.

'What are you thinking?' Skye asked. 'Because I can almost hear your brain whirring it's working so hard.'

Joe laughed loudly, happy that she felt relaxed enough with him to tease him. He shared his thoughts with her.

'Gosh, I hadn't thought of that.' She frowned. 'I'm not sure if that makes me feel more inclined to find him or more anxious about it. I've never really had anyone, parent-wise, putting any pressure on me. My mum was either working or socialising and we rarely spent quality time together. I mostly had the feeling I was a mistake she hadn't banked on, and that she'd needed to make decisions she otherwise wouldn't have made because of me.'

'Like what?' Joe asked, sad to hear Skye think of herself in such a way.

'Don't get me wrong, I know she loved me, but I'm not sure she would have chosen to have a child.'

'Why would you think that?'

She took a moment to answer. 'Because I was mostly left with Gran while Mum was out working, or away somewhere.'

'I'm sure that wasn't the case. Maybe she was just very busy.' He gave her comment further thought. 'Or perhaps your mum just wasn't that good at showing emotion to someone else.'

'I suppose so.' She gazed at him for a moment. 'Thank you, that was a kind thing to suggest. I think I'm going to try and believe that was Mum's way with everyone, not just me.'

'Good.' Joe was relieved to have helped her even in this small way. 'With regard to your father, I'm sure we'll find him some-how, even if it takes a bit of time.'

Skye smiled at him. 'Gran will be thrilled if I do locate him. I can't help sensing that she feels a little responsible for not thinking to push my mum to tell me more about him, even though I don't blame her.'

'It sounds as if you have a lot of love and care from your grandmother.'

Skye gave his comment some thought, then nodded. 'I do. She is an amazing woman and has always wanted the best for me, and for Mum.'

'I'm glad.' She gave him an odd look and, not wishing to say the wrong thing again, Joe changed the subject away from her mother and grandmother. 'I think the first thing we need to do is check out the hotels that were open when your parents worked here and look on social media for any information or photos about their staff, or even people who are posting about them. You never know, if you find your mother, then at least you'll know where your father worked and we can take it from there.'

She beamed at him. 'Now that is a good plan. I'll get on to it first thing in the morning.'

18

SKYE

That night as she lay in bed trying to decide how best to start her search, all she felt like doing was crying. What was wrong with her? She wasn't a crier, not usually. Maybe it was because her search seemed so hopeless. What she did know though was that she would never forgive herself if she didn't take this opportunity to do something about it. But if she wanted to find information about her father, or anything to do with her mother's younger life when she was working on the island, then she needed to get a move on and do it.

Deciding the best way to calm herself was to read through more of her mother's notebook, Skye plumped up her pillows, rested back on them and opened the book. Then, realising she hadn't opened the window, she threw the duvet back and got out of the bed. She heard a thud but couldn't see what it could be from, so opened the window and turned to go back to her bed.

Spotting the notebook lying opened and face down on the floor, she picked it up and noticed for the first time that there was a space between the cover and the spine.

'What's this?' she murmured, holding it up to the light and

peering in, certain there was something there. Breathless with excitement, Skye went to her washbag and rummaged around for her tweezers, then carefully inserted them into the space and slowly withdrew a folded piece of paper.

Her heart pounded and she could barely think. 'What didn't you want anyone to see, Mum?' she whispered as she checked there was nothing else secreted away, put the book down carefully and unfolded the small piece of paper.

C. Ferreira. If I could have my time again… A x

Skye gasped. Could C. Ferreira be her father? And what would her mother do if she had her time again? Would she find him? Or maybe her mother would tell her about him, if he was her father. She liked to think that she would.

At least she now had a name. Even if this wasn't her father, it was someone important to her mother and something that could lead to Skye finding out valuable information about her mother's past. Everything was up to her although she still worried about going to the effort of searching for him, finding him and then being rejected. After her strained relationship with her mother and then losing her, Skye wasn't sure she could cope with him deciding to have nothing to do with her.

Then again, what if he was interested in forming a relationship with her? She might have siblings for all she knew. Excitement shot through her. After spending her life without siblings or any other relatives apart from her grandmother, the thought of having a family, people she was biologically connected to, was tempting. She leant against the windowsill in her bedroom and stared out at the sunny view. She didn't really have a decision to make at all, not if she didn't want to spend the rest of her life regretting not seeing this through.

Whatever she decided to do next could change everything about her life forever. The thought terrified and excited her. At least she had Joe here to help her, and despite their embarrassment about what had happened he really was being a wonderful support. Time was running out though. She had less than four weeks before Lindy and Gareth returned to the island and she and Joe would no longer be needed.

There really was no better time when she was staying at this beautiful farm, rent-free and with a gorgeous, if sometimes annoying, man to help her. She would be mad to not make the most of every second to do something that, whatever happened, would help her find some answers.

Desperate to share this exciting news with Joe, she went to his room and knocked several times.

'Joe?' she whispered when there wasn't an answer. 'Joe?' she repeated louder.

'Uh, Skye?' His bedroom door opened and for a second her heart almost stopped. He must have gone straight to sleep because she had obviously woken him up. His hair was messy and she saw he must have quickly dressed in his boxer shorts because they were on inside out. Skye pressed her lips together, trying not to show her amusement.

'You OK?' he asked, rubbing his eyes.

'I've found something.'

He blinked a few times as she held up the piece of paper. 'C. Ferreira? Who's that?'

'That's it, I don't know.' She explained where she had found it. 'Read the rest.' She watched him do so. 'Don't you think that's intriguing?'

He smiled and nodded. 'I do. You might have found your father, Skye.'

She sighed happily. 'We have something to go on, finally.' Unable to help herself, she flung her arms around him.

'Oof.' He didn't move immediately but then put his arms around her.

She rested her head on his chest, needing to share her excitement, unsure why his heart seemed to be pounding so quickly. 'I'm so happy.'

'I'm not surprised.'

Remembering she had woken him, Skye dropped her arms and stepped back. 'I'll let you get back to bed, but I thought we could start trying to find this man in the morning, if that's OK with you.'

'It is very OK with me.' He smiled.

Feeling slightly awkward for throwing herself at him like she had, Skye waved for him to go back inside his room. 'Get to bed. We can talk about this again in the morning.'

* * *

After barely three hours' sleep, Skye decided she may as well get up. Her mind had raced for most of the night and even though reading usually made her eyes tired enough to sleep and she had tried to focus on reading the Gothic novel she had found on one of the many bookcases in the farmhouse, nothing but exhaustion finally made her drift off.

Relieved to finally get up, Skye showered and was dressing when she heard Joe's car returning from somewhere. Intrigued to know where he had been so early in the morning, Skye ran downstairs to greet him.

'Hey, there you are,' Joe said as Skye reached the door and opened it just as he reached out to do so himself.

She wasn't sure where else he might have expected her to be

because he knew the routine at the farm as well as she did. He did seem a more enthusiastic than usual and she knew it was because of her finding the name.

'Where've you been?' she asked, standing back and holding the door open for him.

He tapped the side of his nose as he passed her on his way to the stairs. 'Put the kettle on while I grab plates for these cinnamon buns I bought from the village bakery.'

'Cinnamon buns?' Skye decided she could get used to eating pastries in the morning. She hoped Joe would continue to go to the village first thing to buy them. Intrigued, Skye went into the kitchen and did as he asked. He fetched two plates and carried the small box of pastries to the living room with her following.

'I thought we might need extra sustenance before we got going this morning.' He looked sideways at her and grinned. 'I suspect you had little sleep after your discovery.'

Skye yawned. 'Not much.'

'Have one of these.' He put a bun on one of the plates and handed it to her. 'I have news, too.'

Excited to hear what about, she made herself comfortable while she waited.

'Well? What is it?' she asked impatiently when he took a bite from his bun without having spoken. He had a drink and leant back next to her on the sofa. 'I have a mate with the same last name as the one you found.'

'You do?'

He raised his hand. 'Don't get too excited; he's away at the moment and not due back for a couple of days.'

'Oh, that's a pain,' she said, not able to hide her disappointment.

'There's more.'

She saw the twinkle in his eyes and jabbed his shoulder. 'Tell me then.'

'It seems that his dad was a porter at the Sunshine Springs for many years. Another chap we know, his mum worked as a chambermaid, then housekeeper at the Bel Amie.'

'This really is a small place, isn't it?'

'Well, contrary to belief, we don't all know each other here in Jersey but the hospitality world here – especially back in the seventies, eighties and nineties – was small and lots of people knew each other.'

Skye couldn't hide her delight. Resting a hand on her chest, she nervously asked, 'Are their parents still alive?'

'Yes, both are,' he replied proudly.

Barely able to breathe, her cinnamon bun forgotten, she asked, 'And do your friends think they'll speak to me?' She gave him a pleading look. 'To us?'

'Us?' He frowned but Skye could tell he was only teasing.

'Well, you're the local boy. I'm clearly not from here with my accent.'

His expression softened. 'It's a beautiful accent.'

'I like it, but that's not the point,' she said impatiently. 'If I'm not from here then maybe they won't be as comfortable sharing their own stories with me.'

He waved away her comment as if he were batting a fly. 'Rubbish. They'll be fine – I'm sure of it.'

Skye took a moment to process the exciting news. 'This is amazing, Joe. Thank you so much.' She didn't want to push him when he was tired, but couldn't help needing to know. 'How soon do you think we could arrange to meet up with these people?'

'Hopefully you won't have to wait too long. Leave it with me and I'll do what I can.'

He gave her a smile that made her stomach flip over. Not wishing to give her feelings away, she took a sip of her tea while she gathered herself.

'That's brilliant, Joe. I really appreciate all you're doing for me. Thank you.'

He stared at her thoughtfully. 'There's no need to keep thanking me, Skye. What are friends for?'

She had to stop herself from admitting she wished they were more than that but forced a smile. 'Yes, of course we are.'

'And supporting each other is what friends do.'

'They do.'

19

JOE

After a chilled morning looking after the animals, followed by both of them searching online to try and find out more about C. Ferreira, Joe suggested they take a walk across the fields.

'I love this place,' Skye said almost to herself.

Joe's hand brushed against hers as they both went to open the lower meadow gate at the same time. He wanted desperately to take her hand in his but didn't want to do anything to cause her to withdraw from him. He cringed inwardly at the thought of how much worse her reaction could have been when he had walked into the shower room.

Joe opened the gate and once they were both on the other side, closed it. He sensed Skye watching him and hoped it was because she was beginning to trust him a little. He was relieved he had been successful in making some headway to locate her father. It wasn't much, but it was a tentative link that he sensed might lead Skye to the man she was longing to track down.

If only she didn't see him as just a friend, although he was grateful for that. Thinking back to how they had first met and then again seeing each other at the farm and realising they would be living and working together, he knew things could have been far worse between them. He might wish there could be more between them but friends was better than nothing and at least they could enjoy each other's company.

He stopped walking and breathed in the fresh sea air. How unfair was it though that only he seemed to feel the chemistry between them? Or was it simply a one-way thing coming from him and there wasn't really any chemistry at all? Probably. Then again, maybe he had been single for too long and had lost the ability to pick up on subtle nuances being sent his way. He looked at her but she was lost in thought about something and by the look on her face it wasn't anything romantic. It was just wishful thinking on his part that there could be anything more between them.

He noticed the slowly rising moon over the fields and was taken aback by the magnificence of it.

'Does the moon look bigger than usual to you?' he asked, wondering if it was one of those Hunter's Moons occasionally mentioned in the newspaper.

'Hmm?'

He realised Skye hadn't heard his question. 'The moon,' he repeated, not wanting her to dwell on whatever was bothering her. 'Do you think it's one of those special moons?'

She looked up and gasped. 'Wow, that is big, even for a full moon.' She stared at it silently for a moment. 'Actually I read earlier that this one is a Flower Moon.'

'It is?' He had no idea what that was and presumed it must be due to the colour. It did seem rather pink, he supposed.

'Apparently, or so it said on the news platform I came across yesterday. Beautiful, isn't it?'

It was. Joe went to take his phone from his back jeans pocket but found it wasn't there. 'I wish I'd thought to bring my mobile to take a photo of it,' he said, disappointed that he must have left it in his bedroom.

'I don't have mine either,' Skye commiserated. 'Not that my phone ever takes decent photos of faraway things like that.'

'Neither does mine, come to think of it. The number of sunsets I've hoped to capture always come across with completely different colours, so I mostly don't bother trying any more.'

'Maybe we're simply supposed to enjoy it rather than try to capture it?'

He liked that idea. 'I agree.'

She was quiet again, staring across the fields and taking in the pink and purple sky to the west. 'Do you really think we'll be able to track down my father?'

'I don't see why not.'

She looked at him and Joe couldn't miss the hope in Skye's beautiful dark eyes.

'It must be strange not knowing what your father looks like,' he said without thinking, immediately cross to have voiced such a thoughtless thing. 'Sorry, that was an odd thing to say.'

'I don't think it was at all,' Skye said, slipping her hand into his and giving it a gentle squeeze.

Taken aback at her unexpected touch, Joe glanced down at their hands.

'Sorry,' Skye said, obviously mistaking his reaction. She snapped her hand away before he managed to think what to say and immediately began walking again.

He didn't want her to get the wrong impression about his reaction and went after her. 'Skye?'

She raised a hand but didn't slow down. 'It's fine,' she said over her shoulder. 'I don't know why I did that.'

Joe caught up with her in a few strides and took her gently

by the arm, pulling her to a stop. 'Hey, I was just surprised, that's all.' When she kept her gaze downwards, he placed a finger under her chin and raised it. 'Look at me.'

It took a few seconds before she did. 'Can we just keep walking?'

Wanting to make her feel better, Joe nodded. 'Of course, if that's what you'd rather do.' Without thinking, he reached for her hand and, after a slight flinch, Skye's fingers closed around his.

'I only wanted to comfort you.' She groaned. 'Well, to show you that you hadn't offended me.'

He tilted his head towards her as they walked. 'And I liked it,' he said quietly. 'It was just unexpected – that's all.'

She looked up at him. 'It's fine. I understand now.'

Joe's heart raced as he watched her. Had something shifted in their friendship? He hoped so. Whatever it was, he liked it.

'Now I know you're happy for me to move ahead with this search for your father,' he said, opting to change the subject onto something she felt more comfortable discussing. He was becoming excited at the next few weeks and what they might hold for Skye. 'It must be fascinating to discover what he looks like.'

'And how much I resemble him.' Her fingers tightened slightly around his in a gentle squeeze. 'I hope so. I'd love to be able to get to know that side of me. I hope he's more open to answer some of the questions I've always had than Mum ever was.' She glanced up at him. 'Mostly I'm initially excited about what he looks like, if I'm honest. I've never had a father and although I've always wondered what it would be like to have one, I'm also used to being independent. I can't help feeling a little unnerved in case he thinks he can step into my life and start taking control of it.'

Joe thought about his own father and thought back to when he was younger and his friends moaned about their fathers interfering in their lives, or giving them ground rules. How much he wished he had a father who cared enough to bother. But this was different. Skye was a grown woman in her twenties and used to making her own decisions. 'I'm sure he won't do that.'

They stopped walking. 'How do you know?' she asked.

He gazed down into her beautiful dark eyes and it dawned on him that the reason she was so headstrong and had initially appeared closed off emotionally was probably because of having to be so strong from such a young age.

'Because we'll make sure he doesn't.'

Skye frowned, looking confused. 'We?'

Joe's heart melted. Did her toughness hide loneliness? She had her gran in her life and prior to that her mother, but by the sounds of things Skye missed the family support network that even he as an only child had experienced thanks to his mother and paternal grandparents being around when he had needed them.

Joe gazed at her. 'Anyhow, I'm here to support you whenever, if ever you need me to. I hope you don't forget that.'

Skye's mouth drew back into a wide smile. 'I won't. And I hope you know I'm here for you, too.'

Feeling a powerful urge to pull her into his arms and kiss her, Joe reminded himself how she saw him as her friend. He had no intention of breaking her trust by overstepping their closeness. He raised her hand to his lips and kissed the back of it, looking over her hand to gauge her reaction in case she thought he was going too far.

'Thank you.' He lowered her hand and continued to walk. 'I

know it's only been a couple of days, but I think we're working well together.'

Skye smiled coyly. 'Yes, I wish I'd had a bit of foresight to give you more of a chance. I might have listened to you more readily the night before at the hotel too.' She laughed.

Taken aback by her amusement, Joe asked, 'What?'

'I thought you were rather pompous that night.' She shrugged. 'And when we were first here at the farm.'

'Me?' He couldn't hide his surprise.

'Er, who else is in this field?' Skye giggled. 'Yes, of course, you.'

'I've never been accused of being that before, ever.'

She giggled. 'Are you sure about that?'

Enjoying their banter, Joe laughed. 'Yes, I am.' Now she mentioned it though, he wasn't so sure. 'In my defence I thought that if you were here then they wouldn't need me and I'd need to find somewhere else to stay. Or return to the bungalow and live with my mother and stepfather again.' She pulled a sad face and made him laugh. 'Are you taking the mickey?'

'I wouldn't dare. I don't want nice Joe to disappear and grumpy, unfriendly Joe to return, now do I?'

He narrowed his eyes, enjoying teasing her. 'If you're not very careful that's exactly what is going to happen.'

She nudged his arm with her shoulder. 'Stop moaning. It all worked out in the end, didn't it?'

It did, he thought gratefully. 'I suppose so.'

She pointed to the moon with her free hand. 'Look at the size of it now.'

Joe did as she suggested and as soon as he did Skye snatched her hand from his and began laughing and running back towards the house.

Joe watched her go, wishing they had longer than a few

short weeks together here. There was something about Skye, apart from the cute way she pursed her lips when she was cross with him, or her determined stance when she was refusing to give about something. He was happier than he could recall being in a very long time and he wished it didn't need to end.

'Hey,' he shouted, enjoying every moment. 'Wait for me.'

20

SKYE

Skye glanced over her shoulder, delighted to see Joe now following her. This was such fun. The freedom from having anything heavy to dwell on for a change was a welcome relief. How could she have ever thought Joe wasn't fun. He was kind and made things fun and she wanted to make the most of every second staying on this amazing farm with these adorable animals and being the only other human apart from Joe.

As she neared the front door she heard the phone ringing. She wondered who it could be and hoped nothing was wrong with Lettie. She opened the door and, presuming Joe might be better answering the call as he knew people on the island, she picked up the phone and held it out to him.

He gave her a confused look before taking the receiver. 'Hello?'

'Joe?'

'Yes, it's me.' Joe pressed the button so the voice was on loud-speaker and she could hear more clearly.

'You are there,' Brodie said, his voice sounding flustered.

Joe shot a concerned look at Skye and cleared his throat. 'Is everything all right?'

Skye's stomach tensed.

'Yes, sorry. I'd tried yours and Skye's mobiles and didn't get an answer so called here. We've had a bit of a drama, but everything is fine now.'

She knew she should have remembered her phone, Skye thought guiltily.

'Sorry, Brodie, we went for a walk and both inadvertently left our phones behind.' Joe looked concerned. 'Do you mean the baby has been born?'

Skye tensed and leant closer to the phone even though she could hear perfectly clearly without doing so.

'She has, I'm relieved to say.'

'She? 'A little girl?' Skye asked, delighted.

'Yes. Sorry, didn't I say? We found out during one of the scans but Lettie wanted to keep it a secret between the pair of us until she was born.'

Skye wasn't surprised, having heard a little from Joe about how despite being a lovely lady, Lettie's mother Lindy liked to take charge.

'That's understandable,' Joe said, giving Skye a knowing smile. 'And Lettie? How's she doing? How are you coping with everything?'

'Lettie is fine, thanks. Tired, of course. She had a shock when she went into labour and everything happened quickly after that, especially as we knew she would need to get to the hospital quickly in case anything went wrong.'

Skye was relieved to hear things had ended up being fine.

'She looks more beautiful than I've ever seen her and insists she's perfectly OK now the baby is here. The baby is perfect.' Brodie sighed. 'I feel so lucky.'

'That's because you are, mate.'

Skye heard a tone to Joe's voice and wondered if having a wife and family was something he looked forward to.

'Skye's here and sends her love to you all, as do I. Remember, if there's anything at all that any of you need, all you have to do is ask.'

'Thanks, Joe. Oh, hang on a sec, Lettie's trying to tell me something.' Skye waited while there were mumblings in the background. Joe pointed to the phone and rolled his eyes. 'Joe, you still there?'

'Yup. What is it?'

'Lettie was hoping you'd find a way to get a message to her parents on the ship. They're not expecting anything to happen for a few weeks yet and were going to be back two weeks before Lettie was due, so they'll have a bit of a shock.' Skye wasn't surprised. 'We've messaged Zac and Melody and my family, but her parents are somewhere in the mid-Caribbean or somewhere else by now. Gareth told her they only turn their phones on every so often as the cost of Wi-Fi is high on the ships, but to be sure to send a message. We've emailed of course.'

'No problem at all,' Joe said. 'Leave everything to us. And don't worry about Derek, he's snoozing in the kitchen with Spud. They're perfectly happy together.'

'Thank you.'

Skye pointed to the phone and Joe nodded. 'Enjoy your quiet time with just the three of you.'

'We will,' Brodie assured her. She could hear amusement in his voice.

'Right,' Joe said. 'We'll let you get back to your new family.'

'Ooh, wait!' Skye took the phone from Joe. 'Brodie, you didn't tell us the baby's name.' She suspected Lindy and Gareth would ask and wanted to be able to pass on that much information.

'Sorry, I should have said. It's Isla.'

'Isla? That's a beautiful name,' she said, smiling up at Joe.

'Thank you. It was Lettie's choice, but I love it too.'

She handed the phone back to Joe.

'I'll update you with anything I think you need to know. Otherwise, just leave everything with us; we've got it all in hand.'

Brodie thanked them and Joe ended the call. He looked at Skye. 'That was unexpected, wasn't it?'

'It was.'

They stared at each other thoughtfully and she wondered whether Joe was thinking the same thing as her. Then unable to help herself, voiced her concerns aloud. 'I wonder if this means our time here will end sooner than we had expected.'

Joe frowned. 'I've no idea, but I hope it won't.'

'I've been working out the time difference,' she said. 'And I think we should try to make contact with the ship as soon as possible before it docks somewhere, and they go out seeing the sights for the day.'

'That's a good idea.'

21

JOE

Joe spent a few minutes searching for contact details for Lettie's parents and then realising he would need to wait until the following morning, had a difficult night's sleep worrying what it meant for him and Skye if Lindy and Gareth returned early as he presumed they would try to do.

Finally speaking to them the next morning, he assured them Lettie and baby Isla were fine and asked if there was anything they needed from him.

'What did they say?' Skye asked when he joined her outside with the alpacas.

'They're going to do their best to change their flights but don't know yet whether there will be availability, or when they might be back.'

Skye smiled but it didn't reach her eyes. 'That's good. I'm sure Lettie will be happy having her parents back home again.'

'Yes, she will.' He watched the woman he had hoped to spend more time with and although he was happy for his friends that their baby had been born, he couldn't help feeling sad that he and Skye would no doubt be parting ways even earlier than either had expected.

Hearing a car, Joe glanced out of the window. 'Who's that?'

They went to look outside.

He recognised the car immediately. It was his grandfather's old Mazda that he had left for his mother and Roger to use. Joe's mood plummeted further.

'Isn't that…?'

'Yes, it's my mother, and by the looks of things she's left Roger behind.' What could she want?

'I'd better go and greet her.'

'I'll leave you to it,' Skye said. 'I need to go and sort out some washing. If you have any, I could put that in the washing machine too.'

'I have a few things on a pile on my bedroom floor that I was going to see to later,' he said, unsurprised that Skye was looking for a reason to be out of the way. They had both had enough excitement for now.

Joe walked outside and forced a smile. 'Mum, I didn't expect to see you today. Is everything OK?' He opened the car door and his mother took his hand and got out. 'Your leg still playing up?'

'No,' she said. 'It's almost back to normal now.' She scanned the area. 'I don't recall coming here before. It's rather lovely, isn't it?'

'It is.'

'Took me a while to find the right farm.' Joe wasn't sure why because there was a sign at the end of the drive. 'I went to the next farm along and met a very nice man, Leonard. He's a farmer too,' she continued. 'And gave me directions here.'

'He's Lettie's uncle. Lettie runs this place.'

Faye gave him a pointed look and Joe knew criticism was

coming his way. 'Maybe if you'd thought to bring me here before, I wouldn't have got lost.'

Joe had no intention of giving in to his mother's sniping. 'You're here now.' He forced a smile and closed the car door. 'Would you like to have a look around now?' he asked, presuming that might be why she was there. 'Or was there something else.'

'Is Skye here?'

Joe wasn't sure his mother was asking because she was interested in seeing Skye again or if she was hoping to find Joe alone to discuss something private. 'She is but she's doing a few chores somewhere,' he said vaguely.

'That's probably just as well.' She didn't move and he realised they were going to have their conversation outside. 'Because I needed to speak to you about money.'

'I see.'

'Well, don't look at me like that,' she snapped.

'Like what?' Joe wondered how long his mother thought this arrangement could continue for. Did she and Roger think that when he was no longer at the farm he could return to the bungalow and the three of them could go back to trying to make things work there?

'Like I make you weary.'

He didn't like to admit that she did when it came to her and money. 'Sorry, I don't meant to.'

'You're irritated with me though,' she said. 'I can tell.'

'I'm not, Mum.'

'But you think I should sort myself out.'

'Did I say that?' Did she blame him? he wondered. He had worked during school holidays at the village pub washing dishes and helping wipe tables from when he was fifteen so that he never needed to ask her for money, aware Faye struggled to make her earnings last very long.

She shook her head and folded her arms. 'I told you about Roger and me being financially embarrassed at the moment. We can't live off fresh air and you know he'll pay you back whatever you loan to him.'

Poor man, Joe thought, aware that this conversation would continue in some format until he gave in. 'Of course I'll help out,' Joe said, trying his best not to show his disappointment. So much for his savings increasing until he could replace the bungalow roof and fix the wall near the entrance as he had been planning to do. 'I'll transfer some to your account as soon as I go inside.'

She reached up and kissed him on the cheek, her whole demeanour changing as if she had only just called in to say hello. Joe doubted he would ever see the money again and didn't mind all that much. All he really wanted was for his mother to be happy, but he knew that she would need to change her ways if that was to realistically happen.

'I should leave you to get on with everything.' She opened the car door. 'Do pop in sometime, won't you? Bring Skye with you. I'd like to get to know her a little better.'

He gave a nod and watched as Faye started the car and drove off. He wondered if the day could get any worse.

The house phone was ringing again. Who could that be now? Joe sighed heavily. Today was turning out to be a bit of a lousy one.

22

SKYE

Joe walked up next to Skye and waited for her to finish her call.

She clicked the phone onto loudspeaker as he had done for her and mouthed Brodie's name. Realising Brodie hadn't said why he was phoning and suspecting he might be so filled with love for his fiancée and new baby that he might have forgotten, Skye thought she had better remind him.

'You haven't mentioned why you called, Brodie.' Skye grinned at Joe to show she wasn't bothered by his noisy entrance.

'Yes, sorry. Lettie asked me to let you know she's being discharged tomorrow, so we'll be coming home to the farm tomorrow around midday.'

Skye saw Joe's cheerful expression disappear and felt her own sadness that their happy bubble was about to be burst. Not that they hadn't expected this moment to come, she reminded herself. And it was Lettie's home after all and natural for her to want to return to the place where she lived as soon as possible.

'She must want to get back to her own things as soon as she can,' Skye said, trying her best to sound more cheerful than she felt. She looked forward to seeing Lettie again and couldn't wait to give baby Isla a cuddle, and she felt mean wishing she and Joe could have just one more day alone together on the farm.

When Brodie hesitated, Skye wondered if there was something else he needed to tell them. Surely Lettie would still want her and Joe to keep running the place, for now at least?

Joe crossed his arms, then something seemed to occur to him. 'Ask Brodie whether there's anything you and I should be sorting out here before tomorrow, maybe.'

He was right. Why hadn't she thought of that? Too selfish worrying about her time with Joe being cut short, she reminded herself guiltily.

'Er, Brodie, was there something in particular you needed me—' she saw Joe point to himself '—um, us, to do to prepare for their homecoming?'

'That's just it,' Brodie replied, sounding a little odd.

'Is something the matter?' She pulled a face at Joe, wondering what Brodie was struggling to tell her.

Brodie groaned. 'The thing is, Skye, I was hoping to persuade Lettie to bring Isla to my cottage for a few days.' He went silent for a moment. 'I don't mean to be selfish, but with Lindy and Gareth still away, I was hoping to make the most of the opportunity to keep our little unit to ourselves. Just for a bit longer. Does that sound silly?'

Joe pressed his hand against his chest. 'No, mate. That sounds lovely.'

'Is that Joe?' Brodie asked. 'I hadn't realised he was there.'

'He's just come in.' Skye held the phone closer to Joe's face.

'Hi, mate.'

'Hi, Joe.'

'We're fine here,' Skye assured him, happy to think she and

Joe might have more time alone themselves. 'And what's more, we think your idea is incredibly romantic.'

'We do?' Joe whispered.

Skye noticed the twinkle in his eyes and knew he was teasing her. She stared at him pointedly and mouthed a yes.

'Brodie,' she continued. 'Joe and I think that's a lovely idea and are more than happy to carry on as we are until the pair of you are ready to come back to the farm.'

'We are,' Joe said. 'We'll keep Derek here too, unless you'd rather he come home, and I can drop him off.'

'No, I'll pop over to see him. We both will and Lettie can fetch some things she might want for her and Isla. I haven't broached the subject of her staying at the cottage with me yet, because I wanted to check with the pair of you first. I'm sure she only wants to return to the farm so that you two didn't think she was taking advantage of your kindness.'

'Not at all,' Joe said. 'We completely understand if you want to spent time quietly at the cottage.'

'Thank you. I'll go and speak to her now and assure her the pair of you are happy with my suggestion.'

Skye swapped glances with Joe and was surprised to see he seemed fine about the idea. 'That's great. Whatever you're happy doing is fine with us. Isn't it, Joe?'

'It certainly is. We'll see you tomorrow.'

'Thanks, guys, I really appreciate this,' Brodie said, sounding very happy as he ended the call.

Skye replaced the receiver back into the holder on the small hall table.

'Is it wrong of me to be this happy about my close friend and her baby not coming home just yet?'

Skye studied Joe's handsome face. He didn't sound as if he felt guilty, but she now knew him well enough to believe that it didn't sit right with him that he felt the way he did. She thought about the situation from Brodie and Lettie's point of view. 'No, it isn't.'

'You don't think so?'

She shook her head. 'How can it be wrong when we're making Brodie and hopefully Lettie so happy? We're giving them time alone together to get used to being a new family with the baby. There's nothing bad about that.'

Overcome by a sudden rush of courage, Skye decided to be completely honest about her own feelings. 'He's also making the pair of us very happy.'

Joe stared at her intently. As the seconds passed, Skye wondered if she had taken a step too far and unnerved him. She opened her mouth to try and make what she had said seem less threatening to him. The last thing she wanted to do was ruin their relationship, as fun and as comfortable as it had become for her at least.

'What I mean is...' she began.

'Please don't try to explain,' Joe interrupted. 'I know exactly what you mean and I feel the same way.'

Surprised and enormously relieved, Skye exhaled sharply. 'I'm glad to hear you say so. For a moment there I thought I'd said totally the wrong thing.'

He reached out and took her hands in his. 'This time here with you has been exactly what I needed.' Spud nudged his thigh, making them both laugh. Joe looked down at him. 'Yes, and seeing you.'

Returning his gaze to Skye, he continued, 'I feel carefree here. I can't remember the last time I felt this relaxed. It's felt like a breath of fresh air spending time here with you. So peaceful and—' he stared at her for a few seconds '—getting to know you has been—' he seemed to struggle to find the right words to explain himself '—joyful, refreshing? I'm not exactly sure what. You're an amazing woman, do you know that, Skye?'

Touched by his words, Skye had to clear her throat to respond. 'Thanks, Joe. I've loved being here with you too. I needed this and I don't think I knew quite how much until now.'

He gave her hands a gentle squeeze. 'Me, too.'

23

JOE

Skye peered past him. 'Has your mother left already?' Skye asked. 'I've put the kettle on in case she wanted a cup of tea.'

'No, she's gone.'

Skye squinted, then placed a hand on his forearm. 'Is everything all right between you both?'

'Was it my scowl that gave it away?' he joked, wanting more than anything to kiss Skye at that moment. Well, he mused, he wanted to do that most of the time, if he was honest with himself. Deciding not to push his luck, he went to speak, then his phone rang. Unsure where he had left it and not liking to ignore a call in case it was his mother having forgotten something, he gave Skye an apologetic smile. 'I'd better see who that is.' He followed the sound into the kitchen and saw that he had left his phone on the worktop. Picking the phone up and looking at the screen, he saw it was Paul, one of his colleagues from work. 'This might be interesting,' he said as Skye followed him into the room.

'Hi, there.'

'Sorry to interrupt you, Joe,' Paul said. 'I've just spoken to my mum about her time working at the hotel and she said she'd love to meet your friend Skye tomorrow morning, if that's possible.'

'I'll ask Skye,' Joe said, unsure how much time Skye and he might take talking with the woman and not wishing to be out when Brodie and Lettie brought the baby to the farm.

'Sorry for the short notice,' Paul continued, 'but Mum is going away for a couple of weeks to stay with her sister, and tomorrow morning is the only time she'll be free until she's back on the island. You mentioned that your friend is only over here for a short time, so I thought I'd better call you straight away.'

'Thanks, that's very thoughtful of you, Paul. Skye is right here.' He muted the call and relayed everything Paul had told him. 'What do you think?'

She seemed startled for a moment before gathering herself. 'Um, yes, I'd love to meet with them tomorrow.'

Glad Skye was taking up the opportunity, Joe said, 'It's very kind of you, Paul. And your mum. Thanks. We do have something we have to be at the farm for tomorrow but that's not until late morning, so could we meet up, say around ten-ish?'

'That sounds perfect. I'll send you the directions to her house.'

Joe thanked Paul and ended the call, excited to share the news with Skye.

'Joe, that's amazing,' she cried her hand immediately covering her mouth in her shock. 'I'll try not to get too excited but I am going to enjoy this moment.'

He rested a hand on each of her arms, wanting to reassure her. 'And you're right to do so. This is a tremendously exciting time for you.'

'And you're helping make it happen.' She beamed at him.

'Do you realise you're the one who is seeing to it that my dream has every chance of coming true? And that's incredible.'

Not wishing to take all the credit, he said, 'We haven't found your dad yet, although I am hoping we do.' A thought occurred to him but he decided not to voice it.

'I can see something's bothering you,' she said, the intensity of her gaze seeming as if she was reading his mind. 'You're worried that I'll be disappointed if he doesn't want to meet me.'

'Maybe.'

'And you'd be right, but I won't let my fear of that happening ruin this for me. I'm going to enjoy every single moment and if I have to deal with it not panning out as I hope, then so be it.'

She was incredibly brave, he decided. 'And you won't have to do it alone because I'll be with you every step of the way.'

The look in her eyes changed and Joe couldn't miss how thankful she was to him. Not wanting her to think too highly of him, because after all wasn't he was only doing what anyone else in his position would do, he said, 'This is exciting for me too, you know.'

'It is?'

Joe shrugged. 'Yes.'

'Why, though?'

'Because it's not every day I get to go on a hunt for a mystery man and try to help someone I like very much to discover more about their history.'

'Aw, that's so sweet of you, Joe.'

He couldn't tell if she was teasing him, then decided this was far too important to Skye to think about teasing anyone. 'I do my best,' he said, giving what he hoped was an angelic expression.

'I know, and I appreciate your efforts.' She raised her eyebrows. 'Seriously. I really do.'

Now she really was teasing him and he was grateful. He didn't want things to become too heavy, especially when neither of them could bank on what the outcome of their search might be.

'We'd better get up an hour earlier if we're to do all the chores before leaving to meet up with Paul's mum,' Joe suggested. 'After that we'll have to race back to be here to welcome Brodie and Lettie.'

'And baby Isla,' she reminded him. 'They're going to make such a cute family, don't you think?'

He thought about it and tried to picture the three of them together. 'I do. Although I'm not sure how they're going to cope if they don't hurry up and decide which house they'll live in.' He thought of Brodie's practice. 'His cottage is right next to his work and Lettie's is at hers.'

'But they're both down the road from each other, so surely it couldn't be too difficult to choose.' Skye wondered what Brodie's cottage was like. 'Surely if Lindy and Gareth return and stay here when they're not travelling, then wouldn't Lettie want to be at the cottage?'

'I've no idea. I do know though that the cottage is tiny and there's barely room for Brodie, so even if they have to share this house with her parents and occasionally her brother and Melody, I have a feeling this is where they'll end up living full-time.'

'I suppose you're right.' Skye sighed. 'After all it's not as if they can leave the animals alone overnight if there's no one else here to take care of things in case of an emergency.'

He saw that Skye was becoming concerned and presumed she was wondering about when she might need to move on from the farm. He decided to change the subject back to her meeting tomorrow. 'I'm sure they'll work it out. After all it's not our problem or any of our business really, is it?'

She pouted. 'No, I guess not. I seem to have forgotten that this isn't my farm, or yours.'

'No.' He grinned. 'We're just here to take care of things for a short time.' He saw her face drop as he spoke and knew he had ruined the mood, so patted her shoulder. 'However, we're here now, and thanks to Brodie, it looks like we'll be able to carry on as we are at least for another week.'

She frowned thoughtfully. 'Unless Lettie disagrees, and they come here tomorrow and move back in.'

He hadn't thought of that happening. 'Ah, that could be a possibility.'

24

SKYE

Skye was glad she wasn't driving to Paul's mother's home. It was difficult enough to concentrate on remaining calm while she tried to decide on the questions she wanted to ask this woman who was kindly giving up her time.

He parked the car and Skye took a steadying breath before getting out of the car.

'You OK?' he asked quietly.

She puffed out her cheeks and shook her head. 'Not really, if I'm honest.' She saw his concern and forced a smile. 'But I will be by the time we reach the front door.'

'You'll be great. And, remember, even if it turns out she didn't know your father then at least you've crossed one person off your list.'

That didn't make her feel much better. 'Off my list of two, you mean?'

'Try to be positive – I'm sure this will be fine.'

Skye wished she had Joe's confidence, but forced herself to seem calm as they stopped at the front door and he rang the bell.

'You've got this,' he whispered.

The door was opened by a man who she soon realised must be Paul. 'Joe,' he said, tilting his head to one side to see Skye. 'And this must be the lovely Skye.'

Lovely Skye? She wasn't sure what he meant by that, but smiled and shook his hand. 'It is. Thanks for inviting me here today, I'm really grateful for any help searching for my father.'

'I can imagine you must be.' He stepped back and waved them into the hall. 'I was happy to help in any way I could when Joe told us your predicament.' He led the way into the home. 'Mum is this way.'

Skye walked into the living room where a woman who seemed to be in her fifties went to stand. 'Please, don't get up on my account.' Skye walked over to her and shook her hand. 'It's very kind of you to invite Joe and me to your lovely house.' Realising she hadn't introduced herself, Skye added, 'I'm Skye by the way.'

'I thought you might be.' The woman laughed, looking from Skye to Joe. 'I've met this handsome chap a couple of times before. Hello, Joe. How are you doing?'

'Fine, thanks.'

'I'm Sandra,' Paul's mother said. 'Paul will make you teas and coffees if you'd like them. We have biscuits too.' Before Skye could answer, she added, 'I'm sorry everything is a bit of a mess. I'm preparing to fly out this afternoon on a trip.'

'We're fine for drinks, thanks,' Skye said, looking at Joe to check he agreed. 'We have to return to the farm to be there when our friends come from the maternity wing at the hospital with their new baby.'

'How exciting.'

'It is,' they said in unison.

'They know you don't have too long to chat either, Mum,'

Paul explained. Then looking at Skye and Joe, indicated the sofa. 'Please take a seat.' Skye happily sat down next to Joe.

'And it's very kind of you to fit in seeing us when you're so busy,' Skye said when she was settled.

Sandra waved away Skye's comment with a friendly smile. 'Now I've been through some old boxes of photos from the two seasons I worked at the Bel Amie Hotel.' Skye leant forward to see the photos as Sandra laid them out on the coffee table in front of her. 'I was looking at them last night and became very nostalgic for those busy but fun days. Seeing them again brought back so many wonderful memories I'd forgotten. It was rather bittersweet. Made me wonder what had happened to all those people I expected to be friends with forever.'

Touched to think how emotional this must be for Sandra, Skye said, 'I suppose I should start by telling you Mum's name really.'

'Yes, do.' Sandra rested her hands in her lap and listened, waiting for Skye to continue.

'Well, she was called Annie.'

'Not Annie Sellers? From Edinburgh?' Sandra interrupted, leaning forward eager to hear more.

'Er, yes. That's her.' That was surprising, Skye thought, feeling a little shell-shocked that all she had mentioned was her mother's first name for Sandra to remember her. 'Did you know her well?' she asked, doubting it to be the case. Surely it couldn't be this simple, could it?

'We were roommates,' Sandra said, her voice filled with emotion. 'But Paul said your mother had passed away and that's why you need to trace your father, knowing so little about him.'

Skye saw the distress on Sandra's face and wished she could tell her otherwise. 'I'm afraid she did. Quite a number of years ago too.'

Sandra gasped and glanced at Paul, who immediately stood behind her chair, his hands on her shoulders to comfort her. 'But she must have been very young.'

Skye nodded and felt Joe move slightly closer to her, comforting her with the reminder that he was there. 'She was barely forty.'

'Oh no. That's so sad.'

Skye hoped Sandra wouldn't cry, because if she did Skye wasn't sure she would be able to retain her own self-control. 'It is. Very sad.'

She felt Joe's hand rest lightly on her thigh, distracting her from becoming too emotional by the warmth of his touch. Skye cleared her throat. Wanting to know as much as possible about her mother and hopefully her father while she had the chance, Skye said, 'I'm sorry to give you such sad news.'

Sandra dabbed at her eyes with a tissue. 'It's not your fault. I suppose I mostly feel guilty.'

'About what?' Skye asked, confused.

'Annie and I were almost the same age. We were very close, once. I feel guilty not having kept in contact with her.' She stared at Skye, her eyes watery with unshed tears. 'I should have kept in touch with her, found out about you. Spent time with her.' Her voice trailed off but before Skye could think how to respond, Sandra continued. 'I suppose we never imagine people's lives will be cut short.' She sighed heavily and dabbed at her eyes again. 'Always assume we have all the time in the world to contact people.'

Hating to see the poor woman so upset on account of her visit, Skye moved forward to the edge of her seat and reached out to take Sandra's hand. 'Please don't upset yourself. I under-stand what you're saying and have felt that way, many times, but have come to the conclusion that regret is a waste of emotion.

Anyway—' she forced a smile '—Mum would have hated to think of anyone she was close to feeling badly.'

Sandra nodded and, believing the woman was feeling slightly better, Skye sat back in her seat again.

'Well,' Sandra said, seeming much more in control. 'You're here to find out about Carlos Ferreira.'

Who? 'Do you mean that's the name of my father?'

Sandra shrugged. 'I presume so. As far as I'm aware.' She raised a finger. 'And I was the closest person to Annie while she was in Jersey. He was the only man she ever spent time with.' She thought for a moment. 'Or showed any interest in, come to think of it.' She narrowed her eyes and studied Skye's face before smiling. 'And looking at you now, with your dark hair, dark eyes and that beautiful bone structure of yours, I'm 99 per cent certain he must be your father. He was a very handsome man, was Carlos,' she said, her voice taking on a slightly dreamy tone that made Skye wonder if Sandra could have had an interest in the man too.

Did something happen between the women involving him to cause a rift? Now wasn't the time to ask for too much information, Skye reminded herself. She was here to focus on her father and discovering all she could about him.

Her stomach fluttered with excitement and nerves. She looked at Joe and saw excitement in his eyes. So she had been right to think C. Ferreira could be her father. And now they had a first name, too. 'Carlos Ferreira,' Skye whispered, saying the name for the first time. 'It's a nice name.'

'He was a nice man,' Sandra said. She leant forward and, moving a few of the photos around, found one she was looking for and tapped on it several times. 'There he is with Annie.'

Skye gasped, aware she was about to look at the most important photo she would probably ever see. She glanced at Joe, unsure why she was hesitating. This was too immense a moment to grasp.

'Go on,' he encouraged.

She picked up the photo with shaky fingers and took a calming breath before looking at it. Skye studied the young couple sitting on a beach, leaning against the sea wall, and struggled to keep her emotions in check. Carlos had his arms around Annie's shoulders. Both were laughing at something someone, probably the photographer, had said.

'I took that photo,' Sandra said, her voice shaky. 'That wasn't long before Annie left, probably only a few weeks. They were very happy and seemed deeply in love.'

'Seemed?' Skye was confused by the use of the word. Looking at the happy faces she would assume they didn't have a care in the world.

'Yes. But if they really had been then why would Annie have upped and left like she did? It doesn't make sense. Unless...' She narrowed her eyes and gazed at Skye. 'When were you born?'

'January 1999.'

Sandra gave her answer some thought then nodded. 'That makes sense. She must have been three to four months pregnant in this photo.' Sadness washed over her face. 'I never knew.' Then looking into Skye's eyes, she asked, 'Why do you think she never told me?'

'I've no idea,' Skye said, honestly wishing she had answers for the poor woman. 'Have you any idea what happened to Carlos?'

Sandra shook her head slowly. 'We didn't keep in touch.'

'Do you know if he still lives on the island?' Skye asked, her mind racing with unanswered questions. 'Was he even from here?'

'I don't know whether he's still here or not, I'm afraid.'

Deciding to bring the conversation back to her mother and Sandra's friendship, Skye asked, 'Mum never gave any reason for leaving then?'

Sandra thought for a moment. 'She asked for permission to return home for a couple of days, I seem to recall. Something about her mother being unwell and needing to see her.' She shook her head. 'But she never came back. I did write a couple of times, then when she didn't reply became angry and...'

Her voice petered off and Skye wondered what it might be that Sandra wasn't comfortable sharing with her. 'And, what?' she asked, desperate to find out more.

Sandra looked down at her hands clasped together in her lap. Then, without speaking, rested one hand on Paul's and glanced up at him. As if a secret code had passed between them, Paul moved to the side of Sandra's chair.

'I'm sorry, but Mum really needs to get on with the rest of her packing.'

Skye knew he was protecting Sandra from becoming too upset and didn't want to outstay her welcome, especially when the pair of them had been as kind and generous with their time as they had been.

Skye got to her feet at the same time Joe did. 'Thank you for giving me so much information, Sandra, and to you, Paul, for arranging for us to meet. I'm incredibly grateful.'

'I'm sorry I couldn't tell you more,' Sandra said, sounding as if she meant it.

Skye realised she was still holding the photo and went to place it down on the table.

'No, please keep it,' Sandra insisted. 'It's yours.'

Skye gasped to have been given such an unexpected treasure. 'Really? You don't mind?'

Sandra smiled and shook her head. 'No. You don't know how

happy I am to be able to help you in this way.' She stared into Skye's eyes for a few seconds, making Skye wonder what it was that Sandra was withholding from her, because whatever it was seemed to trouble her for some reason. 'I feel that by helping connect you to Carlos that I've helped my dear friend Annie in some way.'

'Well, I'll treasure this.' Feeling the need to hug Sandra, Skye said, 'Would you mind if I give you a hug?'

Sandra's eyes filled with tears again and she nodded, opening her arms without speaking.

Feeling as if she was receiving a hug from the next best thing to her mother, Skye stepped into Sandra's arms. It was deeply comforting and Skye suspected by the way Sandra was holding tightly to her, it meant as much to the older lady as it did to her.

As they let go of each other, Skye sighed. 'Well, thank you again and I hope you have a wonderful holiday.'

'Thank you, Skye,' Sandra said. 'And if I think of anything else I'll ask Paul for your phone number.'

'Yes, please do that. I'm happy to hear anything you can remember.' Aware this could include not so happy memories, Skye added, 'Anything at all.'

They left the house and got into the car without saying a word. Once seated, Joe took her hand in his and turned to her. 'You OK?'

She nodded, unable to speak without crying.

'Good. Let's get back to the farm.'

25

JOE

All the way back to the farm, Joe went over everything that had been said at Sandra's home. He had hoped Paul's mum might be able to give Skye some information but never imagined it would be this much. And she had a photo. He glanced at her and saw Skye studying it. How incredible must Skye feel to be looking at her parents together and happy. He wished he had more photos of his own father and his parents when they had first met, but the only time he had asked Faye about them she had admitted she had torn them up and disposed of them.

'How do you feel?' he asked, happy for her.

She swallowed before speaking. 'I think I'm still a bit stunned.' She held up the photo. 'I never imagined in a million years that I'd find out his name, let alone be given a photo of him and Mum together.'

Joe had a thought and not wanting to upset her in any way pondered whether to share it.

'I can see you thinking about something. What is it?'

He looked at her for a second, then straight ahead. 'I was just thinking that going by the dates Sandra said she took that photo that you're also in it. In a way.'

She held the photo closer to her. 'I suppose I am,' she said, her voice quiet and cracking with emotion.

'Hey, I didn't want to upset you by saying that.'

'You didn't, Joe.' She rested her hand on his briefly. 'What you've just said to me is the singular most amazing thing anyone has ever said to me. These are happy tears. Thank you.'

Relieved, but still unsure he was right to have shared his thoughts with her, Joe glanced at her again. 'You sure?'

'Yes.' She sounded convincing so Joe chose to believe she actually might be fine.

'I was wondering, though,' Skye said.

'Go on, what's on your mind?'

'If my father, or the man we presume to be my father's last name is Ferreira, I was trying to work out where he might be from. I don't think that's a typical Jersey last name, is it?'

Joe shook his head. 'No. I think he's Portuguese, or from Madeira.'

'Really? How would you know that?'

Joe remembered this was Skye's first time in Jersey and that she wouldn't have been here long enough to grasp any of the history of the island's people. 'The island has always had people coming from firstly France, then Italy and then Portugal, or Madeira to come and work during the summer seasons here.'

'Really? That's fascinating.'

'As you probably know, the island initially was known for its farming, hence French people coming over to work the land on farms. When the tourist industry picked up in the late fifties and early sixties, quite a few Italian people came to work in hotels and restaurants, then when the island's tourism was at its height in the sixties and seventies people came over to work the seasons in the hotels. I presume that's what your father or even his family might have done. Many people settled on the island and are now part of the local community.'

'I suppose it does make sense that my father was Portuguese going by my hair and eye colour.'

Joe was relieved to see that Skye seemed to like the idea and began to relax slightly. It had been a concerning time at Sandra's and for a while there he had wished he had considered more the repercussions of him introducing Skye to anyone who knew her family.

Then again, he mused, making emotional discoveries could be extremely painful and life-changing but once you came to terms with that new knowledge things became more settled. Or it had done in his experience. Not that his parents' divorce or his ex's decision to dump him was the same as the situation Skye currently found herself dealing with.

'They're here,' Skye said, pointing to the windscreen.

His thoughts returning to the present, Joe peered down the drive and saw Brodie's ancient Land Rover drawing into the yard.

'We made it just in time,' Joe said, glad they hadn't spent any longer at Sandra's home. Even if Lettie expected him and Skye to have time away from the farm she wouldn't be impressed if they both were absent from it for too long.

'I'm so excited to meet baby Isla,' Skye said, opening the door before he had completely stopped the car.

'Hey, be careful. We don't need you hurting yourself.'

She ignored him and after getting out of the car ran over to wait for Brodie to unstrap the baby and lift her carefully out of the car seat. Joe waited for Skye to hug Lettie, then did the same.

'It's great to see you looking so well,' he said to his friend, surprised to see how relaxed Lettie seemed after the dramas of her going into labour early.

'I'm fine, Joe,' she assured him, hugging him tightly for a few seconds. 'You two have been amazing, by the way. Isla and I thank you.'

'So do I,' Brodie said, handing the baby into Skye's waiting arms and giving Joe a pat on the back.

'Now you've got your sweet family and so much to look forward to,' Joe said, smiling.

They began following the women into the house. 'I'm a very lucky man,' Brodie said quietly. 'I never expected to have all that I do.'

'You deserve your happiness,' Joe assured him. 'As does Lettie, and I'm thrilled for you both.'

'Thanks, mate.'

Skye opened the front door and within seconds Spud and Derek bounded out to greet them, tails wagging, whining in excitement. Derek pushed his head against Brodie's thigh, making him laugh. Joe watched his friend bend down to greet his beloved dog and realised how much he must have missed him. He had only adopted Derek the year before when the elderly lady who had taken him on from a neighbour who had had to move couldn't cope and the two had become firm friends.

'I'm going to have to introduce you to baby Isla,' Brodie said as he patted the dog's rump.

Spud was just as excited to greet Lettie, but Joe was relieved to see Skye take his attention and give him a pat.

'Come along, boys, let's get you both a treat for being so well behaved while we were out,' she said.

After settling down in the living room with cups of tea and some biscuits Skye found in the cupboard, Lettie stroked Isla's head as she lay in Brodie's arms. 'I'll come and have a look around after we finish these drinks,' she said. 'Before that I thought Brodie and I should speak to you about our plans for the next few weeks.'

Joe swapped glances with Skye, hoping Lettie had given in to Brodie and agreed to spend some time with him and the baby at the cottage in the village.

'You both seem to be getting along well,' she said, giving each of them a searching look in case they had anything to share with her.

'We are,' Joe confirmed.

'Yes, everything is going swimmingly so far,' Skye agreed.

Lettie beamed at them, then at Brodie. 'You were right after all.'

Joe laughed. 'So what is it you're about to tell us then?'

'Well, Brodie and I thought that if both of you were happy for us to do so, that the three of us would spend a couple of weeks together with Isla living in his cottage.'

'Our cottage,' Brodie corrected.

'Yes, well, as opposed to this house,' she said. 'We thought it would be perfect timing to be by ourselves with the baby and make the most of having the space to do that, at least until Mum and Dad return from their trip. I should be feeling ready to come back to running this place and when Mum is here, she'll no doubt want to be hands on with her first grandchild.'

Joe pictured Lindy's excitement. She would definitely want to take over and he completely understood why Lettie was happy to go along with Brodie's suggestion.

'Sounds like a brilliant idea to me,' Skye said.

Joe heard the joy in Skye's voice that echoed his own. 'I agree. Anyway, you should have some time by yourselves, never mind having at least a few weeks' maternity leave.'

'That's also what Brodie said,' Lettie said, patting Brodie's knee. 'That's not all though.'

Joe tensed but tried to look as if he was completely relaxed. 'Go on.'

She looked from one to the other of them, her expression serious. 'I'm not sure how desperate you both are to return to your normal lives, but Lindy called earlier to confirm she and Gareth will be home a week today.'

'A week?' Skye asked, sounding as alarmed as Joe felt at the news.

'You don't seem as happy as I expected,' Brodie said.

'It's fine,' Joe assured him, turning to Skye when she didn't immediately reply.

'What? Oh, yes, of course it is. They must be dying to meet their new granddaughter.'

'You're both welcome to stay at the farm for as long as you wish to though,' Lettie said.

Relieved not to have to cut short his time with Skye, Joe nodded. 'Thanks.'

Skye hadn't spoken again and he wondered if she was thinking about her meeting with Sandra and presumed she must be.

'You two have been so good accommodating us and all our changes.' Lettie puffed out her cheeks. 'You're amazing, do you know that?'

Feeling slightly guilty that someone was grateful to him when what he was doing benefitted him and gave him the chance to spend quality time alone with Skye, Joe shook his head. 'Don't give it another thought,' he said, unsure what else to say.

'Joe's right. We're happy to do whatever you need us to,' Skye said, giving him a quick look out of the corner of her eye.

Joe noticed Lettie frown thoughtfully for a second. Isla began moaning and distracted her, so he looked at Skye and gave her a relieved smile. He knew his friends wouldn't resent him becoming close to Skye, but what was happening between them was new and both were treading into unknown territory. Who knew if anything would come from this, or if either of them would be hurt by the other. He hoped what they had would grow but for now was happy to keep their relationship, as fresh as it was, just between him and Skye.

Lettie bent down to sniff near Isla and grimaced. 'She needs a nappy change.'

'I'll do that,' Brodie said, standing as he held the grumbling baby. 'Why don't you go and have a wander around the farm, give your animals a cuddle, and I'll see you back here. Then we can go home to the cottage.'

Hearing Brodie's eagerness to go home with his fiancée and baby, Joe waved for Lettie to join him. 'Come along then. Skye and I will show you what we've been doing and how well we're looking after your animals.'

Lettie laughed. 'I wouldn't expect you to do anything less.'

26

SKYE

'Let me carry those bags for you,' Joe said, coming up to join Skye and Lettie in the bedroom where Skye had packed up a few of Lettie's clothes while her friend packed up her baby's things ready to take to the cottage.

Lettie waited for him to pick up the bags containing her clothes then took the two she had been holding with spare nappies, bottles and various other bits and pieces she had no idea what were used for and followed Joe and Lettie downstairs to where Brodie was cuddling a tetchy baby Isla.

'Is she OK?' Skye asked, wondering why the baby was unhappy again.

'She's tired, I expect,' Brodie suggested.

Lettie took the baby from him. 'We may as well get going. The sooner we're at the cottage and settled the sooner we can relax,' she said as Brodie got to his feet.

Skye joined Joe carrying the bags out to the Land Rover, handing them to Brodie when he unlocked the door.

'It's been good to see you both again,' Brodie said.

'It has,' Lettie agreed. 'And thank you from the bottom of my heart for all you're doing for me and this place.'

'Don't give it another thought,' Joe said. 'We're coping just fine. Aren't we, Skye?'

'We are.'

Brodie whistled for Derek, surprising Skye.

She looked at Joe. 'I thought we were keeping him for a bit?'

'I'd presumed the same thing.' Joe turned his attention to Brodie. 'You're more than welcome to leave Derek here for a bit longer, you know?'

Brodie shrugged. 'I had wondered if it was the best thing to do but...'

Lettie interrupted. 'I know how much Brodie's missed his dog and after discussing it we both feel it's better to get the dog used to having Isla around as soon as possible.'

'I suppose you're right,' Joe agreed.

Skye agreed but noticing Spud's tail drop felt sorry for the dog that his friend was leaving. She patted her thigh and Spud slunk over to her side. 'It's OK, boy. He'll be back to visit you again soon.'

'He will,' Brodie assured them, shutting the back door of the vehicle as soon as Derek had jumped inside.

Skye stood next to Joe as they waited for the couple to strap the baby into her car seat and get into the vehicle. She couldn't help thinking how wonderful it had been to finally be able to cuddle baby Isla. It was also an enormous relief to know Lettie was satisfied with the way she and Joe had been caring for the animals and the crops.

She and Joe waved them off as Brodie drove out of the yard and down the long driveway.

'That went well,' Joe said sounding as relieved as Skye felt. 'At least we now know we're doing everything as we should be.'

'I agree.'

Joe rested his hands on his hips. 'I suppose we should get on with the rest of our work now they've gone.'

'We should.'

They walked over to the barn to fetch barrows and spades.

'Seeing them pair of them here reminded me that our time on the farm is limited,' Skye admitted miserably. 'I've loved being here, and to think I'll soon be leaving all this makes me sad.'

Joe stopped walking. 'I was thinking the same thing.' He reached out and took her hand in his. 'I'm going to miss working here with you, do you know that?'

Skye was delighted to hear it. 'I'll miss being here with you, too. We've made rather a good team, despite everything.'

Joe laughed and, letting go of her hand, folded his arms. 'And what exactly do you mean by that?'

She could tell he was teasing her and was happy to tell him. 'Let's face it we didn't exactly start off as friends now, did we?'

He shook his head. 'Maybe not.'

'And you can't deny you were unimpressed to discover you wouldn't be living here alone.'

'That bit is definitely true.' She went to speak but he grinned and raised his hand to speak. 'However, I soon realised that running somewhere like this needs two inexperienced people working together if they are to keep on top of everything.'

'You have experience though – you said so.'

'Only a bit and always focusing on the heavy work lifting and shifting for my uncle. Never running anything, or having to keep an eye on stocks running low, reordering stuff, that sort of thing.'

'Makes sense, I suppose.'

His cheerful expression vanished. 'If this is coming to an

end, we really need to make the most of every second we still have here.'

She liked his sentiment. 'I agree. And that's what we'll do.'

They walked on again but despite her agreement to Joe's comment, Skye was at a loss as to how he supposed they would do that. She already enjoyed waking each morning in her beautiful room, gazing out of her bedroom window as the sun rose or set, and never failed to be cheered up by seeing all the animals and walking in the fields relishing the glorious views over the pretty landscape and out to sea on one side of the farm. She knew that whatever happened in her life this part of it was something she would always be grateful for and would never forget. Especially getting to know Joe and spending so much time alone with him.

27

JOE

That evening, Joe was just getting out of the shower when his phone rang. Towel-drying his hair and drying his hands, he answered the call to find it was his friend Bruno.

'Hi, Joe, I've spoken to my dad and he's happy to meet up with you and your friend tomorrow morning if that suits you both. Around eleven-ish? We thought we could meet you for coffee at one of the cafés in St Aubin and tell you both about the Ferreiras he knows who live on the island.'

Now that he and Skye knew that her father had worked at the other hotel, Joe wasn't sure whether the meeting would be worthwhile. He hoped he was doing the right thing arranging for Skye to meet them. It occurred to him he hadn't mentioned the first name of the Ferreira they were looking for, just in case it did happen to be Bruno's father's name.

He puffed out his cheeks, concerned. He was getting ahead of himself. There was no sense in getting carried away with different scenarios at this point. At least if Bruno's father did turn out to be the man Skye was looking for, Joe mused, then it would be up to the older man to decide how much information he wanted to share about himself.

Anyway, he thought, Bruno had gone to the effort of making arrangements with his father and he didn't want to appear rude. There was no harm him and Skye meeting the two men and for all he knew Bruno's father might have some information that could prove useful for Skye.

'Sounds perfect.' He finished drying himself and dressed. Skye was already in her bedroom having showered before him and he wasn't sure if she would still be awake or whether he should wait until the morning to let her know he had heard from his friend.

He walked out of the shower room and into the hall. Then spotting a light under her bedroom door, walked over to it. Knocking lightly in case she had fallen asleep, he half expected her not to reply.

'Yes?'

'It's me,' Joe said, feeling a little silly and aware it would hardly be anyone else. 'I've had a call from my mate and hope it's OK but I've agreed to meet up with him and his dad tomorrow at eleven. Their last name is Ferreira, and I thought they might be able to offer more information that could hopefully lead you to finding your father. What do you think?' When she didn't reply, he added, 'If you'd rather have more time to think about it I can always call him back and postpone everything.'

'No, don't do that. Look, this is odd talking through a door. Come in for a bit.'

Joe opened the door and, not wishing to breach any boundaries, leant against the doorframe. Skye was sitting up in her bed looking so pretty in her faded cartoon T-shirt, a book resting on her lap, that he wished he could kiss her.

Get a grip, man, he told himself, feeling like a teenage boy rather than someone who had enough experience to know better. 'Sorry to make arrangements without speaking to you first, but it's late and I thought it best to firm a time and place before speaking to you.'

She smiled. 'It's fine. Better than fine actually.' She placed a bookmark inside her paperback and closed the book, placing it on the bedside table. 'I'm aware I need to make the most of every opportunity, however small, if I want to find him.' She bit her lower lip, looking anxious for a moment. 'They have the same last name, you say?'

He nodded. 'I'm not sure how many Ferreiras there are here, but Bruno insists his father will know most, if not all, of them.' He shrugged. 'I thought it was an opportunity we shouldn't miss.'

'I agree. I'm a bit nervous though, if I'm honest.'

He hated to think she might be but understood why she would feel that way. 'There's no need to be. I'll be there with you. Unless you'd rather meet them alone?'

'No,' she said, sounding panicked. 'I'd rather you were there. At least with two of us there we'll have more chance of thinking to ask the most pertinent questions. It's all a bit surreal, to be honest.' Skye smiled. 'I don't think I could have done this without you.'

He shook his head, trying to hide how much it meant to him that she thought so. 'I'm happy to be of help to you. It might have taken longer seeing as you don't know anyone here, but you're resourceful and determined.' He gave her a wink. If there was one thing Skye was, it was that.

She laughed. 'I hold my hand up to being that person.' She sat back against her pillow.

Joe's eyes locked with hers and for a moment he couldn't

think. She looked so beautiful sitting in her bed. He cleared his throat. 'We should get some sleep. Don't fret about tomorrow.'

'Yes, you're right.' She smiled at him, happy once again. 'Thanks, Joe. Sleep well.'

She lay down on her side and reached out to turn off the light before he had even left the room. Joe stared at her back for a couple of seconds. Then realising he had no way of knowing what had just happened to change the atmosphere between them, left the room, closing the door quietly behind him.

He got into bed and stared into the darkness, playing their conversation over and over in his head. He really hoped he was doing the right thing and not about to put Skye in an awkward position with Bruno and his father. He groaned. He was over-thinking things. What was the chance of Bruno's dad being Skye's father anyway?

Not daring to continue with that thought, he lay down and closed his eyes.

28

SKYE

Skye walked with Joe, unsure how her shaky legs were managing to carry her along Le Boulevard to meet his work colleague Bruno and his father. She still couldn't quite get her head around the fact that the man she was about to meet might know her father. It had occurred to her that he could even be the man in the photo and the one Sandra had told her about. But more than likely this Mr Ferreira would turn out to be a different Mr Ferreira. But what if the man she was about to meet was her father? How would she react if he was the man who had been in love with her mother and such a huge part of Annie's life? Even if their relationship had only lasted several months, Skye believed after seeing the photo of Carlos and Annie together on the beach that at least some of those months had made her mum very happy, and for that she was also happy.

'We're here,' Joe said, stopping at the entrance to the café. 'How are you doing?'

She tried to steady her breathing, aware it was shallow and she was giving in to her panic.

Joe took her hands in his. 'Take a long slow deep breath,' he soothed, looking deep into her eyes.

Aware she needed to calm down before entering the café, Skye focused on gazing up at Joe and did exactly as he suggested, feeling instantly calmer.

'That's better. Now, don't forget they are here to meet you, that's all. No one is judging you, or your mum and this is bound to be unusual for them as well as you.'

He was right and the reminder calmed her further. 'They're probably just excited to be helping me by offering whatever information they might have about the man I'm looking for,' Skye suggested.

'Exactly,' Joe agreed. 'After all, I'm sure people don't often meet up looking for help finding a long-lost father.'

'I wish I wasn't so nervous though.'

'You'll be fine, I promise.'

Soothed by Joe's reassurance, Skye pushed back her shoulders, wanting to get on with what they were here to do. 'Take no notice of me, Joe. I'll be fine, but you go in first.'

Of course she would be, she told herself as she followed Joe into the pleasant café, its wooden floors and pale blue panelled walls welcoming them.

Joe stopped and Skye stood next to him, scanning the busy room. She was glad it was relatively noisy and that others wouldn't be interested in listening to their conversation once it got going. In an island of this size she imagined many people knew each other and Skye didn't like to think news of her situation might circulate without her being aware.

'There they are,' Joe whispered, raising his hand in a wave before striding over to a table where two men sat chatting.

Bruno stood and smiled briefly at Joe as they made their way past the tables. Then his attention turned to Skye. She pictured the man in the photo with her mother. The resemblance to him and this guy was incredible and she was almost giddy with shock and excitement that she was eye to eye with the man she now realised could be her own brother. It was a strange sensation and her heart raced so rapidly for a moment she thought she might pass out. She had grown up believing she was an only child. It seemed that she might have a sibling after all.

Bruno's face broke into a smile. 'Skye?' She nodded, unable to speak. He stepped forward to embrace Joe briefly, then turned to Skye. 'I'm Bruno and this is my father, Carlos. It is good to meet you.'

'Lovely to meet you, too,' Skye said, finally able to find her voice.

She watched as Bruno stepped aside to reveal his father. 'Dad, this is my friend, Joe from work.' He waited for them to shake hands. 'And this is Skye, the lady I asked you to come and meet. As you know, she's looking for information to trace her father.'

Skye's eyes met Carlos's and it was as if the rest of the world vanished. Gazing into his dark brown eyes was like staring into a mirror and she knew without any doubt at all that this man was her father. She was barely conscious of any sound, or even of her own breathing as she tried to take in every detail of his face. It was a kind face and still recognisable from the one in the photo Sandra had shown to her.

'Skye?'

Hearing Joe's voice as if from far away, she eventually managed to force her eyes in his direction. 'Yes?'

He gave a nod and she realised Carlos was waiting for her to shake his hand.

'It is delightful to meet you,' the older man said, staring at her as if he was as mesmerised as her.

Does he recognise himself in me? she wondered, wishing she could gather herself a little better.

'Sit here,' Joe was saying, his hands lightly on her upper arms as he steered her to a chair.

Skye sat automatically, unable to think what to say. She was vaguely aware of Bruno saying something then felt Joe's hand take hers under the table and give it a gentle squeeze. She glanced up at him and remembered to concentrate on her breathing and to be calm.

Able to focus again, she listened as Bruno explained how fascinated he had been when Joe had told her about Skye looking for her father on the island. 'I remembered Dad talking about working at the Sunshine Springs Hotel many times and even recall going there a few times for an ice cream. It's a shame it closed down a few years ago.'

Skye thought about Sandra saying she and Annie had worked at the Bel Amie Hotel. She knew she should mention it.

'We met with Paul's mother, Sandra, the other day and she told me that she and my mother, Annie, worked together at the Bel Amie Hotel.'

Unsure how Carlos might react, she was taken aback when his eyes widened, and he covered his mouth with his hands.

'Dad? Are you all right?' Bruno rested a hand on his father's shoulder. 'What's the matter?'

Carlos took a deep breath and, looking at Skye, said, 'You say your mother's name was Annie?'

'That's right.' He remembered her mum, Skye thought, relieved.

'And that she was close friends with a girl named Sandra?'

'That's right,' Joe said, still keeping hold of Skye's hand.

She could barely breathe, sensing this was something momentous for her and Carlos.

Carlos raised both hands slightly and shook his head, giving a shocked laugh. 'I remember them both well.' He seemed to be struggling to remain calm.

He rested his hands on the table and took a deep breath. 'I did work at the Sunshine Springs for three years,' he said, without taking his eyes from hers, 'but before then I worked for one season at the Bel Amie Hotel.'

Skye's heart raced as he spoke, not daring to interrupt him.

Carlos's gaze shifted down to his hands.

'It's fine, Dad,' she heard Bruno say, his voice quieter than before. 'I'm ready to hear anything you have to tell us.'

Skye pressed her lips together, not daring to make a sound as the realisation of who she could be to them dawned on Bruno, and his father realised he was about to share some of his past his son clearly hadn't known about.

She watched as Carlos looked from his son to her and seemed to brace himself. 'The reason I left the Bel Amie was due to a relationship that ended badly.' He appeared to struggle to retain his emotion briefly before continuing. 'The lady in question's name was Annie.' He looked at Skye but she didn't dare speak. 'Her best friend was Sandra,' he added, his voice quieter and his hands clasped together. 'There was a...' he hesitated '...misunderstanding. Annie left without saying goodbye.'

Carlos stared silently at Skye, the misery still clear in his eyes. There was something else, she realised, unable to decipher what it might be. Recalling seeing a similar look in her mother's eyes over the years, Skye realised it was regret. Feeling sorry for Carlos now and the young man he had once been and how much she must have suffered such a deep and lasting pain, Skye said, 'You're not the only one Mum did that to,' she admitted, wishing she didn't feel like a traitor saying it.

Carlos cast his eyes downward again. 'I'm sure she had her

reasons for doing so.' Wincing, he looked Skye in the eyes once again, embarrassed. 'For leaving me, I mean, not you.'

She smiled to show she understood and hadn't taken his words out of context. 'Please, carry on with what you were saying.'

'I admit I struggled to come to terms with her going like she did. It affected me for many years afterwards.'

It clearly still did, she mused, miserably. How much lasting damage had her mother's decisions left on him, herself and even her grandmother? Skye wondered. She realised he was staring at her and sensed he was building up to ask her something.

'Please, ask me anything,' Skye said, willing him to share what was on his mind.

Carlos looked at his son. 'Go on, Pop. I'm happy to hear anything there is about you.'

Carlos sat up a little straighter. 'May I ask when you were born?'

'Of course.' She told him her date of birth and watched as he mentally calculated back nine months. Skye watched as he registered what she already suspected and stared at her as no doubt what the consequences of what happened between himself and her mother meant to Carlos, Bruno and no doubt the rest of their family. And to her.

'I believe I must be your father,' he whispered, covering his mouth with one hand while reaching for Bruno's with the other. Skye watched as Bruno, who she realised had also been staring at her, spotted his father's hand searching for his and quickly took it in his own.

Bruno was the first to react. 'It seems so, Dad.' His face was expressionless for a few seconds and Skye wondered what his next reaction might be despite his bravado before, insisting he was ready to hear anything his father had to share.

Bruno's gaze moved to Joe. 'Well, mate, when you mentioned your friend was looking for her father, I'm not sure why but it never occurred to me that it would be mine.'

Skye felt Joe's fingers twitch slightly before he spoke. 'I probably should have thought this out a bit better,' he said apologetically.

Bruno shook his head. 'How were you to know?' He turned his attention back to Skye. 'It seems likely that you're my big sister.'

Breathless with shock, even though she had half expected this to be the result of their meeting, Skye swallowed. 'It does, doesn't it?'

As if they had shared the same thought, Skye moved her gaze from her half-brother to her father. 'This must be a big shock for you, er, Carlos,' she said, wondering why she was asking such a silly question. Of course it was. 'How do you feel about it?'

He rubbed his face with his hands and didn't reply immediately. 'I'm shocked. Stunned. Happy to know I have a daughter.' He grinned. 'You have two more brothers to meet, but I shall leave that up to Bruno and Joe to arrange if I may.'

'Of course, Dad.'

Carlos reached out to take Skye's hand. 'Mostly I think I'm sad to have not been able to share any of this with Annie. Or to have missed so many years of your life.'

The depth of the sorrow in his voice threatened to make her cry, but aware she needed to lead this conversation in some way and keep it as the happy reunion she wanted to memorise and share with Gran, Skye forced herself to stay calm.

'We have missed a lot,' she said as his fingers held on to hers. 'But we have time, thankfully, to make up for some of those lost years.'

'No time to waste, though,' Bruno said.

Fearing she was about to be told she would soon be losing her second parent so soon after meeting him, Skye forgot to hide her shock. 'Why? What's happened?'

Bruno gave her an apologetic look. 'Sorry, I just meant—'

'What Bruno is trying to say,' Carlos interrupted, 'is that I suffered a heart attack last summer.' Skye's heart ached to hear such a thing. Carlos raised his hand. 'It's fine. I've needed to change my diet, take up a bit of exercise and get used to taking pills, but if I take care of myself there's no reason why I can't live for many years yet.' He smiled. 'We will have time to get to know each other, I promise you.'

'I can't tell you how happy that makes me,' she said truthfully.

'And me. I have many questions to ask you about your life. About dear Annie.'

'Maybe we should arrange to meet up with Sandra when she's back from her mini break,' Skye suggested, liking the idea of learning about her mother's earlier life from the pair who seemed to know her so well.

'I'd like that idea very much.' He patted her hand. 'May I hug you?'

Skye couldn't think of anything she would like better. She stood. 'Of course you can.'

They walked around the table to each other. She stepped into Carlos's open arms, trying to take in the unusual sensation of being held by the man who was her father. Committing every sense to memory, Skye didn't think she could ever find the words to share how this felt with anyone.

Skye wished she knew whether he was married to Bruno's and the other boys' mother. Where did he work? What had his life been like for the past twenty-plus years? She knew so little about this man they all now assumed was her father and she had so many questions she needed to ask him, but now wasn't the time. All she needed to do right now was make the most of this first time with him and hope that there would soon be another opportunity to sit with him and find the answers to all the questions racing through her mind.

'Thank you for finding me, Skye,' he whispered as he hugged her.

Skye's throat tightened with emotion.

They let go of each other and moved slightly back.

'We will meet again very soon,' Carlos insisted. 'I'm sure you have many things you want to know about me as I do about you.'

Skye sighed. 'So many.' She laughed.

Joe stepped forward. 'Bruno and I can liaise with each other and sort something out for you both if you like?'

'Sounds good to me,' Carlos agreed.

29

JOE

They walked hand in hand past the harbour then the parish hall towards the car park behind it, where Joe had parked his car.

'That was more emotional than I expected. Although I suppose after listening to what Sandra told us I should have expected it to be that way.' Joe held Skye's hand in his, enjoying that it felt natural for them now as they walked back to the car. When she didn't reply, he looked down at her, trying to gauge whether it had been too much for her. 'Are you OK?'

She smiled up at him. It was a shaky smile. Her eyes were filled with unshed tears and she seemed to be struggling to keep control of her emotions.

Pulling her closer, Joe let go of her hand and put his arm protectively around her shoulders. 'You did amazingly back there. That can't have been easy for either of you, especially when Carlos realised who you were to him.'

'I can't help feeling badly that it was such a shock to him. Maybe we should have tipped Bruno off about me finding the name in Mum's notebook and then Sandra telling us that Carlos and Mum had been in a relationship years ago.'

Joe was about to agree with her then realised why they hadn't. 'How could we know whether Carlos wanted his son to know about your mum and the time they spent together?'

'True.'

'At least this way it was up to Carlos to come to whatever conclusion he wanted to. He was the one to mention Sandra, don't forget. And your mum, for that matter. For all we knew, he could have had a girlfriend waiting for him somewhere, maybe Bruno's and his other sons' mum. It wasn't for us to share information that Carlos wasn't ready to discuss with his family.' He realised what he'd said and added, 'The *rest* of his family.' Hugging her closer, Joe thought about what this must mean to Skye.

'You're right,' she agreed. 'I'm glad it panned out the way it did though. At least we gave Carlos the option to share or keep secret anything he chose to.'

'I'm happy about that, too. He'll probably need some time to get his head around everything he's learnt today.' Joe wondered how Carlos must feel discovering what happened to Annie after all those years. 'I felt sorry for him, learning about your mum passing though.'

'Poor man. All he expected to do when he came out for coffee with Bruno this morning was to try and help a stranger find out more about her parents.' She groaned. 'He'll probably never trust anyone again after things turning out so differently.'

'He seemed happy enough by the end to have met you though, don't forget.' Joe sensed her emotions racing and wished she was back at the farm already and able to either be comforted by him or spend some time alone to process what had happened at the café. 'This must all be very strange for you,' he said. 'Unsettling.'

She slipped her arm around his waist. It felt good to be this close to him.

'Ever since Sandra told us about Carlos and Mum my world seems to have flipped upside down. I thought that was a lot, but meeting him has made everything seem much more real somehow. I can't quite get my head around it. I...'

She didn't continue her sentence and, intrigued, Joe said, 'Go on. What is it?'

She cleared her throat. 'I just wish Mum was here to know I did find him and that he's lovely.' She sniffed. 'That he still remembers Mum, and fondly too.' She took a tissue from her jeans pocket and blew her nose. 'I hate to think how confused he's been all these years.'

'I know that was horrible to hear. But,' Joe said, wanting to keep the mood as upbeat as possible and hoping to help Skye remember this day positively. 'We know he didn't spend all these years alone and miserable. Don't forget he married, or at least had a relationship with someone who bore his three sons. He's not alone and seemed happy enough.'

'Before we told him our earth-shattering news.'

'This exciting, amazing news that he has a daughter. Something, or should I say someone, who will always be a reminder of that young love he and your mum shared.'

'I like that idea. Thank you.'

They reached the car and Joe unlocked the doors. The drive home was only ten minutes and he took them the scenic route down La Pulente Hill and all the way along the Five Mile Road to the very end at L'Etacq. They could have turned off earlier but he wanted to show her something.

'Is this the right way?' she asked, pointing up the hill that would take them to St Ouen's Village.

'There's something I think you should see.'

He drove around the cliff, past the fisheries, then began the descent of the steep hill. Then, slowing, pointed out of the driver's window. 'Look at that,' he said. 'It's my favourite view of anywhere.'

She peered past him at the expanse of the entire bay they had just driven along, with the rolling waves halfway down the beach. The beauty never ceased to take his breath away, whatever the weather.

'Wow, that really is stunning.'

'I thought you'd like it.'

'I sense there's a reason you're showing me this today.'

He hadn't realised it before now, but knew she was right. 'I thought I'd bring you to the place I come to when everything gets a bit overwhelming.' He indicated left and two minutes later was parked in the small car park near Battery Moltke, a tourist attraction that made up a section of a series of bunkers and gun placements for artillery to the south of Les Landes, built during the occupation of the island during World War Two.

They got out of the car and Joe led her the short way down a path through the gorse to stand on the top of a ridge. 'There,' he said, pointing proudly at the same view he had just driven past. 'This is a better viewpoint.'

He waited while she stared at the incredible view with Corbiere lighthouse at the other side of the bay, the several Napoleonic granite towers dotted along the coast all now standing behind the sea wall built as part of Hitler's Atlantic wall.

'It's so incredibly beautiful,' Skye murmured. 'And wild. I can see why you love it so much.'

'And maybe why it reminds me that my problems really aren't that big after all. There's so much more to the world and our place in it than me. I always feel better seeing this.'

'And listening to the waves at night?' she asked, gazing up at him.

He liked that she had thought of that. 'Yes, that too.' Deciding he should probably get Skye back to the farm, he took her hand. 'Shall we go back now?'

'Yes,' she said. 'I think I need some time to sit quietly and think about everything that's happened this morning.' She looked up at him with an intensity in her face that made his stomach clench. 'I really appreciate everything you've done for me, Joe. And for being with me every step of the way. I couldn't have done this without you.'

He put his arms around her. 'You could have. You're certainly strong enough, but I'm glad you don't have to.'

'So am I.'

30

SKYE

Skye sat in her room, staring out of the window at the view across the fields. What a morning it had been. Life-changing. Wanting to share her news with Gran, she decided to give her a call.

'But that's incredible,' Gran exclaimed when Skye finished telling her all about meeting with Sandra and then with Carlos. 'To think that he knew nothing about you all this time. Although, I hope you don't mind me saying, but I think that was unfair of Annie not to have told him she was pregnant with you. Or even after you were born, or when you were little. It doesn't sound like her and I can't help wondering what happened between the two of them to make her keep your birth a secret from the man you say she seemed so happy with, at least in that photograph Sandra showed you.'

Skye had been thinking exactly the same thing. 'It doesn't sound at all like Mum.' She gave her comment further thought and, recalling all the times her mother changed the subject or got miffed when Skye broached the subject of her father, began to change her mind. 'Actually, I think Mum made up her mind when they broke up that she was going to keep me for herself. And that's exactly what she did.'

Neither of them mentioned how often Annie forgot about spending time with her when she was a little girl, or when she was older for that matter. 'Who knows.'

'The most important thing you need to focus on,' Gran said, 'is your relationship with Carlos going forward. No one can change the past, so it's pointless fretting about what-might-have-beens.'

'That's true. Oh, and did I mention I have three half-brothers? I've only met Bruno, of course, but he seemed lovely and not fazed about discovering he has an older sister.'

Her gran didn't reply immediately and Skye was about to ask her what was on her mind, when she spoke. 'I presume you'll ask Carlos or Bruno to take a DNA test, just to be certain?'

'I suppose so,' Skye said. 'But if Carlos was the only man in Mum's life back then I'm not sure whether it's necessary.' She told her grandmother about finding his name in the notebook.

'Ah, I see. That does change things then.'

She thought so too. 'I wish Sandra was back from holiday so I could ask her more questions about Mum.'

'Try not to expect too much. It's clear your mum kept things from those close to her.' Skye knew her gran probably struggled to accept that Annie had kept so much from her. 'She probably kept more secrets from Sandra.'

'True. I'll try to keep a check on my expectations.'

'I don't want to put a downer on things, sweetheart. I'm just trying to think of all eventualities so you can protect yourself against getting hurt. Your mother did enough of that to you while she was here.'

Skye knew that if anyone else heard Gran speak in this way they might think it harsh, but she was used to her directness and preferred people to say what was on their mind. After so many years of her mother avoiding awkward conversations, it was the way she preferred people to deal with her.

'I know, and I love you for caring about me so much. Thank you.'

'No need to thank me, love. You're a wonderful girl and deserve only the best.' She hesitated, then added an obvious smile in her voice. 'Talking about the best, how are you getting along with that firefighter chap? He sounds as if he's taking good care of you.'

'He is,' Skye said, her heart racing at the thought of him. 'Although, as you know, I'm perfectly capable of taking care of myself.'

'That you are, Little Miss Independent,' Gran said, making Skye smile. 'I'd better go, dear. I have a pie in the oven and I have a horrible feeling it's catching. I've invited a couple of friends for supper and they won't be impressed if I serve up burnt offerings. Much love and call me again soon. Keep me up to date.'

'I will. Bye, Gran.'

Skye ended the call and sat back on her bed. She felt much calmer now, having shared the events of the morning with her grandmother. It was time to go downstairs and continue her work on the farm.

She bumped into Joe as she entered the barn, catching him as he was about to exit.

'Oof, sorry,' Skye said as she slammed into his chest. 'I should learn to look where I'm going.'

'It's fine. Anyway I could say the same thing.'

She sensed something was a little off and realised he didn't seem as cheerful as he had done earlier. 'Is everything all right?'

Joe leant against the doorframe, resting the palm of his hand on the top of the broom he had been using to sweep the cement floor. 'It is really.'

'You don't look fine.'

He sighed. 'I suppose I'm aware that as each day passes this bubble you and I are living in is closer to bursting.'

She folded her arms. 'I know what you mean.'

His expression brightened. 'You mean, you're dreading Lettie and Brodie returning to the farm as much as I am?'

Skye narrowed her eyes. 'I'm not much of a mind-reader so don't quite know how deep your dread is and even though me not looking forward to them coming back here makes me feel guilty I also don't wish what we have going on here to end.'

He gazed into her eyes for a couple of seconds, then said, 'And what do we have going on here?'

How to put it into words, Skye wondered. 'I'm not sure,' she replied honestly. 'But just being here with you and the animals has been amazing. I've loved every second of it and...' She wished she could just say how she felt. How much she fancied him, wanted him to kiss her. 'Oh, you know what I mean,' she added hopefully.

He lifted the hay bale he had just filled, flipped the end of the rope through a ring and tied it securely, causing his T-shirt to rise and expose his toned stomach. 'I think I do,' he said, checking the net was secure.

Her stomach did several somersaults and she couldn't tear her gaze from him.

He lowered his arms and pulled his top back down automatically. 'Is everything all right?'

Realising he wasn't sure why she was staring at him like she was, Skye closed her mouth. 'Er, fine. Sorry, were you saying something?'

'No.' He seemed unsure.

Her heart racing, Skye decided one of them needed to make the first move and, feeling brave after such a challenging yet incredibly surprising morning, she reasoned that now was as good a time as any to take a chance. It wasn't as if they had time to waste if they hoped to make the most of being here by themselves. Anyway she would rather be rejected than regret missing the opportunity to move her friendship with Joe to a more romantic level.

The image of his toned stomach fresh in her mind, Skye stepped forward and slipped her arms around his waist. Hearing Joe's sharp intake of breath before he smiled down at her, Skye didn't need to wonder if she had made the right choice to go with her instincts.

'So we are on the same page then?' he said, taking her in his arms.

'It seems so.' When he didn't say anything else, or make a move, Skye wondered why not. 'Are you going to kiss me then, or not?' she whispered, taken aback that she had voiced the words instead of keeping them in her head.

Joe didn't speak but, putting one of his hands behind her head, pulled her gently towards him as he lowered his lips to hers.

31

SKYE

Skye felt a surge of excitement as she thought about their kiss. She tried to focus on refilling the honesty box with freshly harvested carrots, broad beans, beetroot and bags of Jersey Royals she had picked after leaving Joe grinning in the barn. She felt a warm glow as she recalled how it felt to be in Joe's arms, his lips against hers. He was a great kisser. She couldn't wait to kiss him again.

'I said do you have spring greens yet?'

Shocked to hear an elderly man's voice, Skye spun round, cheeks flaming from being interrupted as she reminisced about Joe.

'Sorry, I didn't see you there. No, I'm afraid not. I think it'll be a couple of weeks yet before we have any of those to sell.'

'That's a shame. My wife loves spring greens.' He gave her a wave. 'Never mind, I'll try again in a few weeks.'

Her thoughts returned to their kiss and how they had almost got carried away. She wasn't sure whether she should be grateful to the postman who'd arrived with mail, including a postcard addressed to them from Lindy and Gareth from Sint Maarten.

She walked slowly back to the yard.

Joe waved at her, looking as if he wanted to tell her something.

'What is it?'

He held up his phone. 'Just had a call from Bruno asking for your number to check if you would like to join him and Carlos for dinner.'

She wondered why she hadn't thought to ask for Bruno's number so she could call him herself. 'Can I see his number and I'll call him back now.'

'Here you go.' Joe brought up his contacts on his phone and held it out so she could see the screen.

She typed Bruno's contact details into her phone, pressing Save. 'Thanks.'

His phone rang again. He looked at the screen and scowled. 'Sorry, I need to take this.'

She hoped nothing was wrong but Joe hadn't seemed all that happy to get the call. He went to the kitchen and Skye focused on phoning Bruno. Her mind raced. Everything was happening so fast she could barely process all the changes in her life.

'All good?' Joe asked when she found him again in the kitchen with the dogs.

'Yes, I'm meeting them tonight. Bruno suggested booking the table for seven-thirty at a restaurant in St Ouen's Bay.'

'Sounds good.'

'It does,' she said, feeling excited yet a little nervous. 'I wonder when I'll get to meet my other two brothers? Or either Carlos's or Bruno's partners.'

'They probably want to take things slowly,' Joe suggested. He gave her a hug. 'You OK?'

'I'm fine.'

'I would offer to come with you but I've been called in to do a shift this evening.'

'You have? But I thought you were given time off work.'

'I was, but staff numbers are low and there have been a few larger emergencies recently and they need to make sure the crews have enough time off between shifts. I don't mind.' He shrugged. 'I could still drop you off later though still if you want?'

She shook her head. 'No, thanks. Bruno said they would give me a lift.'

He smiled at her. 'If you're sure you're OK, I'll go and pop in to see my mother and Roger now before getting ready for work. Apparently there's some issue with my hot water tank they need me to sort out.' He rolled his eyes. 'Funny how they only call me when something is wrong.' He laughed. 'I shouldn't moan, I've been happy enough to let them get on with things while I've been here.'

'I hope it's not difficult to sort out.'

'If it is, I'll call in the professionals.' Joe pushed his phone into his back pocket and pointed to ominous-looking clouds out to the west of the island. 'Looks like there's a nasty storm coming our way this evening.'

Skye wasn't sure that going to the bay to eat would be the best decision. 'Will it be OK eating at the restaurant so close to the sea wall, if you think the storm will be bad?'

Joe laughed. 'It'll be fine. I always enjoy watching a storm from inside, and the place they suggested going to has large windows so there'll be a great view as everything rages outside.'

Skye liked the sound of that. 'All right then. Shall I meet you back here afterwards?'

'Perfect. I'll look forward to hearing all about it.' A message pinged on his phone and Joe sighed. 'I'd better get going. Have a great time.'

'I'm sure I will,' she assured him.

Skye watched him leave, excited to have something to look forward to that evening. She supposed Carlos might be ready for her next load of questions for him and decided to think about the ones she most needed answers to as she worked.

* * *

The storm was already fierce when they ran from the car to the restaurant, getting fairly wet in the short time it took. She asked Carlos more about making this island his home all those years ago, thinking how right Joe had been about the restaurant's location. She hadn't realised the restaurant was right up against the promenade on top of the sea wall. It was too dark to see too much thanks to the driving rain and heavy sky but the sound of waves crashing, rain hitting the window next to them and the roar of the wind were dramatic nonetheless.

'Joe was telling me that many people moved here from Madeira since the sixties and seventies,' she said. 'Did you always mean to settle here, or did it just sort of happen?'

Carlos smiled thoughtfully. 'Initially I only meant to work here for a few seasons. My cousin already worked here. It was he who recommended the Bel Amie to me. After Annie left though I was intending to leave at the end of that season. I did return home to my family in Madeira and my mother talked sense into me, telling me that I had the opportunity to make a good life for myself working in the hotel. So the following season I returned but to a different hotel.'

Skye thought about all the places she had visited and how

each made her feel. 'This is a beautiful place to live. I'm not surprised you changed your mind about leaving.'

'It was two years later that I met my late wife. She's from the island.'

Late wife? Hoping she hadn't upset him by encouraging him to reminisce, Skye knew she had to address his situation.

'I'm so sorry. I wasn't sure whether you were still married or not.'

Bruno took a drink from his glass of lager. 'Mum died ten years ago now,' he said, glancing at his father. 'It was a dark time for us all.'

'It was,' Carlos agreed.

She could well imagine how he had felt. Unsure whether to ask but believing it mattered, Skye said, 'Would she have minded about me? Do you think?'

Carlos shrugged. 'I don't know for sure, of course, but I believe she would have been happy to meet you, Skye. My Della was a kind person and would never have felt threatened by any women who came into my life before we had met.'

Skye heard sirens in the background but didn't take any notice. Although she hadn't heard them much at all since her arrival on the island, she was used to hearing them back at home and presumed there must have been an accident of sorts along the lengthy road behind the restaurant.

'Della sounds like she was an amazing lady,' Skye said, turning her attention back to the conversation. She was relieved to hear it that Della would react that way and hoped that if both Carlos and Bruno believed this then her other brothers would also be open to getting to know her. 'I wish I could have met her too.'

Carlos swallowed, then nodded. 'I would have liked that very much.'

She noticed Bruno staring at something outside a little way along from the restaurant. 'Is something wrong?'

'I'm not sure yet,' he said, squinting out of the rain-soaked window, his face the picture of concern. He stood and walked to look out of another window, coming back shortly after. She saw him check his phone.

'What's happened?'

'There's something going on,' he said. 'I've seen blue lights so the emergency services are already there but I doubt it's a car accident.'

She stood next to him and leant closer to the windowpane to peer out, but it was almost impossible to make out what was happening. 'Why don't you think it's a car crash?'

'Because the ambulance is nearer to the sea wall than it would be if the incident was on the road.'

'Is it a fire?' she asked, unsure how anything could burn with this amount of rain.

He shook his head. 'I spotted the RNLI out there. Someone must be in difficulty.'

Skye shuddered, hoping there was a positive outcome for whoever was involved. She felt her appetite subside and wished they hadn't already ordered. 'I wonder if there's something we could do to help?' she said, unsure in what way.

Bruno frowned. 'Sorry, Dad, Skye, would you mind very much if I go and have a closer look?'

She could tell there was something on his mind and that he wasn't simply being nosy. 'Not at all.'

Carlos shook his head. 'You go. Try not to be out there too long, and stay back from the sea wall – you don't want to get hurt.'

As soon as Bruno left, Skye kept Carlos busy by asking more

questions about his first season on the island. 'It must have been quite different here back then.'

He clasped his hands together and gave a wistful smile. 'It was more different than you would probably imagine. More hotels, the waterfront wasn't completely developed then and there were many more cafés and bars.' His gaze slid to the door. 'I hope he's not too long out there. This storm is bad.'

They spoke for a little longer when the door opened and Bruno walked in, soaked. He took off his coat and hung the dripping item on a hook with other damp outerwear.

'What's happened?' Carlos asked.

Skye saw Bruno look at her with a strange expression on his face, before replying to his father. She realised he was trying to work out how to tell them something.

'What is it?' she asked anxiously, unsure what could concern him when she hardly knew anyone on the island. Then it dawned on her. 'Joe's out there, isn't he?'

He sat down next to her. 'Try not to worry,' Bruno said. 'They're all professionals out there.'

Skye went to stand but he pressed his hand against her arm. 'No, there's nothing you can do. We're helping far more by staying in here out of the way.'

'But Joe.'

He sighed. 'I know but he's not alone and Joe is tough. I'm sure we'll soon hear from him.'

What choice did she have but to concede? 'I suppose so.'

'He'll be fine,' Carlos assured her. 'These men are well trained.'

Skye forced a smile. 'I'm sure he will be,' she said, hoping they were both right.

32

JOE

Joe stood on the sea wall, glad he was wearing his helmet when several pebbles and other debris from the sea slammed against the ground next to him as yet another wave crashed below him. If the swimmer had being caught out with the tide further away from the sea wall the RNLI rescue boat would have been able to help him. But the storm was even more dramatic than he had expected and, as it was, the rocks next to the wall and the fierceness of the waves made that impossible, which was why he and three others were doing their best to see that the man didn't drown.

He helped his colleague on the railing on the sea wall as they both struggled to keep hold of the rope attached to a colleague who was battling to reach the swimmer. He wondered why the man had been swimming with the sea so treacherous. From the call they had received, the man was in his mid-thirties and Joe assumed he must now be frozen and at a risk of developing hypothermia.

Another wave slammed both swimmer and firefighter

against the rocks. Joe winced. This was bad. He peered through the driving rain and for a moment thought he noticed his colleague's arm at a strange angle. Damn, he hoped it wasn't broken.

Grateful that this sort of rescue wasn't something they often were called to help with, Joe caught a movement to his left and saw a man videoing the rescue and another taking photos.

'Get back,' he yelled. 'These waves have stones in them and could kill you.' If a wave didn't drag them into the sea first, he thought.

The one taking the photos looked askance at this information but immediately did as he was asked, while the other chap only stepped back a few feet.

Not wishing to risk missing the signal to enter the water to assist, Joe turned his attention back to the rescue.

'I think he's hurt,' Nicki, his fellow firefighter holding on to the rope attached to his colleague's uniform, yelled. 'Dan, that is.'

Their senior officer, Mac, waved for Joe to go over to him. Checking Nicki was coping with the weight of their colleague, he went to see what Mac wanted.

'Do you need me to go in?' Joe asked.

'You're the best swimmer here,' Mac shouted back. 'And most experienced in the sea, what with all those years' surfing. Dan's hurt but I know him, he's not going to give up unless someone takes over from him. We can't let this guy drown and by the looks of him he hasn't got much strength left. We need to get him out of the water.'

'No problem.' Joe immediately went down the steps into the water, his breath taken out of him as he was slammed against the step railings. He was glad to be wearing protective clothing. Despite being used to the power of the sea and prepared for the cold thanks to his experiences as a surfer, he struggled to make the short distance over to Dan. This was bad.

He swam as hard as he could, but it still took minutes for Joe to reach the man who was at the mercy of the waves and now being thrown about like a rubber toy in a child's bath. The poor guy was ashen and visibly shaking, no doubt from fear and the effects of the cold. After several attempts, Joe managed to grab him, waving for Dan to get to the steps and out of the water. Then holding tightly to the swimmer, Joe felt the rope pull him slowly back to the steps as he helped manoeuvre them both through the rolling waves.

Finally, they reached the steps and his own sheer exhaustion after twenty minutes fighting against the current made Joe wonder how the swimmer could still walk at all. Mac stepped down and took the man's arm, helping Joe get him out of the water to safety where an ambulance crew were waiting to take over.

'You OK?' Mac asked.

'I will be. Though do we know why the swimmer was in the water in the first place?'

'I gather he and a friend had thought it a good idea, but when he got into difficulty and his friend was unable to reach him he wisely went for help.'

'That was sensible,' Joe said, shivering.

'Dan's arm needs attention.' Joe had thought as much. 'I need you to come and help Nicki and I to assist with the equipment. Then we can get you both back to the station. I don't want the pair of you going sick, especially as we're already short-staffed.'

Joe's adrenaline was racing and he was glad to have something to keep him busy while it calmed down.

As he worked with Nicki and two others, he thought of how

differently the night could have turned out for the swimmer and possibly for Dan and was grateful the rescue had been a successful one. He hoped Skye's evening was going well and was relieved the station didn't need him to work again the following day.

33

SKYE

Skye was listening to Carlos reminisce when she heard Bruno groan.

'What's wrong?' Carlos asked.

Bruno looked from his father to her and she knew instantly it was something to do with Joe.

'What is it?'

He glanced at his father as if trying to make up his mind whether to tell her but Carlos gave a nod. He held up his phone, but it was too far away for Skye to see.

'Is it what's going on outside?'

Bruno gave the phone to her. Skye watched the drama unfold, feeling sick at the image of Joe going into the raging sea. She bit her lower lip to stop from making a sound. Why did he do such a dangerous job?

She handed the phone back to Bruno and stood. 'I'm sorry, I can't sit here while Joe's out there risking his life.'

Bruno looked alarmed. 'He knows what he's doing, Skye. He's trained for this sort of thing.'

'I thought he was trained to fight fires, not risk drowning in the sea,' she said, struggling not to raise her voice. 'I need to go there. Joe's life could be in danger.'

Bruno stood. 'And what do you think you can do to assist in any way?'

She knew he was right but refused to change her mind.

'I'm not sure it is the right thing to do,' Carlos said quietly as he stared at Bruno.

Bruno rested a hand on her arm. 'Even if we do go there we won't be able to get too close.' When she didn't stop putting on her coat, he added, 'All right, but I'll come with you. And you must promise to do as I say and keep your distance. Getting close will only hinder the operation.'

Relieved, Skye nodded. 'I promise I'll do as you say.'

'I'll pay and meet you and Dad in the car.'

'The car? It's not that far away.'

'Maybe not, but by the looks of things Dad is planning on coming with us.' Skye noticed Carlos was also putting on his coat. 'I don't want him standing out in this weather when it's not necessary.'

'Of course.'

It only took Bruno four minutes to pay and drive them to the rescue site where a fire engine and two ambulances were parked near to a place she presumed was another restaurant or some sort of club. He parked the car and Skye went to get out.

'No,' Bruno shouted. 'We wait here. There are boulders in those waves and other debris. That's why I'm parked back here.'

Terrified and feeling sick with desperation for Joe's safety, Skye couldn't help but find the feed on her phone and watch from the back seat. She presumed the taller man was Joe, or at least she hoped that was him because the other one seemed hurt. Poor swimmer, she thought, with no protective clothing covering him. What could he have been thinking going into the sea in the first place?

'They've got him out,' she heard Bruno yell in excitement.

She leant forward from between the two back seats to watch as two of the firefighters helped the man wearing only trunks slowly make their way up the granite beach steps. The man was exhausted. They all were by the looks of things. Paramedics hurried forward and wrapped a foil blanket around the man and led him into the back of an ambulance, while the firefighter with the damaged arm was led to the other ambulance.

Skye watched Joe speaking to the firefighter who had been holding on to the rope attached to his uniform and, seeing her taking off her helmet, realised it was a woman. Envy washed over her as she wished she had been more use other than a spectator sitting in the comfort of a car.

Joe helped the woman clear the equipment away with another two men. Then seeing a couple of other firefighters talking to each other, she realised Joe was standing alone. She forgot her promise to stay in the car and got out, running through the driving rain to reach him. She called out his name a few times before he heard her.

Joe looked in her direction, a surprised expression on his face and, seeing her there, hurried to meet her.

'What are you doing here? You could have been hurt. There's debris everywhere.'

'I'm fine,' she insisted. 'I've been in the car the whole time,' she said, indicating Bruno's car over her shoulder.

She looked him up and down, noticing how drained he appeared. 'Can you come back with us to the farm, or do you need to stay here with your colleagues?'

'I'll need to go back but I'll see you at the farm as soon as I can. Don't wait up for me though. I might be longer than I expect with all that's happened.'

'You did very well to save him,' she said, aware her voice was loud to be heard against the wind and driving rain. 'You were incredibly brave.'

He seemed embarrassed by her comment. 'It was a team effort. I couldn't have done anything without the other guys. We're trained to work together.'

Her respect for Joe and those he worked with grew massively. 'I'll leave you to it then,' she said, before running back to the car.

'He's OK?' Bruno asked.

'Yes, he's tired but seems fine other than that.' Realising she had done the opposite of what she had assured Bruno she would do, Skye leant forward in her seat. 'I'm sorry for getting out. I know I shouldn't have done, but I sort of forgot myself.'

She saw Bruno's eyes crease in a smile in the rear-view mirror. 'I'm sure he didn't mind all that much.'

Embarrassed to have behaved like she had, Skye hoped she hadn't made things awkward for Joe when he returned to his shift the following day. 'He wasn't impressed to see me there,' she said, hoping to put the onus back on her.

'Don't worry,' Bruno said, starting the car. 'I promise I won't say anything to wind him up.'

Skye sat back against the seat as Bruno drove them to the farm and thought about how these people risked their lives each day and how incredible they were to be so selfless and brave. She thought of her mother and her absent father gone from her for different reasons, but a loss to her nonetheless. She needed to stop whatever this was between her and Joe before she fell too deeply for him. His job was a dangerous one and if tonight had shown her anything it was that she wasn't ready to lose another person in her life.

The outcome of the rescue might have been a positive one, but she saw how easily his colleague had been damaged and knew how easily the three men in the sea could have died. Whatever she thought of Joe she couldn't bear the thought of him being badly injured or, worse, losing his life. She wasn't strong enough for that emotionally, not after all she had been through in her life. No, she decided as much as she liked him, and she did, a lot, she couldn't face losing him. There was nothing else for it but to stop whatever had been going on between them immediately.

34

JOE

Joe arrived back at the farm exhausted but relieved that everyone had survived pretty much intact after the dramatic rescue. Dan was still at the hospital waiting for a scan on his arm but his wife was with him now and Joe had been told to go home, so after a hot shower at the station and changing into dry clothes, he had driven home looking forward to spending time with Skye and having something to eat.

'You're back,' Skye said as he walked in through the front door. Spud pushed past her to give their usual excited, waggy welcome and he crouched to pat and cuddle the dog before standing slowly. 'You must be hungry, or have you eaten something?'

He wasn't sure if it was his imagination but she seemed out of sorts. 'Starving but it's late. I can get something myself. Why don't you sit and tell me how your meal went with Carlos and Bruno. Did you have a good time getting to know them a bit better?'

'I did, thanks, but I'm more interested in how you are after your evening.'

'Not much to tell,' he said, unsure of the undercurrent he was picking up from her. 'Are you OK? You seem a little...' He wasn't sure what.

'I'm fine. I suspected you might need something to eat so took the liberty of ordering a delivery,' she said. 'I wasn't sure what to get so took a chance and chose for you. Go and get comfortable in the living room and I'll sort out the plates.'

He hoped the drama of the evening hadn't caused Skye's meal to be interrupted. 'Didn't you three get to eat at the restaurant yet?'

She shook her head. 'The food hadn't arrived when Bruno noticed something happening and soon after I insisted on coming out to see what was going on.'

'How did you know? I would have thought it was almost impossible to see with all that rain and sea spray.'

'Someone was filming it and live-streaming. Bruno found it and shared it with Carlos and me.'

Why had Bruno done that? Joe mused. Surely he must have known that Skye would be concerned. Maybe it hadn't occurred to him.

Wanting to placate her, Joe did as she asked. He sank back into the comfortable sofa and noticed she had also lit the fire. It was a sweet touch and made him smile. This was the difference between being with someone and living alone, he reminded himself, deciding he could get used to this sort of welcome.

She carried in a couple of drinks and a bowl of crisps and set them down on the table. 'There you go,' she said, indicating the nibbles. 'Something to keep you going until the food arrives.'

'Don't you want any?'

She shook her head. 'I might have a little something but I'm not that hungry.'

Rain pattered against the windows and the wind howled

outside. 'I'm glad we brought the animals inside earlier today,' he said.

'So am I. It was a good thing you suggested it. The weather was so lovely this morning it never would have occured to me that a storm might be on its way to the island.'

He saw her staring at the fire and assumed she was worried about the rescue. 'Hey, you all right?'

She snapped out of her reverie. 'What? Of course I am. You're the one who was in danger, not me.' There it was again, he noticed. That tone. It wasn't her usual way, but there was something wrong. He wondered if it was simply that Skye wasn't used to the intensity of watching a rescue. He realised she was still speaking. 'Tuck in. You don't want my culinary delights getting cold after all the effort I went to taking the packet out of the cupboard and opening it to pour these tasty morsels into the bowl.'

Joe laughed. He was being oversensitive. He was tired after all, he reminded himself. Skye was great company and the perfect tonic after what he had faced earlier. 'Heaven forbid.'

She sat back on the sofa and he smiled at her, enjoying the two of them being in the warm, cosy living room. The storm hadn't abated at all; in fact he suspected it was still getting worse.

The dogs were snoozing in front of the fire and when the rain increased against the window, Spud opened his eyes, his ears pricked in case of any emergency. Then seeming to presume there was no cause for alarm, he settled back down again.

'How are you feeling?' she asked, her face the picture of concern.

'This is exactly what I needed,' he said. 'You, the dogs chilling and crisps.'

'Don't forget the Chinese food we have to look forward to.'

'Oh, I haven't. I'm looking forward to tucking into that lot very much.'

Skye sat closer to him, sighing happily when Joe put his arm around her shoulders and pulled her gently against him. He suspected she needed the comfort of them snuggling up to each other as much as he did right now.

Certain there was nowhere else he would rather be, or with any other person, Joe closed his eyes. He felt Skye's head rest against his shoulder. 'Are you sure you're all right?'

She took a deep breath. 'It was scary knowing you were in that water tonight,' she said quietly.

'It was for me too, if I'm honest. Thankfully this situation is rare for us, which is a relief.'

They sat in silence for a while and he wished the evening could last forever.

'It's far nicer being warm in here than outside in that dreadful storm,' she said quietly, making him wonder why she was talking about the weather. 'Lettie and Brodie will be back here in a few days when Lindy and Gareth return from their trip.' She snuggled closer to him and sighed.

He looked down at her. 'I suppose we should be grateful we've ended up getting along well. I'm beginning to feel as if I've known you for months rather than days.'

'Me, too,' Skye said, sounding sad. He sensed she was trying not to let the emotion of the evening take over.

He closed his eyes again, but sensing he was being watched, opened them and looked down at Skye, surprised to see her beautiful face turned up to his, studying him. He wanted desperately to kiss her, but was nervous about taking things too far, or too soon.

Suddenly Skye moved back from him and knelt next to him.

Leaning forward, she kissed him. Joe took a second to gather his thoughts, then immediately took her in his arms and kissed her right back.

He was surprised but happy he must have been wrong to sense an atmosphere between them. The touch of her perfect lips against his own sent sensations through him, and he slipped his arms around her and pulled her against him. Hearing a barely audible groan escape Skye's lips, it dawned on him that she might have been waiting for this to happen again, just like he had been. Could that be why she had been acting oddly since he got back?

Skye pushed him back onto the sofa and, lying down, he drew her on top of him, grateful that they were the only two people on the farm and wouldn't be disturbed. Her lips moved from his and she began kissing his neck, then undid his shirt and kissed his chest.

Not wishing her to stop, Joe reached up and pushed his fingers through her hair. Then, feeling stirrings in his body he wasn't sure Skye might be ready for, he drew her up so her mouth was level with his and kissed her again.

A loud banging on the door set the dogs off barking and made them both jump. Skye leapt back from him as if a switch had been flicked.

'That must be our food,' he said, trying to gather himself. 'I'll go and see to the delivery.'

'Yes,' Skye said, looking as shell-shocked as he felt and smoothing down her hair. They stared at each other for a second before she stood and followed him out of the room. 'I'll get some cutlery and plates out ready.'

Joe reached the front door and exhaled sharply, unsure whether he was glad of the interruption or infuriated by it. He wanted Skye, very much. He knew that much but wasn't sure how to read the undercurrent between them. He was going to have to say something.

Discovering Skye had paid for their food over the phone, he withdrew a tip from his back pocket and opened the door to greet the delivery person.

Thanking the delivery guy, Joe took the bag from him and handed him a tip before closing the door again and taking the food to the kitchen. Skye had her back to him and was busying herself setting up two trays.

'I thought we could serve ourselves in here,' she said. 'Then take this through to the living room and watch something on TV.'

Amused, Joe laughed. 'I thought you weren't hungry?'

She pulled a face at him. 'I've changed my mind. It smells delicious and far too tempting for me to be able to resist eating some of it.'

Happy to have the distraction of food and television, Joe agreed. 'I'm not sure what's on, but there's bound to be something.' He placed the bag of food on the worktop and stepped back to let her choose what she fancied to eat.

'Did you know there were only three channels when my parents were younger?'

Skye stopped taking packets from the bags and looked over her shoulder at him. 'Sorry, what did you say?'

Assuming she must have been focusing on the food, Joe shook his head. 'Nothing. I was only talking nonsense. Found anything you fancy pinching from the food you ordered for me?'

He watched as she sorted out the boxes and removed two of the lids. Pointing at them, she grinned. 'I thought I'd have the boiled rice and this.'

Joe laughed and walked to stand next to her. He peered down. 'Ah, the Kung Pao chicken.'

'You can have it if you want? I really don't mind.'

He shook his head. 'No, it's fine. I'm happy with whatever's left.'

'The, er, chow mein?'

He nodded, amused. 'Or the dumplings.'

'Well, it all looks delicious,' she said, looking him in the eyes for the first time since they had kissed. 'You're being very generous with your food. I should really have ordered something for myself too.'

'It's fine. Anyway, I feel happier with us both eating.'

'That's sweet of you.' She served her food and, picking up her tray, turned to him. 'I, um...'

Seeing how awkward Skye seemed and that she was struggling to put something into words, he said, 'Why don't you carry yours through to the living room and get started eating? You don't want your food to get cold and it's never as hot as it is in the restaurant when it's been delivered. I'll join you in a couple of minutes.'

She stared at him briefly then nodded. 'OK.'

He watched her walk out the kitchen, his heart racing. Never mind Skye feeling awkward, he was behaving as if this was his first encounter with someone from the opposite sex. Why was he acting so oddly? Why was she?

Forcing himself to focus on his food and not wishing to make the atmosphere between them any more uncomfortable than it already seemed, he began serving chow mein and dumplings onto his plate. Then placing a couple of boxes of the other food she had ordered onto the side of his tray, he carried them through to join Skye once more.

'Good?' he asked, happy to see her tucking into her food.

She finished chewing her mouthful and nodded. 'Delicious.'

He rested his tray on the edge of the coffee table, moved the boxes from the tray to the table and sat down next to her, pulling his tray onto his lap. He breathed in the smell of the tasty meal in front of him. 'It certainly smells good.'

They ate in silence for a while and he wondered if Skye was as relieved as he was to have something to focus on to escape the awkwardness that had fallen over them.

He wondered what was going to happen next though, because as much as he would like things to continue this way, there seemed to be something on Skye's mind.

He noticed she wasn't eating much and was playing with her food, seemingly lost in thought. Unable to stand it a moment longer, Joe turned to her. 'What's the matter, Skye? You seem troubled by something, or am I imagining it?'

She stared at him, looking sad. When she didn't speak he tried to work out what might be wrong. He watched as she placed her tray on the coffee table and waited for him to do the same. A sense of dread coursed through him.

'There's something I need to speak to you about, Joe.'

35

SKYE

He gazed at her, looking worried, and she felt her insides melt as his eyes locked with hers.

Studying his handsome face gazing down at her, his wavy black hair falling forward slightly over his face and his deep, navy eyes gazing intently at her, all she wanted to do was kiss him again.

Not that she should have kissed him earlier. It was unfair of her to do what she had done when she had intended on speaking to him about her concerns, but stupidly she couldn't seem to help herself. Now she was probably going to ruin what could have been a perfectly lovely end to their eventful evening. But he needed to know how she felt and the sooner the better before she did anything silly like kiss him again.

'Skye? Are you going to tell me what's bothering you?'

She closed her eyes, trying to think clearly, which wasn't easy when she was so attracted to him. Everything about him was perfect, apart from him doing a dangerous job.

'I'm sorry I kissed you earlier, Joe.'

He frowned. 'You are? Why?'

'Because it wasn't fair of me.'

His face clouded over and he stared at her for a few seconds without speaking. 'Why?'

She looked away, unable to bear the confusion on his sweet face.

'Skye,' he said gently. 'What's the matter? I hope you know you can tell me anything.'

Why was this so difficult? 'We can't carry on as we have been, Joe.'

He shrugged. 'I'm not sure what you mean.'

She explained about seeing him at the rescue earlier. 'It gave me such a shock to see how dangerous your job is.'

He smiled. 'It's not always like that. And that's the first sea rescue I've been involved in.'

'But it is a dangerous job, isn't it?'

'I suppose it can be, but we're well trained and we have the right equipment.' He narrowed his eyes. 'What's this really about, Skye?'

She groaned. 'I've lost too many people in my life to bear the thought of getting close to you and risk losing you too.'

She waited for him to react but he just stared at her looking bemused.

'Joe?'

He shook his head. 'I'm not sure what I can do about that. It's what I do. What I love doing.'

'Yes, and I would never presume to expect you to change that, but I'm not sure I can stand being with someone and not knowing whether they'll come home in one piece at the end of a shift.'

Hearing herself saying it out loud gave her worries gravitas, but he didn't agree with her. She waited for him to speak and hoped he could understand.

'I see where you're coming from, but surely everyone takes risks constantly in their lives. You do with all your travelling. All your plane trips. The vehicles you must have ridden in when you were away.' He shrugged one shoulder. 'The train trips back in Scotland. Car trips. Do you worry about those each time you embark on one?'

She shook her head slowly. 'I suppose not.' She began to feel a little silly. What he said made good sense.

'Skye, I don't know about your feelings for me and I know we've only known each other a short while, but I find myself liking you more each day. Of course I'll understand if you decide you don't want to take what we had together any further. If you do though, I'm happy to try and find a solution.'

She hadn't expected this and wondered what he would say next. 'Like what?'

'I'm not sure yet.'

She stared at his mouth as he spoke and wanted more than anything to erase the conversation she had just instigated and kiss him. Be carefree for once in her life and not try to control the outcome to a relationship that had barely begun.

'What are you thinking?' he asked, narrowing his eyes, his mouth turning up at the sides in a smile.

Unable to help herself, Skye pushed aside all thoughts of being sensible and pushed him backwards before leaning into him and kissing him.

He reacted instantly and for a moment Skye lost herself in the thrill of kissing him again. 'Sorry,' she said, sitting back slightly. 'I don't know what's got into me tonight. I seem to be suffering a roller coaster of emotions.'

'Don't stop on my account.' Joe leant back on the sofa,

clasped his hands together and stretched his arms above him. 'This has been an eventful evening in one way and another.' He sighed happily.

Skye wished her eyes weren't immediately drawn to the space between the bottom of his T-shirt and the top of his faded jeans. What was it about his slightly tanned, taut lower stomach that sent her crazy? Surely sexy parts of his body was the last thing she needed to be staring at when she was trying to be sensible for both their sakes.

She sensed him looking at her and saw him lower his arms, pulling his top down slightly, probably confused by her erratic behaviour. Embarrassed to have been caught staring at his lower abdomen, Skye reached out to collect their plates but before she could touch them, Joe rested his hand on her arm, sending tingles like electric raindrops flickering through her body.

'We don't have to clear those away just yet, do we?'

Unsure why she seemed to have forgotten how to speak, Skye shook her head slowly and cleared her throat. 'Um, I suppose we don't.'

What was she thinking? Of course they didn't. It wasn't as if anyone else was even in the house. Feeling his palm against her forearm still, she looked into his eyes and a pang of lust hit her deep in her stomach.

'Would you mind if I kissed you?' Joe said, his voice barely above a whisper.

'Er, no.' Why had her voice come out all squeaky?

Joe didn't appear to have noticed and, taking his hand from her arm, moved closer to her, turning his body fully to face her. She leant into him, unable to help herself. After a brief kiss, Joe took her into his arms, kissing her, hard.

This time though he was the one to suddenly stop, disappointing Skye. She wasn't ready to stop kissing this gorgeous guy. He moved a few inches back from her and gave her a half-smile that seemed to her to be something of an apology.

'I'm sorry,' he said, as if sensing what she was thinking.

'Is everything all right?' Skye asked, not able to tell him she had been hoping for more.

He kissed her lightly on the lips, his hand running down her hair. 'Nothing is wrong. In fact I don't think anything has ever felt this right to me.'

'Me, too,' she admitted, her voice barely above a whisper. She didn't understand his reluctance to continue and hoped he would enlighten her a little more.

Without taking his eyes from hers, Joe said, 'I worry if we start something here what might happen when you leave the island.'

'You're worried about my feelings?' She was about to tell him she was a big girl and could take care of herself. 'I'm not that fragile, if that's what you're worried about.'

He stared at her, a slight frown crossing his face briefly. 'It's not just you I'm worried about.' A loving gaze radiated from his blue eyes. 'I'm also worried about me.'

'You are?' She wasn't sure why she was surprised to hear him speak like this. Perhaps she had presumed a gorgeous man who looked like Joe must be tough, but clearly there was a much gentler side to him. And tonight she had been saying one thing and acting in a completely different way. She knew she should be relieved he wasn't too fazed by her erratic behaviour, but it didn't help her frustration that she really wanted more from him.

'Does that make me sound ridiculous?'

Hating to think she had made Joe question his reaction

when all he was doing was try to stop either of them being hurt, Skye took one of his hands in hers.

'No, of course it doesn't. You're a lovely guy and you care about others' feelings.' Forcing a smile, Skye raised his hand and kissed the back of it. 'I did enjoy kissing you though. Maybe we could have just one more?'

36

SKYE

Skye lay in her bed the following morning, thinking back over the previous night.

She thought how supportive Joe had been to her, yet again. How understanding when she had acted like a right weirdo. He really was a thoughtful man. Kind. That's what he was, she decided. Above all else Joe wanted to see people happy. Skye decided she wanted to do something nice for him.

She could begin showing her appreciation by getting out of bed and making him a cooked breakfast before they started their day. It would soon be time for the pair of them to set off to work, she realised as she glanced at her phone screen. Gasping in shock at the lateness of the time, she quickly got up, showered and dressed then ran downstairs to get there before he did. She heard him humming to himself before she was halfway down the hallway.

'Why are you up already?' she asked, not expecting him to have got down before her and hoping it didn't have anything to do with her telling him how nervous she was about the job he did. She also couldn't help feeling a little disappointed that her plan to do something nice for him had been quashed. Clearly Joe had had the same idea as she had done. 'Did you sleep OK?'

'I did,' he replied as he cooked. 'You?'

'Sort of,' she said, not admitting to spending the night going over and over how exciting it had been getting closer to him. 'I'm sorry about the way I acted last night.'

He stopped and turned to her. 'You're not sorry about what happened between us, I hope?'

'What? No, not that. That was nice.'

He gave her a cheeky grin. 'Nice?'

'Stop it, Joe. You know what I mean.' She cringed. 'I meant what I said about your job.'

'Ah, that.' He turned back to the cooker and continued what he was doing. 'Do you still feel that way?'

'Yes, it's a concern of mine. But I'm trying to reconsider after what you said about life itself being full of risks.'

'I'm glad.'

'Anyway,' she said, wanting to change the subject. 'I was going to cook for you this morning.'

'Don't let me stop you.' Joe turned, holding the pan in one hand and a spatula in the other. 'Want to take over?'

Amused to see him wearing one of Lindy's aprons, she grinned and pulled out a chair, quickly sitting down on it. 'No, you seem to be doing well. I'm happy for you to feed me.'

'Damn, I should have waited in bed for a bit longer before getting up.' He smiled over his shoulder. 'I won't make that mistake twice.'

'What's the plan for today?' she said, changing the subject. 'The usual?'

'That's right.' He cracked a couple of eggs into the pan next to the bacon and Skye was transfixed by his muscles moving as he did. 'How many?'

Taken off guard for a moment and unsure what he meant, she had to think back to what he had been saying. He looked over his shoulder at her again. 'You OK?'

'Sorry, I was miles away.'

'Everything all right?'

'Yes, just not quite fully awake yet probably. Sorry, what did you want to know?'

'One egg or two?'

'Oh, just the one for me, thanks.'

Having cooked her egg, Joe served their food. Skye thanked him and began eating, relishing every peaceful moment alone with him.

Skye finished her food and leant back in her chair, her hands resting on her full stomach. 'That was delicious, thank you.'

'I'm glad you enjoyed it,' Joe said, putting the last forkful of food in his mouth.

'Do you enjoy cooking? You seem relaxed doing it and certainly know what you're doing.'

She couldn't help thinking that wasn't all he knew about. Then catching him watching her, wondered if he was confused or simply embarrassed by her double entendre.

Skye took his empty plate with hers to the sink and began washing up, hoping he didn't notice how pink her cheeks had become. She turned on the hot tap and squirted some washing-up liquid into the bowl, swirling the water around to foam it up.

Skye sensed an atmosphere between them. She turned slightly to look at him. 'Something wrong?'

He frowned. 'I've just had a really selfish thought that I'm not sure I can share with you.'

Skye forgot her hands were wet and turned to face him, suspecting she might have had the same thought. 'You wish

Lindy and Gareth weren't coming back quite so early, am I right?'

He nodded slowly. 'You are. Is that really selfish of me?'

'No. To be honest I was thinking the same thing. So if you're being selfish then so am I.'

Joe sighed. After a moment's thoughtful silence he said, 'I'm just not ready to go home and live with my mum again, or...'

Willing him to say something about her, Skye said, 'Or, what?'

Joe stood and walked over to her. Skye's breath caught in her throat and she wondered whether he was about to kiss her. Her excitement petered away when he took her wrists in his hands and gently moved them over the basin. 'You're dripping all over the floor.'

Cringing inwardly, Skye hoped he hadn't seen the look of longing that she was sure had been on her face. 'Ooh, sorry about that.'

'No worries.' He went to the utility room so Skye finished the washing-up, realising for the first time that the tops of her feet were wet from the drips. What a dope she was. She really needed to focus more on what she was doing.

Seconds later, Joe returned with the mop. 'Can you move over for a moment?'

She did as he asked, drying her hands on the nearby towel. 'Thanks. I should be the one doing that though.'

He mopped the area where her feet had been. 'I don't see why.'

'Because I was the one to make the mess.' She laughed, picking up the first plate to dry it.

Joe stopped and looked at her. His face was inches from hers and Skye could almost hear her breath, the air between them had become so still.

She wanted to kiss him so badly. She was deciding whether to when his face moved closer to hers and their lips connected.

Joe must have rested the mop against something to free his hands, because immediately after that he had one arm around her back and the other took the plate she had forgotten she was holding from her hands. She was only vaguely aware of him placing it on the draining board next to them as his lips pressed against hers once again.

Loving being in his arms, Skye gave in to her instincts and slipped her arms around his neck, making the most of being alone with him in the house and free to kiss him.

A few seconds later, their kiss over, Joe leant slightly back from her, staring at her with such intensity that Skye wondered if it were possible his feelings might mirror her own. She really hoped they were.

'I know we both feel guilty about wanting this...' he hesitated '...whatever this is between us, to last as long as possible. And I know you have your concerns about my work and also that this current situation will soon going to be over when the Torels return, and we'll go our separate ways, but I'm not ready for that to happen. I know it's wrong, but I can't help myself.'

'Neither can I,' she admitted, her voice barely above a whisper as she stared at his perfect lips, missing them being against her own. Not wishing to waste a second longer of the short time they still had to be together, Skye pulled him down slightly until her lips pressed against his again, happy when he reacted exactly how she had hoped he would and kissed her.

37

JOE

All Joe knew was that he didn't want this moment to end. He and Skye might have lives to get back to but right now he wished that wasn't the case. Everything about her was perfect. From the way she kissed, to how her green eyes sparkled every time she laughed at something funny, her love for the animals and well, just everything about her. If only she didn't worry so much about how he earned his living, or even if she lived here and wasn't going back to Edinburgh when this was all over.

He reminded himself that she did have a family here now and would more than likely be travelling over to spend more time with them, getting to know each of them. It wasn't perfect, but it was something, he supposed. And, he realised, there was nothing to stop him going to visit her. But would that be enough? He doubted it would be for him.

Joe felt a nudge against his thigh and glancing down, saw Spud pushing his head against him. Reluctantly he moved back from Skye and peered at the dog. 'What's the matter, boy?'

Derek sidled up to Skye's leg and pushed against her, his eyes gazing up at her as if he was trying to tell her something.

'Something's wrong,' she said thoughtfully. 'His tail is down and Derek's tail only does that when he's unhappy, or worried.'

Joe bent to stroke him. 'What's wrong, little guy?' he asked, cuddling Derek whose tail rose, he was relieved to notice.

Skye gasped. 'We forgot to feed the dogs,' she said guiltily. She looked at the kitchen wall clock. 'It's an hour and a half after their usual breakfast time. Oh, you poor boys,' she said, stroking them both before looking at Joe again.

Unable to help himself, he gave her a quick peck on her lips. 'This means that we're also late to feed the other animals.' He bent to stroke Spud and then Derek who was now wagging his tail, letting it tap noisily against the cupboard door where their food was stored. 'Clever chap.' Joe laughed. 'All right, we get the message. I'll feed you right this minute.'

'How selfish of us,' Skye said, picking up the plate and tea towel to dry up. 'I feel really mean now.'

'Not as bad as me.' Joe fetched the bag of kibble and a new tin of dog food from the utility room and returned to the kitchen. 'All I was thinking of was our food.' He smiled at her, wishing she was still in his arms and recalling how it felt to hold her, kiss her.

Spud nudged him again and Skye laughed. 'You need to pay more attention to him, at least until he's eaten.'

Joe groaned. 'Sorry, Spud. I really am being useless this morning.'

'Oh, I wouldn't say that exactly,' Skye teased, making him laugh.

'I'm glad you think so.' He opened the tin, placed the two dog bowls down, poured in the required amount of food and spooned in some of the tinned meat, mixing them together. 'There you go, lads. Enjoy.'

Hearing vehicles outside, Joe put the food away and went to

see who was there. 'It's some of the lads from Leonard's farm come to help finish harvesting the Jersey Royals.'

'Right,' Skye said. 'I'll go and greet them and meet you in the field.'

'Won't be long.'

He watched her go, waiting for the dogs to finish eating so he could wash up their bowls rather than leave them to attract flies. Skye really was always diligent and he didn't wonder why Melody had thought her the perfect person to suggest for coming over and running the farm.

And he was very glad that she had done. It had been a refreshing time staying here at the farm and getting to know Skye. He had thought himself settled until his mother's arrival and moving to the farm. He'd presumed he was happy with his lot and that having a job he loved and his home meant that there wasn't anything missing. He hadn't noticed anything missing – not before coming here and getting to know her. Now, as he thought of the time they had spent together on relaxed walks on the beach and in the fields, sitting up late chatting; chilled, pleasant times he'd spent in her company, he realised there had been a gaping hole in his life that he now felt an urge to fill.

If only there was a simple solution to making that happen. Even if Skye came over to visit Jersey and spend time with Carlos and Paul, they also had their own lives, and how long could Joe realistically expect her to spend here? He could visit her in Edinburgh, and assumed that as her grandmother lived there that would be where Skye would want to live. Unfortunately, he knew from past experience with his ex that meeting someone under one circumstance rarely ended up working long-term when both parties had to get back to their daily work routines. However he looked at it, a relationship between them would take some thought and a lot of compromise if it was going to work in the long term.

Maybe he wasn't meant to expect this amazing time with Skye to continue after the Torels returned and he moved back home and Skye returned to live with her gran. He was probably being fanciful, romantic even, hoping that they could find a way to make this work.

Hearing the dog bowls clanging against the tiles as Spud and Derek licked them clean, he picked them up and washed them. He caught sight of Skye out of the window striding up from the lower meadow and leading the three rescue alpacas to the field where they would spend the day. She didn't seem to have a care in the world but he now knew her better and understood that there was a lot for her to contend with and get used to, especially after all the recent changes in her life, meeting her father and discovering she had half-brothers. It couldn't have been easy for her meeting Carlos for the first time, discovering more about her mother and learning of experiences her mother had chosen not to share with her.

He dried the bowls and put them away in the cupboard, then went to join Skye in the field. If they only had a short time left together then he needed to make the most of every second with her, because it wasn't long now until Lettie and Brodie would be back.

38

SKYE

A few days later, Skye reread the message she had just received from her father. 'He wants me to arrange for us to meet up with him and Sandra, if she'll be willing to,' she explained to Joe as they watched another trailer load of potatoes being driven away to the docks in St Helier for shipping to the UK. 'Do you think she'll be up for that?'

Joe shrugged. 'I've no idea. I don't see why not though. Why don't you ask her and see what she says?'

Working out that Sandra would have returned from her holiday a couple of days before, Skye decided to contact her. She didn't want to waste any time, so immediately began typing in a message and pressed send before she had a chance to talk herself out of it. 'It's still very early so she might not be up yet,' Skye said, already prepared to brace herself for disappointment. If she could get Sandra to agree then hopefully the two of them would inspire each other's memories as they reminisced and gave her more information about her mother. It was worth a try.

After the previous few days when the tension between her and Joe had been heightened after their intimacy during the storm, she was glad to have been kept busy and now she had this to focus on to stop her mind from tormenting her with constant thoughts about what might happen between them when their time on the farm was over.

'Come along,' Joe called, waving for her to join him in the larger barn. 'Now the last of the lorries has left we should let the animals out into the fields. It's going to be warm today and they've all probably been a bit disturbed by the voices and engine sounds going on for the past couple of hours while Lettie's uncle and his staff harvested the Jersey Royals.'

'Good idea.' Happy to have something to distract her from constantly checking her phone for Sandra's reply, Skye helped lead the alpacas while Joe sorted out the cows and took them to their field.

Her phone vibrated against her buttock and after closing the gate to ensure the alpacas were safely in the field, she withdrew her phone and checked the screen. 'She's responded,' Skye yelled excitedly.

'What does she say?' he asked, exiting the next field. 'Has she agreed to join us?'

Skye opened the message and squealed, causing the dogs' heads to turn in her direction, ears pricked. 'Sorry, boys. Yes, Sandra said to arrange whatever we like and she'll fit in with us.' She read on. 'Apparently she has very little in her diary right now.'

She beamed at Joe, realising how excited she was coming across when he laughed. 'Sorry. I'm a bit enthusiastic. I know so little about Mum's life before I was born. Little more than what I've discovered in her notebook, to be honest. I'm desperate to discover anything I can about how she lived. I feel a little as if I'm trying to find all the pieces of a jigsaw puzzle, hoping that once I've found all the bits I'll have a much better understanding of why she made the decisions she did and how every-thing changed her.'

'You don't say,' he teased, walking over to join her. 'Well. When do you want to arrange this get-together?'

'In five minutes' time, if I could.' She laughed. 'Um, would you think it too impatient of me to ask them to join us tonight?'

Joe mulled over her question. 'I think it's a great idea. That way neither will have too much time to overthink meeting up after all these years. Yes, let's make it this evening.'

Delighted that Joe was happy with her suggestion, Skye immediately sent both Carlos and Sandra messages, suggesting they all meet at the farm.

'We can buy some bits to eat in the village.'

'We can,' Joe said, smiling, before returning to the barn to check on the goats.

'I've told each of them to come with their sons. I thought that if they did they might feel a little less strange about meeting each other again after all these years.'

'That sounds like a good plan. At least that way each of them will have someone to arrive and leave with.'

Hearing concern in his voice, Skye wondered if it might be too much for poor Sandra and Carlos. 'Maybe I shouldn't have arranged for them to come tonight. I don't want to make things difficult for anyone and I have a feeling that me delving into their pasts could do just that.'

Joe came out of the barn following the goats. 'Don't worry about it. I'm sure they're fascinated to discover what the other one has been up to.' He pointed to the water trough. 'Check those have enough water in them, will you? Unless you already have done.'

She hadn't, so walked over to the first one and checked the

pipes had automatically filled the trough at the field closest to her. 'This one is fine.'

Giving Joe's comment some thought, Skye reasoned that he was right. She would probably feel the same intrigue to have a reunion with an old friend from years before and felt much better. 'Do you want me to go and buy the food, or should we go together?' she asked, unsure what exactly to buy but not wanting to pressurise Joe into yet another job for her.

'I'm happy to come with you. I love food shopping.'

Skye laughed. 'You love food.'

He threw his head back and laughed with her. 'You're not wrong about that.'

* * *

Later as they sat outside on the terrace for a few drinks with their guests, Skye was glad Joe had thought to light one of Gareth's outdoor heaters. It was much better weather now the storm had passed but there was still a bit of a chill in the air.

She watched as Joe served the last of the drinks and joined her on the seat beside hers. Carlos and Sandra were in deep discussion and seemed to be enjoying each other's company very much, she was relieved to note. Their sons began asking Joe about the rescue but in typical Joe fashion he didn't seem to want to talk about it and turned the conversation to Dan and his broken arm.

Skye took a sip of her wine and watched the man who she now knew was her father. Her dad. How odd it felt to finally know who he was and discover she had an entire other side of her family and siblings that she had never expected to have. She was enormously relieved that not only did he seem like a genuinely kind man but also that he had a good relationship with his sons. As far as she was concerned that said a lot about him, as did his immediate acceptance of her and not holding whatever happened between him and her mother against her in any way.

She was also relieved that Bruno, Paul and Joe got along so well, which wasn't too surprising as they all worked together. But it was an added bonus.

Although, she wondered, as she turned her attention to Joe and the thing that unexpectedly bothered her more than her new relationship with Carlos: what would happen when Lettie and Brodie returned and she and Joe were no longer needed at Hollyhock Farm? Skye supposed he would return to his bungalow and somehow find a way to make the dynamic work with his mother and stepfather, but what would she do? She couldn't stay here, not unless she found somewhere to live and a job. Anyway, hadn't she assumed she would spend a little time with Gran before going travelling again after this ended?

Joe laughed at something Bruno said and Skye's heart ached to think that in a matter of days, she would have to part ways with the man who had brought so much into her life. Hell, he had found her father for her. It was a lot to be grateful for, let alone how it had felt to spend time in his muscular arms. The thought sent a familiar tingle through her body.

She shook her head, determined to focus on the matter in hand. Tonight was about her father and Sandra getting reacquainted, not her fretting about missing Joe.

Bruno and Paul were talking about something, and she realised Joe was watching her. 'What?' she asked, unsure why he had such a strange expression on his face.

His eyes shifted to the side and it took a moment for her to realise he was trying to get her to look at Carlos and Sandra. Confused, she did as he hoped and watched them silently as they spoke. Then it dawned on her why Joe had wanted her to look at them. Their mannerisms, the way they were looking at each other. Carlos's fingers were tapping his knee and Sandra seemed to only be half listening to what he was saying.

She widened her eyes and looked at Joe. 'Do you think they like each other?' she whispered so only he could hear her question.

Joe's mouth drew back in a satisfied smile. 'I think they do.'

They both turned to watch the old friends and Skye recalled how Sandra had been divorced for many years and Carlos was a widower. She thought that maybe she had inadvertently started something exciting between the two people.

She wondered again about her earlier theory and it made her feel even less cheerful. She covered her mouth as she gasped. Could that be why her mother had left Jersey so suddenly? She must have had a good reason never to contact either the man she loved or her best friend ever again.

She felt Joe's hand on hers. 'Shall we go and check on the food?'

She was grateful for his interruption and suspected he might have heard her quiet intake of breath. She knew he would want to find out what it was that had made her react in that way.

'Yes, that does make sense,' he said after she finished telling him her thoughts about her mother's sudden departure from the island when she was pregnant. He opened the oven, pushed his hand into an oven glove and pulled out one of the trays of food. 'This looks about ready to me.'

Only half registering what he was saying, Skye thought for a moment. 'I'm not sure whether we've done the right thing bringing Carlos and Sandra together now. What do you think?'

He shrugged. Then taking the food from the oven, placed it onto the top of the cooker. 'It's too late to do anything about it now. Maybe it's fate and you were meant to meet them both and bring them together. Who knows? This could be how you find answers to questions you never even suspected having.'

She thought about his comment, then nodded. 'Maybe.'

'Right, let's set this lot out in the dining room and call them in to eat.'

39

JOE

He followed Skye with two large plates of food into the dining room. He was going to keep an eye on Carlos and Sandra for the rest of the evening and see if he was right about them having feelings for each other. He went outside to call everyone inside, helping carry Sandra's drink, then when everyone had taken a seat and he and Skye had served them some of the food, he took his seat next to Skye.

'This really is delicious,' Sandra said, having eaten some of the food she had been served. 'Thank you both so much for going to so much effort for us.'

'Yes, thank you,' a chorus of voices added.

'We're happy you're here,' Skye said. 'And I'm glad to have the chance to get to know you all better.'

Carlos finished a mouthful of food. 'I was wondering how long you're over on the island for, Skye. I'd like to spend a bit more time with you when you aren't working, if that's all right with you.'

Joe saw Skye's bright smile and was happy for her that everything seemed to be going so well between her and her father.

'That would be amazing,' Skye said. 'I'm still coming to grips with all that's happened. I'd like you to meet Gran at some point.'

'Your grandmother?'

'Yes.' She hesitated. 'I lived with Gran after Mum died. Well, we lived with her on and off for a few years before that. She's excited to know we've met each other now.'

Joe saw the troubled look on Carlos's face and wasn't surprised. It must hurt to hear that your child had experienced grief at a young age.

Sandra looked perplexed. 'It all sounds rather complicated to me.'

Skye laughed. 'It isn't really, but I can see why it might sound that way.'

Sandra said something to Carlos, and Joe watched as he continued to eat his food. There was definitely chemistry between the pair of them. He wondered whether there might have been something between them all those years ago, too? He hoped not. He was wondering whether to broach the subject in a round-about kind of way when Skye spoke.

'I hope you both don't mind me asking, but do you have any suspicions why Mum left so suddenly?' When neither of them spoke, or seemed to move a muscle, making Joe suspicious that something had been amiss, Skye added, 'She must have had a reason for doing so, surely? I presume it was because she was shocked to discover she was pregnant. Then again, who suddenly leaves the man she loves without any warning, or note about going?' Skye picked up her glass and took a sip, then holding it in Sandra's direction, said, 'Or leave her best friend and flatmate, without giving any reason?'

Joe watched Carlos and Sandra stare at Skye. Neither spoke but he could tell they were trying to think what to say in reply.

Then Carlos looked at Sandra and she at him for a few seconds before both turned their attention back to Skye.

'Do you want to speak?' Carlos asked Sandra, without turning to her.

'All right.'

'What is it?' Skye asked, her hand closest to Joe finding his and taking hold of it.

Joe's heart raced, hoping that what Skye was about to be told didn't ruin the newly discovered relationship with her father.

'Well,' Sandra began. 'It was like this...'

40

SKYE

Skye's stomach tensed as she waited for Sandra to share what had happened. 'Please, go on.'

Sandra clasped her hands together on the table and stared at them briefly before continuing. 'I don't know for sure, of course, but I believe Annie might have got the wrong idea about Carlos and me from something harmless. Annie had been working a late shift and Carlos and I had gone out to the pub with a few friends.' She sighed. 'It was something we all did several times a week, so nothing out of the ordinary. Anyway, I invited a few friends back to the flat.' She shrugged one shoulder. 'It was really only a largish room rather than a flat, but it was bigger than most of our friends' places so they tended to congregate back at our place after the pub closed.'

Anxious to hear more, Skye watched as Sandra took another sip of her wine. 'Go on.'

'Yes, well, it was the usual fun and laughter, then the others left and Carlos wanted to wait to see Annie.' She turned to him. 'Isn't that right?'

'It is,' he said earnestly to Skye.

'I'm not sure what happened, but I seem to recall that one of the earrings I was wearing got caught up in the lace curtains on the window as I leant out to close it slightly to keep out the midges. Carlos came up to me and tried to untangle it, and to see what he was doing, he had to move his head very close to mine.' She sighed heavily. It was a sound filled with regret, Skye realised.

Carlos nodded. 'It was then that Annie arrived back. We didn't hear her until the situation made me then Sandra laugh.' He frowned. 'It was the embarrassment of having to be so close to each other, I think. I felt awkward and clumsy not to be able to release the curtain from her earring.'

'Yes, and I was embarrassed to have caused the situation in the first place.'

Wanting to know more from Annie's side, Skye asked, 'What did Mum do?'

'That's the thing,' Carlos said. 'Nothing. As far as I recall, one of us realised she was standing there just after Sandra managed to remove her earring.'

'That's right. We turned and Annie was standing there. I saw something was wrong but it never occurred to me until afterwards that it could be the earring incident that caused it. I asked her if everything was all right.' She swallowed. 'I think I probably suspected she might be pregnant but was worried how she would react if I did ask her. Now I wish I had done, especially after what happened.'

Carlos looked so sad that Skye wished she could hug him. Not before finding out everything though, she decided. 'Then what happened?'

'Nothing,' Carlos said. 'We had a few drinks. Sandra went to bed and left Annie and I alone together for a short while. I recall her saying how tired she was and that she needed to go to her bed. So I left.' He didn't speak for a moment. 'The following day while Sandra and I were working our shifts, Annie left. That night was the last time I saw or heard from her.'

'Me, too,' Sandra said miserably. 'I did write several times, but the letters came back marked, "Return to Sender". I tried to phone but was told by a woman I presumed was your gran that Annie no longer lived there. I had no other way of tracing her, so lost touch.'

It was all so sad, Skye mused. How different all their lives might have been if her mother had asked what was going on, or hadn't walked in at that moment.

Sandra gasped when a car alarm began sounding outside. 'Is that your car?' she asked.

Bruno stood and peered out of the window. 'It sounds like it. Sorry, if you'd excuse me for a minute?'

They watched him go.

'So much unnecessary sadness for so many people and all because of a silly misunderstanding,' Skye said, desperate to hear more about her mother's story while she had the opportunity.

'I agree,' Carlos said. 'So you see, Annie got the wrong idea. I was devastated for years after that. Still am, if I'm honest. I met my lovely wife and married and had the boys, but there was always something missing for me.' Skye watched him look over his shoulder towards the door and assumed he was checking that Bruno hadn't already returned. 'I don't mean to discount my life with my boys and my dear wife,' he said, his voice low, 'but I want to be honest.'

'It's fine, Dad,' Bruno said from the doorway.

Skye realised he must have come back into the house and heard at least some of what Carlos had said.

'Son, I—'

'It's fine, Dad,' Bruno repeated, resting a hand on his father's shoulder. 'I want to know everything about you and Annie.' He looked over at Skye. 'I sometimes wondered what it might be like to have a sister instead of just brothers and would have happily swapped both my brothers for one many times over the years.'

Unable to help herself and despite worrying that it might be inappropriate to do so, Skye laughed. For a second she presumed she might have offended the others at the table. Then Bruno laughed and the rest of them did too, breaking the tension in the room. It was a relief.

Carlos looked briefly at Sandra then turned to Skye. 'I felt guilty about what had happened,' he said, giving Sandra an apologetic smile. 'Even though nothing untoward had happened between the two of us.'

'No, it hadn't,' Sandra agreed sadly. 'In fact I was tormented for years about how different all our lives might have been if Annie hadn't walked in just at that moment.'

'Or misconstrued why the pair of you were so close at that point,' Skye said thoughtfully, wondering the same thing. She might have had her father in her life and not wasted twenty-plus years. Her mother would probably have been much happier having a steady partner in her life. She sighed. 'Who knows, I could have grown up here.'

Carlos's eyes lowered. 'I would have loved that,' he said wistfully. He looked at her again. 'I feel guilty for so many things. Not only what happened with Annie, or you, even though that is my biggest regret.' He looked at Sandra. 'But because of Annie leaving as she did I felt I couldn't continue my friendship with you.'

Sandra nodded. 'Same here. I hadn't even realised you were keeping your distance from me because I was determined to have nothing to do with you in case anyone did suspect that there was something secretive between us.'

'It's all so sad,' Skye said miserably. 'So many if onlys.'

Hearing this story was also enough emotion for one day and she was happy to let the matter drop. She had watched Carlos's and Sandra's faces intently as each spoke and relayed their part of the story and whether she was right to or not, she didn't know, but she did believe both of them. She loved her mum deeply but knew her well enough to know she could misconstrue people's actions, especially when she was in a sensitive mood, which was more often than not.

Typical too of her mum to act impulsively and want to run away from the situation, although she didn't blame her for wanting to return to Gran and hear her words of comfort. It can't have been easy to believe your boyfriend and best friend had betrayed you, especially when she was at her most vulnerable.

She heard someone clear their throat and realised it was Joe. 'I think, for what it's worth, that there's been far too much misunderstanding, upset and unnecessary feelings of guilt after that night.' He looked from one to the other of them slowly while they watched him in silence. 'What do you all say to finally putting all this behind you? Let's face it, nothing can change the past, however much we might wish it. Choices made back then were made for a reason whether we agree with them or not.'

'That's true.' Sandra tilted her head to one side questioningly. 'Move on, you mean?'

'Yes,' Carlos agreed, nodding. 'Joe's right. We should focus on what we can do going forward.'

Skye loved that idea. 'I agree.' She looked at Joe and gave

him a grateful smile. 'You can be rather wise sometimes, can't you?' she said quietly.

He laughed. 'Er, thank you?'

'I thinks this makes good sense,' Bruno said.

'Me, too.' Paul groaned loudly. 'What a relief. I was beginning to worry where all this was leading to. Mum has had enough to deal with in her life, and from what I've gathered, so have you, Carlos. You both deserve to be happy.' He raised his glass to Skye. 'You all do.'

Bruno raised his glass. 'I say we toast to happiness and moving forward and then I'm going to have to call it a night.' He grinned. 'Some of us have an early start tomorrow.'

'So do we,' Skye said, glad to know she and Joe would soon be alone together so she could process all that had happened during the evening.

Bruno laughed. 'I was referring to you two.'

41

JOE

Joe busied himself in the top field a few days later while Skye weighed and bagged the vegetables she had harvested that morning to refill the honesty box at the roadside. He was wondering how she was getting on, relieved earlier that week had ended up going well, when his phone rang.

'Lettie! How's motherhood treating you?'

'I'm exhausted and think I've aged a hundred years.' He was about to commiserate when she added, 'But I'm loving every single second of it. Apart from the lack of sleep.'

It was good to hear her so happy although the tiredness in her voice was unmistakable. 'I'm glad you're enjoying it. What can I do for you?'

'I just wanted to let you know Brodie and I will be moving back into the farmhouse tomorrow. I'm loving it at the cottage but can't help feeling badly that I've left you both to just get on with things.'

Tomorrow? Joe felt a pang of misery to hear her say as much. 'We don't mind,' he said honestly.

'I'm sure you don't, but Brodie is also missing Derek,

although I imagine the dog is perfectly happy being with you two and Spud.'

She was right. 'He's having a great time. I'm sure he'll be delighted to see Brodie though.'

'Is that OK with you and Skye, do you think? I still won't be able to do very much, I'm afraid, but I felt that I should get back to the farm and some semblance of normality before I get too used to just being with this little one all the time.'

He adored Lettie, and as much as he was aware she and Brodie would be returning soon, he had somehow succeeded in pushing the matter to the back of his mind. Tomorrow seemed far too soon. He wasn't anywhere near ready to burst the happy bubble he and Skye were inhabiting.

Reminding himself that this wasn't his farm and forcing himself to sound positive, Joe said, 'Of course that's fine. It's your farm and you can come back here whenever you want.'

'I'll soon be back to full strength and when Mum returns she's insisted she'll be only too happy to take care of Isla while I'm out of the house working.'

'That's good.' Joe hoped his replies didn't sound too robotic. He realised Lettie was still speaking.

'You and Skye will soon be able to go back to living your own lives. You've both been brilliant stepping in and taking on the farm as capably as you have done, and I'm very grateful.'

'We've loved every minute,' he said, realising that more with each passing second just how precious a memory living with Skye on this beautiful farm had been.

'Every single one?' Lettie teased.

He laughed. 'Well, maybe not initially,' he admitted. 'But once we got to know each other better we both began to enjoy it far more. Skye really is an amazing woman.'

Lettie didn't speak and he realised what he had said. 'Er, Joe?'

'Yes?' He cringed. Why hadn't he thought before speaking? Lettie knew him well enough to pick up on what he had said.

'Am I right to suspect there might something between the pair of you then?'

There was but he wanted so much more. Not that he had any intention of sharing that nugget of information with his friend. 'She's fun and we do get along well.'

'Hmm, I see.'

'You don't,' he said, trying to deflect. 'Right, I don't know about you but I have hungry mouths to feed here and not just one of them either,' he said, stroking the nose of the nearest alpaca who had come over to the fence to see what he was doing.

'I get the message.' She giggled. 'We'll see you both sometime tomorrow morning.'

'Great. See you then.'

He ended the call and looked in the direction of the driveway. Now he needed to share this latest news with Skye. He was fairly sure she was going to be as miserable as he was about it.

'What?' Skye said after Joe finished telling her the news. She sat on the grass in the meadow where he had come to meet her. 'I'm not ready for this to end though.'

Joe shook his head, feeling her pain. 'Neither am I, but there isn't much we can do about it.'

Skye got to her feet. Joe looked up at her, wondering where she was going. 'What is it?'

She had a mysterious look on her face as she held her hand out for him to take. Joe took her hand in his and stood. 'What are you thinking?'

'We might not be able to do anything much about Lettie and

Brodie returning to their home, but we can make the most of the time we have left alone together.'

Was she thinking what he hoped she was? he wondered, his mood lifting dramatically 'Go on.'

Skye began leading the way to the house, through the hall to the stairs and ascended them, still holding on to his hand.

'Skye Sellers, where are you taking me?'

'If you haven't worked that out yet, Joe, then I'm surprised.' They reached the attic floor. 'Your room or mine?'

'I don't care. You choose.'

Seeing her face light up in a smile, Joe felt her hand grab his belt before she pulled him towards his bedroom door. 'Then we'll go to yours,' she said as she led him inside and closed the door. 'I haven't really been in here before. Not properly.'

Joe saw the look in Skye's eyes as she led him to the bed. He wanted this, very much, but was confused about her concern not to become too involved with him because of his work. Should he say something?

She gazed up at him. 'I know what I said about us,' she said as if she had read his thoughts. 'But I've decided that with Lettie and Brodie coming back tomorrow and us having no idea what will happen next, I don't want to miss this opportunity to be with you.'

'I'm glad,' he said, hearing the huskiness in his own voice. 'Do you mind if I kiss you?' he asked, desperate to take her in his arms.

'No,' she whispered, moving closer to him and slipping her arms around his neck.

He stared at her perfect mouth, waiting for his to press against it, and took her in his arms, his excitement intensifying as she gave a gentle groan.

Kissing Skye seemed like the most natural thing in the

world. They seemed to know exactly how to react to each other, almost as if they had been intimate with each other for months.

She moved away and for a moment Joe presumed Skye wanted to stop what they were doing, until she took off her T-shirt and unclipped her bra, dropping it to the floor. He stared transfixed as she pushed down her shorts, then her pants and stepped out of them.

'Well? Aren't you going to join me?' she asked, grinning at him.

'Yes.' He unbuttoned his jeans, letting them drop to the floor before kicking them to the far corner.

Skye laughed, obviously enjoying his awkward fumbling as he struggled to remove his briefs. 'Let me help you with those,' she said, her amusement making him aware that this was a scenario neither of them would be forgetting for a very long time.

Finally free of their clothes, she pushed him onto his bed and climbed on next to him. The next thing he knew she was moving one leg over his thighs, sitting astride him.

She beamed at him. 'That's better,' she said quietly in a low voice that made him wonder why he hadn't fallen in love with her the first second he set eyes on her. Or maybe he had and had been too stubborn and wrapped up in his own exhaustion to realise it. 'Now, where were we?'

Joe didn't allow himself to think, he just put his arms around her and pulled her against him as they began kissing again. His breath caught in his throat as she moved lower and kissed his chest.

He had been intimate with other women, but none of those experiences felt nearly as good as being with Skye. Any further thoughts vanished as he gave in to the sensations.

42

SKYE

As they welcomed Brodie, Lettie and the baby back to Hollyhock Farm the following morning, Skye had to concentrate on staying focused on the present and not walking around the farm with a silly grin on her face. She still couldn't believe that she had instigated what had happened between her and Joe. All her mind and body wanted to do was go back a few hours to being in bed with Joe. It had been the most amazing night of her life and as awkward as she had initially felt leading him up to the attic, she was relieved she'd had the guts to do so. Joe was too much of a gentleman to take the initiative after what she had said about not seeing a future for them, she now realised.

She gave his hand a gentle squeeze, waiting for Brodie and Lettie to take the baby from the car. 'Are you OK?'

'I am now.' She looked up at him just as he gazed down into her eyes. 'I wish we had more time alone here though.'

'So do I.'

Brodie opened the boot of the car. 'I'd better go and help,' Joe said.

Skye agreed and let go of his hand, immediately going to see what she could carry for Lettie. 'We have everything ready for you,' Skye said, glad to have spent some of the morning with Joe vacuuming and dusting the place in readiness. 'I wasn't sure where Isla would sleep, so thought you could let me know if there's anything you need me to set up for you.'

'We have her moses basket. Brodie will bring that in. Her bedding too and some of her clothes and all the other paraphernalia babies seem to need. It's a lot for such a little person.'

Skye laughed. 'It does seem like quite the rigmarole.'

They walked into the house. 'Do I sense a change in atmosphere between the pair of you?' Lettie said, leading the way straight upstairs to her bedroom on the first floor where she, Brodie and the baby would be sleeping for the next couple of weeks.

Skye didn't know how to answer that comment. She wasn't ready to be open about her feelings for Joe, not to Lettie when her reason for being on the farm was to work there, not develop feelings for her colleague.

She thought of how baby Isla must have changed Lettie's life already and wondered if she would ever be in that position. Having babies was something she had never really considered before. She wasn't sure if it was because she hadn't ever been settled enough with anyone to plan a future, or if she was simply unused to having siblings and mostly only having just herself and Gran to consider as she grew up. It was an odd realisation. She immediately thought of Joe, then pushed the thought from her mind. All she wanted from Joe right now was to spend as much time with him as she could and enjoy their new relationship while they were in the same place.

'Sorry,' Lettie said, placing the baby onto the bed and looking concerned. 'I hope I didn't say the wrong thing.'

'No, why?'

Lettie studied her face, making Skye feel a little vulnerable. 'You seemed sad there for a moment.'

Skye shook her head and smiled. 'I'm fine.'

Lettie began changing the baby's nappy. 'You don't want any?'

'Babies? Maybe.' Did she? 'I'm not averse to the idea, just not anywhere near ready to want one yet.'

Lettie cleaned the baby and took a fresh nappy from a bag she had also brought upstairs. 'And Joe?'

What? 'What about him?'

Lettie glanced over her shoulder and grinned before turning her focus back to the baby. 'I meant, how are things between you two? When we pulled into the yard, I noticed you were holding hands. I presume you must have become closer to want to do that?'

Skye didn't want to appear as if she were avoiding the issue. 'We have become closer. He's a really great guy. I'm glad I realised it while we were still here together.'

Lettie finished changing the nappy and buttoned up the baby's Babygro, then lifted her and gave her a cuddle before turning to face Skye. 'I'm glad too. I was a little concerned when I first left you here and wouldn't have been surprised if either one of you had decided not to stay. Then I saw you were both handling running this place well and it was an enormous relief, I can tell you.' She gave a knowing smile. 'I'd love for the pair of you to become an item.'

Skye knew Lettie meant well. 'I wouldn't be averse to it myself,' she admitted quietly. 'However, we both live in different places and as soon as I've spent a little time with Gran after I leave here, I'm going to set off on my travels again.'

Lettie's face fell. 'That's a shame.'

'Not really. I'm looking forward to going away.' She realised what she had said and hated to think she might have given the wrong impression to her friend. 'Not that I haven't loved being here, because it's been amazing, and I would do it all over again in a heartbeat.'

'You would?'

'Absolutely.'

'What about Joe? Do you think he might be up for it?'

'It depends what *it* is,' Joe said from the bedroom door, making them jump.

Skye turned to face him, unable to hide how happy she was to see him. He gazed at one then the other of them. 'We thought we were alone in the house.'

'Now I'm even more intrigued to know.' He studied her face, his eyes twinkling in amusement before he looked at Lettie. 'What are you up to?'

Lettie laughed, her expression one of innocence.

While she waited for Lettie to answer him, Skye wondered whether he would want to repeat the experience looking after the farm and why Joe suspected their friend was up to something. 'I don't think Lettie is up to anything at all. Are you?'

Lettie shrugged, grinning at them both. She handed the baby to Joe. 'Hold her while I sort this lot of nappies out. Skye, would you mind passing me those baby clothes while I put them away in the drawer here?'

'Of course.' Skye could tell Lettie was stalling and sensed Joe knew it too.

'You're such a little cutie,' Joe said to baby Isla. 'She's seems very good.'

'She is most of the time, thankfully,' Lettie said, placing the last of the baby clothes neatly in the drawer and pushing it closed.

'Right,' Joe said, arching an eyebrow as he held the baby in his arms. 'Now your attempt to distract me hasn't worked, maybe you'd like to share what you were wanting to know about me.'

Lettie shrugged. 'Fine. I wanted to know whether Skye thought you'd be up for helping to look after this place again. I mean, if my parents were away at the same time Zac was.'

'What?'

'Don't look so startled, I don't mean now, but at some point in the future. You know, if Brodie, Isla and I want to get away for a few days or a couple of weeks.'

Skye knew Joe's reaction was excitement rather than being shocked and loved that he was happy at the thought of returning. 'I'd do it happily.'

'Thanks, Skye,' Lettie said, folding her arms and staring at Joe. 'And how about you?'

Skye felt him look at her and hoped he would agree too. Even if the pair of them were soon to go their separate ways it would make parting from him so much easier if she knew there would at least be a chance to do this all over again at some point in the future.

'If Skye is happy to do it, then I'll be willing to do it with her again.'

Skye struggled not to show her delight. She saw the glint in Lettie's eyes and realised that Joe had just given her the answer she was hoping for.

Joe handed the baby back to Lettie and shook his head, amused. 'Are you doing your best matchmaker impression?'

Lettie cuddled her little girl. 'Why wouldn't I?' She gave Skye an apologetic smile. 'I admitted to Skye just before that I saw you both holding hands when Brodie and I arrived.' She pressed a hand on her chest. 'You looked so sweet together.'

'Sweet?' Joe sounded aghast at the suggestion.

'Well suited then. It was lovely to see.'

Joe glanced at her then back at Lettie. 'We have got to know each other quite well while we've been here, haven't we, Skye? It's been...' he hesitated '...nice.'

Nice? She wasn't sure whether to be pleased or insulted but reasoned that he was keeping what happened between them private.

'Nice?' Lettie snapped, clearly having the same reaction to her, Skye noted, with amusement. 'I was hoping for more.'

Joe moved closer to Skye and took her hand in his. 'It's been amazing.' He looked Skye in the eyes and she sensed he was about to say something meaningful to her. 'Special actually.'

Her stomach flipped over and wanting him to know she felt the same way, said, 'It has been for me, too.'

Joe grinned at her. 'I'm glad.'

Skye heard a cough. She and Joe turned to Lettie.

'Sorry,' Joe said. 'I forgot you were there for a moment.'

'I did wonder whether you might have done.' Lettie motioned for them to leave the room. 'Off you go then, you two. I need to give this little one a feed and I'd rather do it quietly in here.'

Happy to oblige, Skye led Joe from Lettie's bedroom. 'Let us know if you need anything.'

43

JOE

Skye went to go downstairs, but taking the initiative, Joe held her back, deciding he would rather spend this unexpected time alone with her in the attic where they wouldn't be interrupted.

'Let's go this way first,' he whispered when she seemed surprised about him stopping her from going down to the lower floor.

'Why?' she asked, giving him a knowing grin.

'Because I want to be alone with you,' he whispered, aware she knew perfectly well what his motives were. 'Unless you have other ideas?'

She shook her head. 'Nope,' she said so he led the way up the stairs to their rooms.

As they went upstairs Joe wondered what might have happened if he had decided on that first day here to change his mind and leave Skye to run the farm by herself. No, Joe decided, he was a gentleman and would never have done that to her. Or to Lettie and Brodie. It was strange how things worked out though, and this time he was relieved how amazingly well they had turned out for him.

At the top of the stairs, Skye pulled him into her room. His breath became shallow as he stared at her. Not wanting to presume anything, Joe waited for Skye to close her bedroom door behind them.

They stared at each other and Joe waited for her to make the first move, working out that Brodie and Lettie's bedroom might be right under this one. His mood dipped slightly.

'You do know that Lettie's...'

'Yes,' Skye said quietly. 'I worked that out too. But that doesn't stop us from kissing.'

Pleased with her suggestion, he smiled. 'No, it doesn't.' He took her into his arms. 'You really are the most gorgeous woman,' he murmured, kissing her mouth then her neck before gazing into her eyes. 'In so many ways.'

'I'm glad you think so.' Skye slipped her arms around his neck and kissed him.

Not caring about anything else, Joe lost himself in the sensation of kissing this woman he might never have met if it hadn't been for Brodie speaking to Melody. She pressed her body tight against him and he wished they were alone in the house once more.

Eventually, Skye moved slightly back and looked up at him. 'I wish we could have had longer by ourselves here.'

'I was thinking the same thing,' he admitted. 'This isn't over yet though.'

'I'm glad.'

Hearing Brodie call for the dogs to take them walking, Joe thought they should probably go down and see if they were needed for anything. He went to speak, but Skye began kissing him again and, not wishing for the moment to end, he pushed everything else to the back of his mind.

The dogs began barking excitedly outside just as Joe heard a car coming down the drive.

'Who can that be?' Skye asked, hurrying over to the bedroom window. She gasped. 'It's a taxi. You don't think...'

'What?' *Please don't let it be Lindy and Gareth already*, he thought. They must have caught an earlier flight than he and Skye had supposed, and this was their home.

'It is. It's Lettie's parents.' Skye turned to him, a slight frown on her face. He assumed she was thinking the same thing as him. 'That means Lettie and Brodie won't be needing our help any longer, doesn't it?'

It did seem that way, Joe thought miserably. 'They're not going to expect us to leave straight away,' he said, trying to make Skye feel a bit better. 'Although I do have my bungalow to return to, if necessary.' He thought of living with his mother and Roger again and withheld a groan of regret. 'They won't send you away early though, surely?'

She stared at him and sighed. 'But it won't be the same here without you.'

'Nothing will be the same as it has been.' He pulled her back into his arms and held her tightly. Her hair smelt of summer days and her warm body pressed against his, making him wish he never had to let go of her again. To go from the high of them sleeping together to having to face parting with no idea what future they might be able to make together, if any, was too depressing.

'Hey, where are you all?' Brodie yelled from somewhere downstairs. 'You're never going to believe who's here.'

Joe stared silently into Skye's dark brown eyes. 'We'll think of something. Our time isn't finished yet.'

'Do you promise?'

She had such a look of sadness on her face that he felt compelled to comfort her, desperate to make her feel better. 'I do.'

'Joe, Skye, Lettie, where are you all?' Brodie bellowed.

'I think we've got too used to being alone here and left to our own devices.' Joe reluctantly let go of Skye and saw the regret on her face that mirrored his own. 'Come along,' he said. 'We'd better go and greet them.'

'I suppose we should.' Skye took a deep breath and smiled widely.

Amused by the comical look on her face, Joe asked, 'Are you attempting to look happy?'

'I most certainly am.' She nudged him in the side. 'I suggest you try to do the same thing.'

He noticed her lips, slightly swollen from all the kissing they had been doing recently. 'You look very pretty, you know?'

Her fingertips went to rest on her lips. 'Yes, I know I look as if I've had a filler of some sort.' She laughed. 'In fact, I now know that if I'm ever tempted to have any that all I need to do is find a cute man to have a kissing session or two with.'

He narrowed his eyes and kissed her again. 'In that case, can I volunteer to be first in line?'

'If you like.'

'Where are you all?' Brodie was beginning to sound exasperated. Lindy was a lot to deal with especially when she was excited, Joe knew. 'I think Brodie needs our support.'

'Let's go and put the poor man out of his misery.'

'I suppose we should. Otherwise, poor Lettie is going to have to cut short little Isla's feed and that really wouldn't be fair of us.' As much as he would love to remain alone with Skye he couldn't in all good conscience do that, he decided.

They hurried downstairs without saying anything further. 'Brodie, what's the matter?' Joe asked as if he didn't already know.

'It's Lindy and Gareth,' Brodie said, quietly motioning for them to follow him to the front door. He stopped with the door half open and turned to them.

'Lettie loves her mum but knows how Lindy will try to take charge from the moment she's home, especially with Isla being her first grandchild. I have a feeling she's going to be even more determined to have her own way than she usually is.'

'Where's my grandbaby?' Lindy bellowed from outside, pushing the front door open seconds later and stopping in front of the three of them. She peered around them. 'Where's Lettie and the baby?'

'Um, they're in our bedroom,' Brodie replied. 'Lettie's feeding her.'

Lindy beamed at him and then, when he didn't immediately move out of the way, she gently pushed past him, Joe and Skye. 'Sorry, no time to waste. I need to have a hold of that little angel.'

The three of them looked at each other.

'We should go and help Gareth with the luggage,' Joe suggested.

They found Gareth standing among four large suitcases with two smaller cabin bags, an expensive-looking carrier bag and Lindy's handbag.

'She doesn't travel light, does she?' he whispered to Skye as they waited for Gareth to settle with the taxi driver.

'I suppose they have been away for a while,' Skye said thoughtfully. 'And visited lots of places. Lettie told me that they have balls and smart dinners on board, as well as needing casual clothes for everyday lunches, visiting places and that sort of thing.'

Joe wasn't sure he would be suited to going on a cruise if that was the case. 'I wouldn't have enough clothing in my entire wardrobe to fill one of these cases.' He gave her a questioning look when she didn't immediately reply. Skye had only come with a small bag of clothes, and he couldn't imagine her having a massive wardrobe full of clothes back at her gran's. 'How about you?'

Skye laughed. 'No. I'm far too uninterested in clothes shopping to own anything other than what I usually wear.' She shrugged. 'I could probably do with buying some new stuff though, now I think of it.'

'Why? You always look lovely.'

She pulled a face. 'You've only ever seen me in one of my two pairs of shorts, or my jeans. I can look well turned out if I try.'

Unsure why she was reacting in this way, Joe said, 'I can well imagine. I didn't mean to infer that you didn't bother, you know. Only that...' What had he been trying to say? He wasn't exactly sure. 'I suppose I'm just taken aback that anyone can own as many clothes as Lindy.'

The taxi driver drove away, leaving the four of them standing in the yard.

'Here,' Brodie said, going over to Gareth and picking up the first two heavy cases, his face reddening and cheeks bulging when he felt the weight.

Aware he needed to do follow suit, Joe did the same. 'Oh my word!' he exclaimed as he lifted them.

'Heavy?' Skye asked, looking sympathetic. She went to pick up the two cabin bags.

'No, I'll take those,' Gareth said. 'You take Lindy's bag, if you will. I'm bound to put it somewhere I shouldn't and annoy her.'

Joe followed Brodie into the house and wondered how well Gareth and Lindy got on during their trip. Both had always spent their lives working in different areas of their farm, Lindy taking charge of the house, guests and her baking while Gareth took charge of the farm animals and crops. Spending weeks together, with no family to distract them, must have been interesting.

'Leave one of the cases at the bottom of the stairs, both of you,' Gareth said. 'I'll take them up to the bedroom afterwards.'

'It's fine,' Brodie called from halfway up the first flight.

'Yes, no worries.' Joe was glad they had stopped at the four cases. 'We'll have these up there for you in no time.'

He followed Brodie into the bedroom and placed the cases he carried next to Brodie's.

'Hell, those were heavy,' Brodie grumbled, shaking his hands. 'I'm sure I've damaged the circulation in my hands.'

Joe laughed. 'You're not the only one. What have they packed in them, lead weights?'

They were still amused as they reached the ground floor and found Skye in the kitchen chatting to Gareth as he waited for the kettle to boil.

'It sounds amazing,' she said. Then noticing Brodie and Joe enter the room, added, 'Gareth has been telling me all about their transatlantic journey, then stopping at ports along the east coast. It sounds incredible.'

'It was astounding. The beauty we've seen and the magnificence of some of it.' Turning to Brodie and Joe, he asked, 'Tea, coffee or beers for you lads?'

'Coffee for me, please,' Brodie said. 'I have to get back to the surgery.'

'Yes, I'd better only have a hot drink too,' Joe said. 'I'll have coffee as well.'

'I wonder how Lettie's getting on?' Brodie said, half to himself. Then appearing to realise Gareth was in the room and how what he'd said might sound, added, 'Sorry what I meant was—'

Gareth laughed. 'It's fine. My wife is ecstatic about her granddaughter.'

'Our granddaughter, Gareth,' Lindy reminded him as she and Lettie entered the room.

He pulled a face filled with sarcasm. 'Yes, I know Isla is our granddaughter, Lindy. I'm also not kidding myself that I will have to take a step back and wait my turn when it comes to giving her a cuddle.' He rolled his eyes and smiled. 'As I was trying to say to our family and friends here, I never imagined you would cut short our trip even for this adorable baby.' He addressed everyone else. 'But my darling Lindy insisted she couldn't wait to get back.'

'Neither could you, Gareth. Don't make out this is all me.' She sighed. 'We're sorry it took as long as it did for us to arrive back here though,' she said to Lettie and Brodie.

'Don't be. We understood, Mum.' Lettie kissed her mother's cheek.

'Of course we did,' Brodie agreed. 'We took the opportunity to spend some time by ourselves at the cottage and made the most of Joe and Skye being here to look after everything.'

'And we were happy to do that, weren't we, Skye?'

'We were.' She gave Joe a look that to anyone else might just reaffirm what she had just said, but Joe read the meaning in her eyes and it made his stomach clench.

He wished his mother had found somewhere else to live so he and Skye could move to his bungalow for a while, at least until she decided to return to Edinburgh. Realising the others were watching him and probably waiting for him to speak, he added, 'It's probably worked out well for everyone that things turned out this way.'

Gareth spooned coffee granules into two mugs. 'Everyone except my bank balance,' he said, laughing. 'Those extra flights cost a fortune.'

'Oh, Dad, stop teasing.' Lettie laughed. 'We all know you were happy to pay whatever it took to get back here.'

'Maybe,' he said, giving her a wink.

44

SKYE

Skye opened her eyes and groaned. Her head was pounding and she worked out that she had not enjoyed nearly enough sleep. Her bedroom was directly over Lettie's, and the baby had cried on and off during the night, keeping poor Lettie and Brodie awake, as well as herself. She wondered if Joe had managed to sleep through it and hoped he had done.

The past few weeks had been a whirlwind of changes. First with her grandmother handing her Annie's secret book, then meeting Joe and then again at the farm and thinking him insufferable only to discover he was pretty much the man of her dreams. Never mind meeting her father, who she was relieved to know was a kind, sweet man who had never known she had existed. It was a lot to process.

She stared out through the open windows at the blue sky and shuddered despite the warmth of the morning at the thought of all she would have missed out on if she hadn't taken Lettie up on her offer to extend her stay on the island.

'How did you do it?' she asked Joe across the breakfast table as they each ate a couple of slices of toast alone, the others still up in their rooms. Lettie and Brodie were catching up on much-needed sleep and Lindy and Gareth were dealing with their jet lag.

He gave her a questioning look, still looking sleepy. 'Do what?' he asked before taking another mouthful of his toast and Jersey honey.

'Sleep through the baby crying and poor Lettie doing her best to soothe her. It must be a special talent,' she added, marvelling at his ability and wishing she could do the same.

Joe shrugged. 'Sleeping through noise is something I've learnt to do.'

'Really?'

'I need to grab a few minutes' sleep whenever I can if it's been a long night, or I've missed out on my sleep for some reason.'

'I wish I could do the same,' she groaned, 'but I've always been a light sleeper.'

Hearing heavy footsteps, they stopped talking and waited to see who was coming along the hallway.

'Good morning,' Gareth said, looking bleary-eyed. 'Get any sleep last night, either of you?'

Amused, Skye shrugged. 'A little.' She didn't want anyone to feel bad on her account. 'I suppose the baby is getting used to a new house.'

Gareth walked over to the kettle and switched it on. 'Let's hope it doesn't take her too long.'

'I hope poor Lettie and Brodie managed to sleep a bit,' Skye said.

'She did eventually.'

Skye watched him make two mugs of tea. 'Lindy insists she needs one of these before she can get out of bed.' He added a little milk into each drink and stirred before returning the carton to the fridge. 'We had the baby in with us for several hours. Lindy was certain she could calm the little one but she only managed to for a short time.'

Skye hoped they had been able to get some sleep.

He raised the mugs slightly. 'Well, I'm going to take these upstairs and try and get back to sleep for a bit. I'll catch up with you both later.' He stopped by the door. 'Unless you need me for anything?'

Skye and Joe shook their heads.

'No,' she said. 'We're fine as we are.'

Skye wished she could do as the Torels were doing and get another hour or two of sleep. She was here to do a job though, despite being exhausted and suspecting she looked as lousy as she currently felt.

The sound of the baby crying rang through the house once again. Skye winced. Poor Lettie.

Joe ate the last mouthful of his toast then finished his drink. 'Right,' he said, placing his empty mug on the table. 'When you're ready shall we get back outside where it's a bit more peaceful?'

'One second,' Skye said, eating her last mouthful of toast and local honey. 'Mmm, that is so good. I'm going to have to pack a jar of this honey when I leave.'

'I'm not looking forward to that happening.'

She gave him a sad smile. 'Me neither.' Not wanting either of them to focus on their forthcoming parting, she stood, finished her tea and took her mug and plate to the sink.

Joe did the same. 'Let's get out of here,' he whispered as they heard Lettie's voice leave the bedroom.

'Yes, let's. I think the rest of the family will be getting up very soon and I'd rather leave them to have breakfast in peace.'

'We need to be quick; I can hear them coming,' he whispered as Brodie called for Lettie to bring the bin bag with dirty nappies. He took Skye's hand in his and led her down the hallway and out of the back door.

Skye wasn't sure where he was leading her and didn't care. She was just happy to be spending time alone with him once again. A surge of panic raced through her. There would be very few moments like these left for them to enjoy before the time came for them to leave. And she hated that thought.

They stopped on the other side of the trees at the end of the garden. Joe led her a short way into the wood and, stopping next to one of the large pine trees, took her in his arms.

'Why have we come this way?' she asked, aware the animals were on the other side of the house.

'I can't wait a moment longer to kiss you again.'

Skye grinned. 'I was wondering how long it would take you.'

'And what would you have done if I hadn't brought you out here?' he teased.

She cocked her head to one side. 'I would have taken it upon myself to show you what you should have been doing.'

Joe laughed. 'And this, lovely Skye, is part of the reason I have the best time with you.'

'Because I'm cute and funny?'

'That too, but mostly because you know what you want and are not shy about making it happen.'

45

JOE

As he walked with Skye around the side of the house to go and feed the animals, Joe still felt the pressure of her gorgeous lips on his. She was such a good kisser, he mused, wishing he had more time alone with her. Then again, they still had a bit more time together on the farm. At least he hoped the Torels wouldn't expect him to leave straight away seeing as they no longer really needed him and he only lived twenty minutes away. Both he and Skye realised that although Gareth was retired he missed aspects of farming and would probably be only too happy to take advantage of the opportunity to step back into his old work boots and start working with his beloved rescues once again.

Joe looked up at the cloudless sky above the pine trees. 'Lovely, isn't it?'

Skye sighed. 'It's a perfect day.'

He heard regret in her voice. 'It doesn't help when we're preparing for our time here ending, does it?'

'No.' Her voice was quiet.

Turning to her, Joe took her in his arms. 'Don't feel too

badly,' he said, wishing he could take his own advice. 'We still have a bit longer.'

She looked up at him, then rested her head against his chest and put her arms around his waist. 'I'm not ready for it to end though.'

Neither was he. He could feel her warm breath through his shirt and wished they could stand together like this all day.

'I am sad about going, but already feel a bit like a guest who's starting to outstay their welcome here.'

She looked up at him and frowned. 'I don't understand. Why?' She continued, 'Now the family are all back together and enjoying baby Isla, the dynamics are different. It's understandable.'

'It is, but don't you get the sense that they don't want to upset us by telling us we're no longer needed here?'

He watched her as she gave his suggestion some thought. 'I see where you're coming from, but I don't think it is like that. I'm sure they would have said something. Anyway, we're both leaving very soon and Gareth and Lindy seem happy not to have to worry about the animals for now.'

She made good sense and Joe felt better.

She laughed.

'What?'

'I was just picturing the Torel family sitting around the baby, gazing at her and swapping thoughts on how clever she is, how pretty and what brilliant career Isla is going to have when she grows up.'

Joe smiled at the thought and wondered if anyone other than her gran had ever done that with Skye when she was small. He doubted it. From what he had picked up, her mum hadn't seemed the type to do that. He thought of Carlos and the terrible misunderstanding that had shaped both Skye's life and those of her parents. It was all so sad and, worst of all, needless.

The thought of Carlos gave him an idea. 'I've thought of something.'

'Go on,' she said, looking intrigued. 'What is it?'

'If you're leaving soon then we should contact Carlos and arrange to meet him for supper somewhere. What do you think?'

'Why have you suddenly thought of my father?'

'I just want to help you make the most of your time left here.'

'That's sweet of you. Thanks, Joe. I really should make the most of having him nearby.'

'Great. When would you like to do it?'

'I suppose I could see if he's free tonight.' She gave a nod. 'I could tell him about the Torels' early return from their cruise and the baby. Oh, and also about my plans to leave the island soon. I could talk to him about arranging meeting up with him and Gran at some point in the future too.'

'Good idea.' He watched in silence as she withdrew her phone from her back pocket.

The call on loudspeaker, Joe listened as the phone barely rang before Carlos answered her call. 'I was hoping to hear from you.' Skye looked at Joe. 'I've got Joe standing with me,' she explained. 'We wondered if you were free for supper tonight?'

'Hello, Joe,' Carlos said. 'I'm glad my daughter is going to bring you along with her. It will be nice to see you again. As it will be you, Skye,' he said cheerfully.

Skye laughed. 'I'm glad to hear it.'

They arranged to meet up at seven-thirty at one of the restaurants in St Brelade's Bay.

'Would you mind if I bring Sandra along with me?' Carlos asked.

Joe's eyes immediately met Skye's. She seemed as surprised as he was. Joe pulled a face. *Interesting*, he mouthed feeling a bubble of excitement expand in his stomach.

'That would be lovely,' Skye said. Final arrangements made, Skye ended the call, her hand holding the phone dropping to her side. 'I wonder if the pair of them have seen much of each other?'

'I was thinking the same thing,' he admitted. 'Wouldn't that be brilliant, if they have been?' She frowned thoughtfully. 'Would you mind?' Joe wasn't sure if the idea might offend Skye in some way, especially now knowing the reason behind Annie getting the wrong idea and running from the island and everything that had happened afterwards.

She thought about his question. 'No. It's not as if Mum is still around to mind. They both seem lovely people and despite their families I did sense a sadness about each of them. A loneliness maybe. Didn't you?'

Joe nodded. 'I did.' He frowned. 'We're getting a little ahead of ourselves. Carlos probably thought it a pleasant gesture to invite Sandra out with the pair of us.'

'Possibly, or,' she added thoughtfully, 'maybe there is something between them now?'

Whatever it was, he sensed they would find out much more when they met up with Carlos and Sandra that evening. 'We won't have much longer to wait, I hope.'

46

SKYE

It was surreal sitting across the table from her father and her mother's best friend again. It was also a relief to have a distraction from her sadness about having to leave Joe soon. Skye focused on making the most of her evening and tried to imagine all the things these people could tell her about Annie and supposed they knew her better in many ways than she had done. It was an odd thought, but nonetheless one that gave her hope that she might be able to learn much more than she ever imagined.

Throughout their first and second courses, Joe had been great at keeping the conversation going, but she sensed that each of them were unsure how deep to take the topics. It wasn't as if any of them knew each other all that well. She didn't even know Joe all that well, she realised, only the side of him she had spent time with at the farm for the past few weeks. Maybe that was all she needed to know about him: that he was kind, generous of spirit and honest.

She felt Joe's hand on her leg when Carlos became lost in a conversation about his sons and gave her a knowing look. It took a few seconds for her to understand Joe's meaning behind it. Then it dawned on her he didn't want her to miss that opportunity to delve more into Carlos's and Sandra's lives when they knew her mother. Joe was right. It was now or possibly never because who knew what would happen once she left the island.

She knew from her travelling experience that promises made to keep in touch were often not followed through, simply due to everyday occurrences or personal situations changing. She gave Joe a slight nod then waited for a lull in Carlos and Sandra's conversation.

Both reached for their glasses simultaneously and Skye took that moment to speak.

Straightening her shoulders and taking a deep breath, Skye spoke. 'Um, I was wondering about my mum,' she said, wishing she had thought how best to broach the subject. 'You both knew her well.' She looked at Sandra. 'Best friends and flatmates know pretty much all there is to know about each other, as far as I can gather. You must have shared stories, secrets maybe, with Mum.'

Then, turning her attention to Carlos, added, 'And you knew Mum well enough for her to conceive me.' She felt her cheeks reddening and wished she might have put the words slightly less personally. 'That is...'

Carlos gave her a gentle, sweet smile. 'It's fine, Skye. I know exactly what you mean. You know, er, knew Annie as your mum. You want to find out more about her from an adult's perspective. Am I right?'

He was. 'Yes.' Not wanting either of them to get the wrong impression of her grandmother, she wanted to explain a bit about their help. 'Gran was always Mum and my go-between. She loved us both unconditionally and always tried her best to be honest with me about why Mum had gone away that time, and why she wasn't there for one of my school recitals, or end-of-year assemblies with all the other parents. However, I know she withheld information to protect me either from getting the wrong impression of my mum, or in case I judged her unfairly, like most children or teenagers with limited life experience sometimes do. Gran, on the other hand, tried her best to fill in the gaps, and still does.' She thought of her mother's notebook Gran had only given her before she left to travel to Jersey. 'I have a feeling she might have kept information about Mum close to her chest, not wanting anyone to judge her wrongly.'

Sandra's right hand went to her ear and for the first time Skye noticed the silver hoop earrings. 'Annie gave me these,' Sandra said, 'for my twenty-first birthday.' She took a shuddering breath before continuing. 'They were the last thing she ever gave me.' She pursed her lips and thought briefly before smiling.

'They're lovely,' Skye said, imagining her mother choosing the plain but beautiful earrings and holding them up before wrapping them nicely for her best friend. 'I love to think that Mum touched them.'

'So do I,' Sandra said, her voice almost a whisper. 'I wear them on special occasions sometimes and always worry I might lose them.'

'I can understand that.'

Carlos leant slightly to his right to peer at them. 'I believe I went with Annie to buy those,' he said, a dreamy quality to his voice. 'She bought them from a small jeweller in the Central Market, if I recall correctly.'

Sandra's hand flew to her chest. 'That's right. I still have the box, and one of the first things I did after she left and I realised she probably wasn't coming back was to walk there and have a look around. I'm not sure why I did it, but it felt good to go somewhere new that we hadn't been together, as if I was retracing her steps.'

Skye listened to them as Carlos carried on telling Sandra about that day, and it occurred to her that even though she and her mother had had their own issues, she always knew she would come back to her, and she always did. Even though she missed her mother every single day, she could see that Carlos's and Sandra's emotions towards Annie and her disappearing from their lives were still incredibly raw. They were the ones who had truly suffered by what had happened, not her. It was a revelation, and she couldn't help feeling deeply sad for the pair of them.

Sandra excused herself and, picking up her handbag, went to the ladies'. Then Carlos, spotted someone he knew and excused himself and went to chat to them.

'So,' Joe asked. 'What do you think of this evening so far?'

'I feel badly that me coming into their lives has opened old wounds. Maybe I was wrong to contact them.'

He stared at her without speaking for a moment, then shook his head. 'If anyone is in the wrong for that it's me. Don't forget I was the one who got in contact with their sons and took the matter further, not you.'

He was right, but she didn't like to think of Joe feeling guilty for doing something in an attempt to help her answer questions about her life. 'Maybe so, but you did it solely to help me resolve unanswered questions in my life.' She took his hand and gave it a gentle squeeze. 'And I can't thank you enough. Meeting Carlos and also Sandra has helped me make sense of many things.'

He frowned. 'Such as?'

Skye gave her answer some thought. 'I now know who my father is, obviously. But meeting Sandra, I also have a more rounded version of Mum to think about. Like hearing about the fun she and Mum had when they worked together. Then how Mum left without confronting either of them and never having contact with them again.'

'I'm not sure how that's helped you,' he said, turning to face her full on and leaning his right elbow on the table.

'Because I always used to think that when Mum ran off for months at a time it was because of something I'd done, because I'd disappointed her, or misbehaved in some unacceptable way.'

He seemed surprised. 'And now?'

'Now I know she also behaved that way towards the man she loved, and with her best friend, too. It wasn't about me, but about her. How she dealt with things.' She sighed. 'How she dealt with those close to her. It was difficult but at least I now know nothing I did would have made any difference to those times she went away.'

He seemed happy with her reply. 'That's good.'

'I sense a but coming.'

He shook his head. 'No. I was just going to add that I wish you'd discovered this about her years ago. I hate to think you've carried the weight of that guilt on your shoulders.'

'But I won't do any longer,' she said, smiling. 'And that is thanks to you contacting Carlos and Sandra, so please don't feel guilty in any way.'

She saw Sandra returning from the bathroom.

'We'd better change the subject,' Skye said. 'But I'm glad we've cleared that up.'

'So am I.'

47

JOE

'Quickly, before Sandra gets to the table,' he whispered, 'I think we're right that the pair of them have become much closer. Watch how they react to each other.'

He watched Skye as she thought about what he had just said. 'The way each smiled when the other spoke is a bit of a giveaway too, unless it was about something sad. Oh, I think you're right.'

He smiled at her then frowned. 'You wouldn't mind that happening, would you?'

'Of course not. They both deserve to be happy. It's not as if Mum is around to mind and anyway her relationship with my father was over twenty-five years ago, so it's not as if she should have an opinion either way.'

'I suppose so.'

Sandra waved at a couple on a nearby table as she walked past, then reaching them pulled out her chair and sat, hanging the strap of her bag onto the back of her seat. 'Sorry I was a little while. I bumped into a friend I haven't seen for ages. We've arranged to meet up for coffee one day this week.'

'That's nice.'

Sandra looked thoughtfully at Skye then Joe. 'Have I missed much?'

'Not really,' Joe said, not wishing to give information that was Skye's to share.

He wondered whether Skye would cave in and admit the subject of their conversation. 'We were talking about you and Carlos.' She smiled. 'Joe and I suspect there might be a little romance going on between you both. Would we be right?'

Sandra's gaze flew to where Carlos was standing and Joe could tell she was happy he and Skye had discovered their secret.

'I think I should wait for Carlos to come back to the table before saying anything.' She laughed. 'But I won't deny you could be right.'

'Did I hear someone mention my name?'

Joe hadn't noticed him returning to join them but was glad he had. He waited for Sandra to explain what they had been saying as Carlos took his seat. He listened to her, not looking remotely bothered, Joe was relieved to note.

'I see,' Carlos said eventually. 'You wouldn't mind, would you, Skye?'

She shook her head vehemently. 'No, of course I wouldn't. In fact I'd be really happy to know the pair of you had found each other again thanks to Joe and I inadvertently bringing you together.'

'I'm glad,' Carlos said, smiling at her.

Relief washed through Joe. There had been a few times when he had worried that by taking on this quest of Skye's he might inadvertently disrupt other people's lives, but this was a wonderful result.

'We've been talking too,' Carlos said, putting his arm loosely across the top of Sandra's chair. 'We know you're going to be returning to Edinburgh soon, Skye.'

'That's right,' she said.

'Obviously Sandra and I need to see where this fledgling relationship of ours leads us, but we both agree that we would love for you to come back sometime soon and spend more time getting to know us both.'

'Yes,' Sandra agreed. 'I'll dig out my old photo albums and see if I can find any other pictures of our time with Annie for you.'

'That would be amazing,' Skye said, turning and giving Joe a beaming smile that made his stomach flip over. 'I couldn't bear to lose contact with either of you now I've found you both.'

'That make me very happy,' Carlos said.

'Me, too.' Sandra took Skye's hand in hers and smiled at her. 'Your mum would be very proud of the young woman you've become, Skye. I hope you know that?'

Skye swallowed and for a moment Joe worried that she might cry. She seemed to gather herself quickly. 'Gran tells me that occasionally, but I often feel that she's doing it to be kind. Coming from you, it feels more like something I can take at face value.'

'Well, I truly believe it.'

Carlos cleared his throat. 'I'm hoping that one day you'll feel comfortable enough to call me Dad.'

Joe wondered how long he had been building himself up to mentioning this to Skye. By the look of concern on Carlos's face it had probably been a while. Joe waited for Skye to react.

'I don't see why not,' she said, clearly touched by his suggestion. 'I think everything is still rather surreal for us all, but I am coming to terms with it. Slowly.'

Joe was relieved the evening had gone so well for Skye and

for the others. Most of all, he was happy Skye had said she would come back to the island. This was brilliant news and exactly what he needed right now. It wasn't perfect, but it was something to cheer him up.

After saying their goodbyes, he drove them back at the farm, tired but very happy.

Skye stopped before walking in through the front door.

'What's the matter?' Joe asked, tensing and preparing for trouble.

'I can hear voices, can't you?'

Joe laughed. 'There are four other adults apart from us living in the house at the moment so that shouldn't be surprising.'

She shook her head slowly and raised a finger. 'There. Did you hear that?'

He had no idea what she was going on about. 'I'm not sure what you mean.'

Skye gasped and ran into the house. Concerned, Joe followed, catching up with her in the living room.

'Melody?' Skye asked, sounding surprised and looking elated. 'What are you doing here?'

'We were going to surprise you all tomorrow,' Zac said from the drinks trolley behind the open door. 'Then Melody found cheaper flights and so we decided to come over this evening.' He held his hands apart. 'Surprise.'

Skye laughed and ran over to Melody, hugging her tightly.

Joe went over to Zac and after a brief hug patted his friend on the back. 'It's good to see you again.' He looked him up and down. 'You have a good tan but you look exhausted.'

'The tour was amazing fun but exhausting. I'm glad it's over so I can catch up on some sleep.'

Melody pushed his shoulder. 'All he's done since he's been back is sleep.'

'I have done other things,' Zac said, an unmistakable twinkle in his eyes.

'Shut up, Zac,' Lettie grumbled. 'There are young ears here.'

Zac looked astonished at her comment, making Joe laugh. 'Letts, the baby is far too young to pick up on anything I shouldn't be saying.'

'Will the pair of you stop bickering?' Gareth grumbled. 'It's been peaceful here until you came back, Zac.'

'Hah,' Zac exclaimed. 'That's not what Lettie's been telling Melody.' He pointed to the baby sleeping in Brodie's arms. 'From what I gather, my little niece has been keeping you all awake with her demands.' He raised an eyebrow at Brodie. 'I wonder who Isla takes after?'

'Zac?' Lindy said in a threatening tone.

Joe felt Skye's arm slip around his waist and draped his arm around her shoulder. Pulling her gently against him, he bent his head and whispered, 'I'm really going to miss this family, you know.'

'I was thinking the same thing.'

48

SKYE

Her last few days on the farm were passing far too quickly for Skye's liking. Even though she and Joe made the most of spending every single second possible together, it wasn't enough. There were far too few times when they were alone, and as much as she would have liked to spend another night with him it didn't feel right now that Melody and Zac were back in the house. Too many people around them to dare risk being overheard.

Gareth and Zac had been helping her on the farm, and Melody when she wasn't helping Lettie by taking the baby so Lettie and Lindy could go out shopping, or into the town to buy things for her or the baby. It was lovely spending time with them all, but it wasn't the same as being alone with Joe.

It dawned on Skye that she had lost track of the days and had now worked her last day with Joe without realising it. She wished she would have known so that they could have marked it in some way. But how? Skye found it more and more difficult to hide her sadness that her time on the farm and being near Joe was rapidly coming to an end.

'What's the matter?' Melody asked, giving Skye a shock and making her drop the broom onto the barn floor. 'Sorry, I didn't mean to startle you.'

Skye bent to pick up the broom handle and stood, giving Melody a reassuring smile. 'Take no notice of me; I'm probably just tired.'

'Rubbish. I know you better than to accept that. You're upset that you're going to have to leave Joe behind, aren't you?'

Melody knew Skye far too well for her to deny what was bothering her. 'You're right, of course.' She rested her hands one on top of the other on the broom handle and sighed. 'I really like him, Mel. He's nothing like I first thought. He's been so amazing helping me find my father and all sorts.'

'What?'

Skye explained what had happened and about Carlos.

'But why didn't you mention this to me when you called? This is massive news, Skye,' she added before Skye had a chance to explain.

'I'll tell you all about it soon, but it's still very new to me. I suppose I needed to come to terms with everything before sharing anything about it.'

'You like Joe though, don't you?'

'I do.' Skye smiled. 'He's a lovely man. And—' she laughed, still unable to quite believe it herself '—I'm not an only child any more.'

'You're not? Wow, that's amazing.'

She thought back to all that she'd learnt about her family. She had three half-brothers who lived off the island. It was strange to think that one even worked alongside Joe at the station. A swell of excitement coursed through her as she thought about these new developments in her life. How lucky was she to have even been able to meet Mum's flatmate from when she worked on the island. Sandra had been so generous with her memories as had Carlos. Skye smiled to herself.

'What's more, I have a suspicion that Sandra and Carlos seem to have struck up a relationship of their own.'

Melody's mouth dropped open. 'You're kidding, right? This isn't some episode from one of those soap operas we used to watch?'

'No, I promise you it's all happened, and all of it is thanks to Joe. He also works with Sandra's son.'

She couldn't help laughing as she watched the expressions on Melody's face go through a mixture of confusion, surprise, astonishment and finally acceptance. 'This really is amazing. So not only have you fallen for the dishy firefighter, slash farmer, but you've also found a family you never knew you had, as well as meeting your mum's best friend. I'd call that one hell of a result, Skye, even by your standards.'

No wonder she found it a lot to take in, Skye thought.

Then, recalling Melody's comment about her falling for Joe, she panicked slightly. 'How do you know about me falling for Joe? I never said anything about that.'

Melody stared at her. 'Seriously, Skye. Don't you think I know you at all? To me it's as obvious as that broom you're holding.'

Astonished that her secret had been discovered, Skye needed to find out more. 'But when did you come to that conclusion?'

Melody laughed and shook her head. 'When you and he walked into the room that first night Zac and I were here. I saw the way you stood next to each other. Arms around one another and the way you were so comfortable with him. Also the way he kept gazing down at you as if he couldn't believe you were standing with your arm around his waist.'

'That does make sense.' She thought back to that night and supposed it was obvious if they behaved in that way.

'So,' Melody said, looking serious for once, 'what do you intend doing about it?'

'What do you mean?'

'If I know you at all, which I do, you will have little intention of letting mere miles get between you and the lovely Joe. Am I right?'

Was she?

49

JOE

'You're looking very pensive,' Joe said the following evening as he and Skye walked the two dogs on the beach. 'If you're anything like me you'll be pondering over what happens when you leave here?'

She picked up the dogs' ball and threw it, laughing when both dogs raced across the sand to try and reach it first.

Skye sighed. 'I am.' She took his hand and looked up at him. 'I'm just not ready for all this to end, even though I know we all need to get back to our lives and I want to spend some time with Gran again.' She grimaced when another dog reached the ball first. 'Oh dear, I think there might be a fight if we don't go and rescue their ball,' she said as Derek and Spud chased the smaller spaniel and he took off across the sand with the ball in his mouth.

'Hey, boys!' Joe bellowed. Neither dog took any notice of him, focusing only on chasing the smaller dog and retrieving their ball. 'Blast.'

He let go of Skye's hand and ran after them, aware of Skye laughing and calling for him to go faster as she followed.

'Spud. Derek. Here!'

'Boys,' Skye shouted, her voice with a sing-song tone to it. 'Who wants a gravy bone?'

She had barely said 'who wants' when both dogs' ears pricked up and they turned and began running to her.

Impressed by her clever thinking, Joe slowed to a walk. 'I hope you have some of those things in your pocket, because if you don't they'll never trust you again,' he said, laughing as both dogs ran to her.

She pushed her hand into her jacket pocket and took out two of the bone-shaped treats. 'Of course I do.'

She looked very proud of herself, Joe thought, impressed. 'Well done.'

Once the dogs reached her, Joe hurried to join them and quickly clipped their leads to their collars. Skye took hold of Spud's lead, and he kept Derek's.

'I think we've lost that ball,' he said, watching as the spaniel followed its owner up the slipway towards the car park.

'Never mind, they have loads back at the farm.' She laughed. 'You're out of breath.'

'No, I'm not,' he argued, trying not to show how right she was. 'Just a little maybe.'

Wanting to change the subject and relaxed now that both dogs were back under control, Joe said, 'Are you still planning on returning to Edinburgh?'

She stopped walking and stared at him thoughtfully. 'I was, because I want to see Gran and tell her face to face about everything, but I'm going to miss you.' She looked at him without speaking for a moment, then clearing her throat continued. 'I thought I'd go travelling again. I'm not sure where yet, but I'll see what flights I can get when I'm back in Edinburgh.'

'Your grandmother will be happy to see you again, won't she?'

Skye smiled. 'She will. She'll be relieved Carlos and I get along and even though I've updated her with some of what's happened while I've been here, I want to sit with her and go through Mum's notebook and add in what I've learnt about her life and how it affects me and everyone else to the back of it.'

'That sounds like a good idea.' Joe was glad Skye was coming to terms with everything she had discovered and knew she was hoping that by telling her grandmother everything it might help her recover from the loss of Annie. He sighed. 'I'm going to miss you.' He opened her arms and Skye stepped into them, her free hand going around his waist.

Skye rested her head on his chest and he tried to set the sensation of having her holding him, her body against his, to memory.

Skye's hands went to his chest. She pushed back from him and looked up, giving him a questioning look. 'So what are we going to do about it then?'

Confused, Joe gazed down into her eyes. 'I'm not sure I know what you mean.' He thought quickly. 'I'm not sure what yet, but we will come up with a plan.'

He saw something in her eyes. She was waiting for him to make a decision but he wasn't sure what she was hoping for. He needed to think and fast. Something occurred to him and his heart raced as his mind did too. 'You mentioned going travelling.'

'That's right.'

'My mum and Roger still don't seem to have any intention to leave the bungalow. I could go home, of course, but they'll have settled into a routine now and I don't think the three of us would work in the same house. I'd feel bad asking my mum to leave though.'

'I can see how that would be awkward,' Skye said thoughtfully. 'So, have you got any ideas about what you intend doing next?'

As they spoke a plan began taking form in his mind. They might not have known each other for very long, but the amount of time they had spent together living in the same house and working side by side day after day must be similar to the time most couples spent dating for several months. Wasn't it? He decided it was.

'I'd love to travel more,' he continued. 'And...' Unsure whether he was about to ruin things by making Skye feel pressurised to agree, he hesitated.

'Go on.' She gave him an encouraging smile. 'What's on your mind?'

He sighed. 'Only that, if you're happy for me to, I'd really love to join you.'

'On my travels, you mean?'

He nodded. 'Would that be something you'd consider? Because I can't think of anything I'd rather do than spend the next few months—' he gave her a gentle squeeze '—or years making memories with you. We could discover new places together. I think it would be amazing.' Aware he was letting his enthusiasm get away from him, Joe forced himself to calm down. 'What do you say?'

She gazed up into his eyes for a few seconds, unnerving him when she didn't immediately answer his question.

'Don't feel you have to agree just to please me,' he said hurriedly. 'It's only a thought. To be honest, this is the first time I'm thinking it through properly.' He was rambling and wished he would stop talking and give her a chance to think. To respond.

Skye beamed at him suddenly. She flung her arms around his neck, surprising him and making him laugh. 'I say let's do it.'

'You do?'

'I said so, didn't I?' She laughed.

Barely able to believe what had happened, Joe wrapped his free arm around her waist and held her against him, kissing her, unable to believe that something that had begun as them both wanting to help out a friend could end up with them finding their perfect partner.

'I have a feeling our story has just begun. What do you think?' he asked, gazing into her eyes.

'I had just come to the same conclusion.'

* * *

The following morning, he left Skye at the farm to go and tell his mother his plans.

'You're leaving? Why?'

'Because I need time away from my job,' he said, repeating what his supervisor had told him when he agreed that Joe was doing the right thing by taking time away to do something completely different. 'You need this, Joe,' he had said. 'I've been worried about you since your grandfather died. You seemed to push yourself harder than ever rather than taking time to deal with your grief.'

'I know that now,' Joe said, finally willing to listen to the man who had tried his best to do the right thing by him. Now, though, he was facing his mother and she was another matter entirely.

'Anyway, Mum, we both know this place is too small for the

three of us and with my boss telling me I can return to work whenever I feel ready, I think this is the perfect time to do this.'

'And are you really doing this for you, or for Skye?'

He didn't like the way this was going. 'I want to keep spending time with her and getting to know her. We both want to travel more, so why not just go for it?'

She shook her head grumpily. 'I've only recently returned and you choose now to leave?'

Joe wasn't sure what to say without being rude but checked himself. 'Mum, I don't judge when you follow your heart, and that's exactly what I'm going to do by going away with Skye. I'll be back at some point and we will stay in touch.'

He went to give her a hug. 'I'll say goodbye now,' he said, hoping to leave before they ended up having a row. He loved his mother and didn't want to leave things with bad feelings on either side.

She reluctantly hugged him back. 'You must do as you wish, I suppose. I'm only your mother. Why should my feelings be considered?'

'I love you, Mum,' he said, refusing to be drawn into an argument, aware that was what she was trying to do to keep him there a bit longer. 'I'll keep in touch.'

50

SKYE

'I'm so excited you've both decided to carry on and go travelling together,' Lettie said as she cuddled baby Isla and walked with Skye to join Joe and Brodie in the yard. 'He's such a lovely man.'

'Who, Brodie?' Skye teased, watching the two men chatting with Gareth and Lindy next to Brodie's vehicle.

'No, silly, Joe.' They laughed and Skye wished she had longer to get to know Lettie and spend time with Melody, but it was time for them to leave and she was excited to give her grandmother a hug after being away.

She saw Joe look their way. 'There they are.' She watched his mouth draw back into a wide smile and the loving look emanating from his eyes and hoped that never changed.

'We're not late, are we?' Lettie asked, handing Isla to Brodie briefly before enveloping Skye in a tight hug.

'No,' Brodie replied. 'But we will be if we don't leave straight away.'

'I'm going to miss you both,' Lettie said, letting go of Skye and hugging Joe. 'You've both been amazing helping like you did, and Brodie and I really appreciate having that time alone with our baby when we came out of hospital.'

'We were happy to do it,' Skye replied, feeling a little guilty knowing she and Joe had enjoyed their extra time alone too.

Brodie handed the baby back to Lettie and kissed the tops of their heads. 'I won't be too long.'

Skye hoped Joe wasn't too upset after Faye's reaction the previous day. He had tried to call her but she hadn't answered. Faye didn't answer. 'You OK?' she whispered as he took her rucksack and put it next to his in the boot of the car.

'Sure. I'll be fine. She does this sort of thing. All it really does is confirm that I'm doing the right thing not moving back into the bungalow with her and Roger.'

She took his hand and gave it a gentle squeeze before they both got into Brodie's car. 'I'll sit in the back,' Skye said, not waiting for Joe to reply before doing so.

'Enjoy yourselves,' Lettie called as Brodie started the car and drove out of the yard.

'Bye, Lettie.' Skye waved to her as the car went down the driveway, sad to be leaving but excited to be taking this next step with Joe by her side.

They arrived at the airport six minutes later and got out of the car. Skye was saying her goodbyes to Brodie when she heard Joe speak.

'I don't believe it.'

She and Brodie turned to see what he was referring to and saw Faye hurrying towards them. Her heart dipped, hoping Joe's mother wasn't about to cause a scene and ruin his departure even further.

'Joe, wait,' she said her heels click-clacking across the zebra crossing from the car park to where Brodie had parked outside the departure terminal.

Joe groaned and glanced at Skye. 'Sorry about this.'

'It's fine – she's your mum.'

'Mum,' he said, going to her. 'What are you doing here?'

Faye pushed her hair from her face. Skye could tell she was a little distraught and felt sorry for her. She left Joe and his mother to some privacy and stayed next to Brodie, out of the way.

'I had to come,' Skye heard Faye say breathlessly. 'I couldn't leave things between us as they were. And I do know it was all my fault.'

'Mum, it's fine,' Joe said.

'It's not. I was selfish. I spoke to Roger and he pointed out a few things.'

'Like what?'

Skye hoped Faye was about to say something to make Joe feel much better about leaving.

'I made a few phone calls and contacted an old friend who has offered me her cottage for a few months. It's not available just yet and I told her Roger and I need to stay in the bungalow while you're away to keep an eye on things, but she insisted that was fine.'

'What are you saying?'

'That I have somewhere Roger and I can move into when you get back. You're right to go away with Skye and see where this relationship leads.'

Skye looked over without thinking and caught Faye's eye. Faye waved. 'Hello, Skye. I hope the pair of you have a wonderful time together.'

'That's very kind of you, thank you,' Skye said, relieved Faye had had a change of heart.

'Thanks, Mum,' Joe said.

'That's not all. Roger also admitted how embarrassed he has

been accepting money from you to keep us going. So we're putting the feelers out for jobs for the pair of us.'

'Really?'

Skye couldn't miss the shock in Joe's voice.

'Yes. We shouldn't be relying on you,' Faye said. 'Basically I wanted to come here and apologise and let you know things will change.'

'I see.'

'And of course to give you a hug and say bon voyage to the pair of you.'

'Thanks, Mum, I appreciate this.'

Skye watched as the pair hugged and said their farewells before Faye gave her and Brodie a wave and walked back to the car park.

Joe took his bag from Brodie and Skye slipped her hand into his.

Brodie held up his car keys. 'I'm going to get a fine if I don't move on from here,' he said. 'Off you go and have a brilliant time, the pair of you.'

'Thanks, Brodie, we'll do our best.' Joe laughed.

'We certainly will,' Skye said, giving his hand a squeeze and leading him into the departure hall.

'I'm looking forward to this,' Joe said as they queued to go through security.

'You're not the only one.' Skye sighed happily. 'I don't think I've ever been more excited about embarking on an adventure than I am today.'

'Me, too.' He bent to kiss her. 'Let's do this.'

* * *

MORE FROM GEORGINA TROY

In case you missed it, the previous uplifting romance in the Hollyhock Farm series from Georgina Troy, *Second Chances at Hollyhock Farm*, is available to order now here:

www.mybook.to/SecondChancesBackAd

ACKNOWLEDGEMENTS

Firstly, my thanks must go to my cousin Chris Sweeny, one of three firefighters, including Jonny Burch and Nick Willis, who were finalists for a national Pride of Britain award for their daring night-time rescue of a swimmer in St Ouen's Bay, in Jersey in August 2023. It was that rescue and their bravery that inspired one of the incidents in this book.

To my brilliant editor, Rachel Faulkner-Willcocks and her help to make *Love Blooms at Hollyhock Farm* the best version of itself. Also my thanks must go to Helena Newton for all her hard work with copy edits and picking up everything I had missed, and my proofreader, Anna Paterson.

Thanks also to the hardworking, endlessly supportive team at Boldwood Books who are a hugely supportive and incredibly inspirational bunch.

I'd also like to thank you, dear reader, for choosing to read *Love Blooms at Hollyhock Farm* and I hope you enjoyed Joe and Skye's story.

ABOUT THE AUTHOR

Georgina Troy writes bestselling uplifting romantic escapes and sets her novels on the island of Jersey where she was born and has lived for most of her life. She lives close to the beach with her husband and three rescue dogs. When she's not writing she can be found walking with the dogs or chatting to her friends over coffee at one of the many beachside cafés on the island.

Sign up to Georgina Troy's mailing list for news, competitions and updates on future books.

Visit Georgina's website: www.deborahcarr.org/my-books/georgina-troy-books/

Follow Georgina on social media here:

facebook.com/GeorginaTroyAuthor

x.com/GeorginaTroy

bookbub.com/authors/georgina-troy

ALSO BY GEORGINA TROY

The Sunshine Island Series

Finding Love on Sunshine Island

A Secret Escape to Sunshine Island

Chasing Dreams on Sunshine Island

The Golden Sands Bay Series

Summer Sundaes at Golden Sands Bay

Love Begins at Golden Sands Bay

Winter Whimsy at Golden Sands Bay

Sunny Days at Golden Sands Bay

Snow Angels at Golden Sands Bay

Sunflower Cliffs Series

New Beginnings by the Sunflower Cliffs

Secrets and Sunshine by the Sunflower Cliffs

Wedding Bells by the Sunflower Cliffs

Coming Home to the Sunflower Cliffs

Hollyhock Farm Series

Welcome to Hollyhock Farm

Second Chances at Hollyhock Farm

Love Blooms at Hollyhock Farm

BECOME A MEMBER OF

THE
SHELF
CARE
CLUB

The home of Boldwood's
book club reads.

Find uplifting reads,
sunny escapes, cosy romances,
family dramas and more!

Sign up to the newsletter
https://bit.ly/theshelfcareclub

Boldwood

Boldwood Books is an award-winning fiction publishing company seeking out the best stories from around the world.

Find out more at www.boldwoodbooks.com

Join our reader community for brilliant books, competitions and offers!

Follow us
@BoldwoodBooks
@TheBoldBookClub

Sign up to our weekly
deals newsletter

Printed in Great Britain
by Amazon

61151856R00171